ABANDONED

BY

W. *William* CLARK RUSSELL

AUTHOR OF

"THE WRECK OF THE GROSVENOR," "MY DANISH SWEETHEART," ETC.

METHUEN & CO.
36 ESSEX STREET W.C.
LONDON
1904

TO

CHARLES J. TABOR, M.B.

OF BATH

WITH CORDIAL GOOD WISHES

CONTENTS

CONTENTS

ABANDONED

CHAPTER I

THE WEDDING

M ISS LUCRETIA LANE stood at the toilet-glass in her bedroom in Chepstow Place, Bayswater, dressing herself for her marriage. She was watched from the embrace of an armchair by a young lady who was to accompany her to the church, and who was dressed for the solemnity. How? In a hat and jacket and skirt, for this was to be a very simple ceremony, and Miss Lucretia was putting on her hat and thrusting pins into it, and toying with it as ladies do with their head-gear when they adjust it, whilst her friend sat and watched her.

Miss Lane was a handsome, tall, well-proportioned, finely-moulded young woman, aged twenty-four, with dark red hair, large shining brown eyes, a little Roman nose, a firm mouth with red lips, a throat of a rich whiteness, close-seated ears, delicately tinted like certain beautiful shells, a low, square, tranquil brow, dark and clearly pencilled eyebrows, white, ivory-bright, even teeth, rather small hands, the fingers long and nervous, and the nails so shaped that, taking them with the ears, and a certain delicacy in the carving of the lineaments of her face, you would have guessed she had a strain of good old blood in her.

The other girl, Miss Constance Ford, takes so small a part in this story that there is no occasion to say more about her than name her.

"You had better make haste," said Miss Ford. "Do you know what the time is? I am certain that was Major Stroud who knocked some minutes ago. What makes you linger and pause so? Don't you feel well, Lucretia?"

Lucretia turned her head slowly, brought her fine eyes to bear upon her friend, and said, with a slight frown and in a note of temper—

"Don't tease me!"

Miss Ford stepped to the window and looked out. It was Wednesday, in September, 1890. Villas over the way, dull sky with shadows of fog looking like rain-clouds hanging over the pointing fingers on the chimney-stacks; a piano organ under the window began to play "Auld Robin Gray." Miss Ford started to sing; she sang audibly, with her face averted and her eyes screwed into their corners upon Lucretia.

> "My father argued sair—my mother did'na speak,
> But she look'd me in the face till my heart was like to break;
> They gied him my hand, but my heart was in the sea,
> And so Auld Robin Gray he was gudeman to me."

Lucretia went on fiddling with her hat. What ailed the girl? Was she going to be married to Auld Robin Gray? Was her heart in the sea? How should a young woman look whilst she is dressing, or being helped to dress, for her wedding? She is taking a momentous step; the event is the most significant that can happen to her in all her days. It is more heavily freighted with consequences than the circumstance of her birth. It is a harbour out of which she will sail into an ocean, wider and more awful in its appeals to, its demands upon, her five mortal senses than the imagined life into which the grave cradles, as the launched ship is cradled, the disembodied, and therefore the function-less spirit. How should a young woman look, then, on the eve of her marriage?

Not surely in the main as Lucretia Lane looked. She was extremely fidgety; the rovings of her fingers were often aimless; she sometimes trembled. Several times Miss Ford had observed Lucretia's reflection in the glass, talking to herself. It might have been sus-pected by a medical observer that had a strong man been rent with the mental conflict which was obviously raging in the heart and in the soul of Lucretia Lane, he would have sweated. Lucretia, not being a strong man, was suffering from the war within her after the manner of her sex, at least of those of them who cannot put down their foot and mean—though their heart break as they resolve—that their yea shall mean yes, and that their nay shall mean no.

"I think I had better go downstairs and tell them that you are coming in a minute," said Miss Ford.

As she spoke, Mrs. Lane entered the room; a comely, clean little gentlewoman, aged about sixty, with the word neatness writ large on every turn of her; a trifle bustling with nerve as she entered in black silk, black lace, and jet cape, black bonnet with white feathers rather rakishly perched on a black comb; a woman of whom you might safely affirm that her bedroom would be a model of folded-up things, a woman to touch and adjust objects into symmetrical bearings; on whose bedroom mantel-piece, for example, the shepherd and shepherdess would be exactly equi-distant from the marble clock and the painted china candlesticks.

She did not seem to observe her daughter's manner, mood, or bearing. Her mind was capable of dealing with one idea only at a time, and the idea that now possessed her was not the face of her daughter as the girl stood before the looking-glass putting on her hat.

"Not ready yet, Lucretia?" cried Mrs. Lane, who always gave her daughter the full pomp of her baptismal title. "The major is downstairs walking about with his watch in his hand. He thought he would be late, and actually ran a part of the way, and has scarcely got his breath yet. You know how impatient he is. All these little retired India men are. And irritable. I think we are most fortunate to have got him to give you away. He is afraid the clergyman won't wait if he's kept. How long are you likely to be, dear?"

"Two minutes," answered Lucretia, without turning her eyes from the mirror into which she was directing their beauty and brilliance, and which was reflecting a countenance glacial in expression. Under that sort of ice of reserve what a vast number of disagreeable and dangerous properties may be floating!

"I'll go downstairs and keep the major company," said Miss Ford; and as she passed Mrs. Lane, she whispered, "Lucretia seems very uncomfortable."

"You are quite happy at heart, my darling, I hope?" said the mother, getting hold of that idea and none other, and approaching her daughter to look at her reflection in the toilet-glass.

"I cannot make haste if you talk to me, mother," answered the girl. "There! this hat must do."

She put on her gloves and went downstairs, followed by her mother, whose face wore an expression of uneasiness and surprise, as well it might.

About the little parlour flitted with agitation the figure of Major Stroud: a shape of bristling whisker and wiry moustache, buttoned up in the form of a cask of ale in a frock-coat, and there was temper in the Indian duskiness of his eye. Miss Ford stood in the window. On the sideboard were displayed the wedding gifts: from Major and Mrs. Stroud a silver tea-service; from Mr. Featherbridge a full-rigged ship under a glass shade; from Miss Giddens a silver-mounted paper-knife; from Miss Ford a set of silver salt cellars; from Dr. Phillips (who could not come) the works of Shakespeare; from an old servant who was married, a biscuit tin; from Mrs. Lane a watch and chain, a diamond brooch and gold bracelet, the gifts of her husband (deceased).

"I am sorry to have kept you waiting, Major Stroud," said Lucretia.

"I'm afraid we shall be late as it is. Are we quite ready?" answered the Major.

But the irritability went out of his eyes as he looked at the handsome girl, bowing to her, and then smiling.

The marriage was to take place at St. Stephen's Church, which is within a convenient walk of Chepstow Place. They might have driven, but they chose to walk. Lucretia walked with her mother, the Major and Miss Ford behind them. Mrs. Lane endeavoured to get her daughter to talk; but the girl was extraordinarily silent. She would answer "Yes," or "No," or "I don't know," languidly, abstractedly, with a visible and indeed pronounced inattention as though she was under a spell, or as if she was in that sort of sleep in which the slumberer responds to questions without recollecting

anything that was said when she awakens. Mrs. Lane
was without much talent, and therefore unequal to the
establishment of any sort of satisfactory hypothesis;
even the intuition of the mother failed her, that marvellous penetration which is Nature's gift of interpretation
without mental effort. In a foggy sort of way she
desired to believe that her daughter was too high-
spirited to appear to be fretting over what was not
indeed to prove an immediate farewell to her mother
and home, but which was, nevertheless, the most absolute
of all solutions of continuity, a complete severance in
effect, though she might continue to dwell for a long
time with Mamma. Mrs. Lane remembered that she had
felt in this way herself when she was married, when she
wanted to cry whilst walking up the aisle on her father's
arm, and made strange faces under her veil to hide
her emotion. Little did she foresee, good woman,
the bolt that was to drop with a meteoric blast at
her feet!

At the church door Major Stroud gave his arm to
Lucretia, who took it with an exterior of frigid impas-
sivity, and together they approached the altar preceded
by Mrs. Lane and Miss Ford. A few spectators spotted
the sittings. Though all ends and parts of London
swarm with business and hurry there are always plenty
of people with leisure enough to make a crowd at a
wedding. Even a walking, and hatted and jacketed
wedding is sufficiently extraordinary (in an age when
of course people are very seldom married, very rarely
born, almost never buried) to delay the yelp of the
milkman, to arrest the motion of the perambulator, to
retard the delivery of Sir Thomas's piece of salmon, and
to bewilder the blind man following his dog upon the
pavement.

Some figures were near the altar awaiting the arrival of the bride. There was nobody answering to the appearance of Auld Robin Gray amongst them. One was a tall, deep-chested, clean-shaven man, with a straight nose, standing a little out in a sort of seeking way, greenish-grey eyes like salt water in soundings, hair parted down the middle, close-cropped, like a soldier's; a rather military-looking man on the whole, with something marine in the motions of his body, as though he was on board ship in a small sea-way. Under thirty years of age. His smile was slow in formation, like that of an actor whose business it is to keep his face. He had very good teeth, which made his slow smile like the gilding of sunshine upon his countenance. He was Captain Francis Reynolds of the British Merchant Service, and he was waiting near the altar in St. Stephen's Church to be married to Lucretia Lane.

His best man stood near him: Mr. William Featherbridge, a brown-eyed, bearded person of twenty-eight, sheep-like in steadfastness of gaze, but with hints in his shape of considerable alertness at the call of duty.

Captain Reynolds, as Lucretia approached, viewed her with a face moving with love, and a smile eloquent of devotion and of manly affection. She did not meet his eye; her face was uninterpretable; you could not have detected the least quiver of lip, the faintest hint of agitation, in any the smallest working of the lineaments of her countenance. The deuce alone knows how it was with her, what she was about, why she was there, why, being there, she did not look the radiant maiden, she did not bear the label of the rosy and modest virgin who was to find a blissful haven for life in the manly

bosom alongside of her.   Some who watched her put it
down to nervousness ; some to that sort of conceit which
makes people superior to any kind of situation they
may happen to find themselves in ; some to acting ;
none, not even the mother, not even the bridegroom,
who, standing next her, looked at her marble-hard face
a minute before the clergyman began to read, attributed
the girl's behaviour to the right cause, which was an
impassioned sense of chastity dominating all other
emotion with the vigour of hysteria, yet without force
of spirit in it to subdue her to the nun-like path she
scarcely knew whether she wished to tread or not. _ She
was in a state of mind that froze the sources of feeling,
that closed the portals of every corridor of the heart
and soul, that numbed the brain till volition was mere
mechanism, till the will might have been compared
to a dumb and stirless raven perched upon a bust,
like that of Pallas in the poem.

The clergyman began to read the service.   The
responses were scarcely whispered by Lucretia.   The
officiating minister, a curate, looked at her over his
spectacles somewhat pointedly, then at the man whom
he was transmuting into the golden state of husband,
God wot!   In the vestry Captain Reynolds took his
wife's hand and, with a face full of love, sought to kiss
her ; but she shrank from his lips, almost shrank indeed
from her mother's, and the name which she inscribed
under that of her husband was scarcely legible for the
tremors that ran through her hand.

Captain Reynolds' face was clouded ; his eyebrows
were arched into a fixed expression of astonishment ;
he was profoundly confused, and looked about him with
perplexity.   In the vestry he received an inquiring stare
from his best man, Mr. Featherbridge, and his answering

glance was as blank as that of the gaze of a man in a black room. He offered his wife his arm, and she took it, and together they walked down the church to the door followed by Mrs. Lane ; the others lingered to join them a little later on. The moment they gained the pavement Lucretia withdrew her hand.

"Mrs. Lane," said Captain Reynolds, "Creeshie will not speak to me. What is the matter? What have I done ?"

"Lucretia," exclaimed Mrs. Lane, who walked on her daughter's right, and who spoke in a voice that showed that tears were not far off, "I cannot understand your conduct. Do you feel ill, my darling?"

"No."

"Does your marriage make you unhappy?" said Captain Reynolds.

She returned no answer, keeping her eyes obstinately bent upon the ground.

"It is such a wretched beginning," said Mrs. Lane. "I gave my sanction. I thought you both wanted this. Whatever is the cause of this change in you, Lucretia?"

"I can scarcely hear what you say, with these omnibuses and cabs and boys whistling," answered Lucretia.

"I do not think it very kind of you, I am sure," said Mrs. Lane, in a whimpering way. "It is very hard upon Frank. I could not have treated your father like this. Certainly not at the very outset. It is incredible," she said, projecting her head past her daughter to peer at Reynolds. "What will our friends think, if you carry on like this ?"

The husband of a few minutes was dredging his wife's face with his eyes, but could find no meaning in it outside its beauty pleading to him. No hint to convey a physical or a spiritual explanation of the mystery of this sudden metamorphosis. He was bitterly concerned. Could it be possible that she was mad? That she had suddenly given life to a latent but pregnant seed of hereditary distemper—a strain in the family that had been concealed from him, a quality of intellectual structure of which the girl, and the mother herself, might have been ignorant as a part of the paternal or maternal legacy? He had kissed her often. She had never repulsed him. They had often sat together alone in the twilight hand in hand. A couple are seldom married without certain happenings having gone before. Memories of the tender green of the May of love were sweet and scented between them. It was not to be supposed that she could forget all of a sudden. She must remember everything, though she gave no visible expression to recollection by dramatization of her mood. He felt that she should know better than to act like this. She was now his wife. She could not get away from that. She had always been very willing to marry him. What in the devil's name had gone wrong with the fine creature? Yet never was his love more consuming than whilst he walked to Chepstow Place with the beautiful, chaste, animated statue he had wedded.

The moment the house door was opened Lucretia passed in, ran upstairs to her bedroom, and locked the door. Captain Reynolds and Mrs. Lane walked into the parlour where a hired waiter was trimming the refreshments—cakes, ices, chicken, sandwiches, fruit, jellies, and so on, with champagne.

"Doesn't she mean to return, do you think?" said Reynolds.

"Oh dear, her conduct is most extravagant and un-intelligible! She ought to be in the drawing-room to receive our guests. I haven't the least idea what to do;" and the eyes of the neat, comely little gentlewoman fairly streamed.

"It must be a passing fit," said Reynolds, in a low voice, frowning, and tapping the floor from the heel with the toe of one boot. "It may be a matter for a doctor."

"I'll go upstairs and see what she means to do," said Mrs. Lane. "Stay in the drawing-room, Frank. If she keeps on like this some excuse must be made. We must say that she's ill. But oh, how silly of her; and what an awful position to place us in!"

And she trudged upstairs to her daughter's bedroom, whilst Frank went to the floor above, where the draw-ing-room was.

"Who's there?" exclaimed the voice of Lucretia.

"It's I, your mother," answered Mrs. Lane, talking at the door-handle which she had turned without producing further consequences. "For goodness' sake unlock the door and let me in that we may talk ration-ally. There is yet time; the people haven't arrived, though they are coming."

"I don't mean to live with Captain Reynolds," said the voice of Lucretia.

A pause followed this terrific remark. The mother scarcely seemed to hear, or hearing to understand. The black bonnet with the white feathers swayed from side to side like the head of a listening hen.

"What!" then gasped Mrs. Lane; and, seizing the handle of the door with both hands, she shook it as though she had got hold of her daughter, crying, "Let me in! How dare you behave like this, Miss?"

forgetting that the Miss was now Mrs. "Do you want to break my heart? Open this door, Lucretia."

"I don't intend to live with Captain Reynolds," said the lady inside, speaking with such deliberation that there was the interval of a pulse at least between the dropping of every syllable.

Now, this girl had sanctioned and expressed delight in Reynolds' arrangements for them after marriage: they were to take a run to Edinburgh and the north for a week or so, and then the bride would return to her mother and live with her until her husband's return.

"Why don't you come out and join Frank and me, and behave yourself properly?" cried Mrs. Lane.

No answer was returned. Captain Reynolds, on the lower platform, came on to the landing to listen. When, as he swiftly did, he discovered that Lucretia did not answer her mother, he called out, in a loud stern sea voice, "She's my wife, Mrs. Lane. She has no right to withdraw herself from me. If she will not open the door I can easily put my shoulder against it."

The house was small, and the captain's voice very filling, and the hired waiter stood half in and half out of the parlour door with his left ear cocked upwards, and a grin of astonishment on his face, while the housemaid, with a nosegay in her bosom, listened at the foot of the staircase. Lucretia could not fail to hear Frank's voice. She exclaimed from her bed, on which she had seated herself—

"You may tell him that if he attempts force I will swallow this bottle of poison I am holding."

Mrs. Lane shrieked. At that moment the hall bell rang, and the house door was hammered upon. With the echo of her shriek, as it might seem, on the expression of her face, poor Mrs. Lane went downstairs, and, with a toss of both hands, cried—

"I can do nothing with her. She threatens to poison herself if you approach her."

"Is it not a case for a doctor?" said Captain Reynolds. "Shall I go for Dr. Phillips, and explain matters, and bring him round?"

"Dr. Phillips can't help us," moaned Mrs. Lane; "if I can't influence her, how should Dr. Phillips?"

"Major and Mrs. Stroud," said the housemaid.

And they entered, and were quickly followed by others of the invited; the curate who had officiated, Miss Giddens, Miss Ford, Mr. Featherbridge, and one or two more.

The major was a little man who asked questions; conversation with him consisted of a series of interrogatories. He was a Paul Pry, always hoping (without saying so) that he didn't intrude, and intruding to a degree that was often offensive. He rather relished the misfortunes of others; he was one of those people who, according to the French cynic, find something that does not displease them in *les maux des autres*.

This major, with all the rest, must instantly have seen there was trouble in the little house; and so, consistently with his nature, he went to work to ask questions.

"Where is Mrs. Reynolds?" he inquired, rolling his eyes over the room as though he expected to see her shape herself out of a cabinet or an armchair.

"She's not very well, major," responded Mrs. Lane, discovering the greatest disorder of spirits, sincere uneasiness, and much misery by her manner.

"Not well!" cried the major. "Why, she was quite well ten minutes ago."

"People sometimes fall ill in one minute," said Mr. Featherbridge.

"What can be the matter?" whispered Miss Giddens to Miss Ford.

"She was very singular before she went to church and very remarkable during the service," was the reply, faintly delivered.

"I am afraid we intrude," said Mrs. Stroud.

"Can I be of any service?" asked the curate, who, stepping close to Mrs. Lane, added in her ear, "I did observe a strange constraint in your daughter's manner at the altar which made me fear she was not quite happy at heart."

"She refuses to live with her husband," said Mrs. Lane, in a ghastly whisper.

The curate, who was blue about the upper-lip and cheeks, and had a face like a beardless saint without a halo in a church window, composed his face into the exact posture of a whistle; the expression arrested the eye of the major, who fearlessly took a step towards the pair.

"Now, what is it all about?" said he. "Mrs. Lane, I plead the privilege of a friend. At your request I gave your daughter away. Why is she not here?"

The poor woman, looking at him under her white feathers, seemed to crack nuts, and rather spelt than pronounced the words, "She declines to live with Frank."

"Oh, that's all damned nonsense!" burst out the major. "She is legally compelled to live with him. What's made her change her mind? They seemed very much in love. I thought she was deuced cold during the service. Where is she? Shall I go and talk to her? I'm not a man to stand any tomfoolery.

If she were my daughter she'd either favour me with a very complete explanation or—shall I go and see her?"

All this he exclaimed in so loud a voice that the whole room was in the secret, and many looks were exchanged.

"I am truly sorry, dear Mrs. Lane," said Mrs. Stroud, very kindly; "our presence can only be an intrusion under the circumstances."

"I am awfully sorry," said Miss Ford, going up to the widow, with her hand extended; "but you'll find she'll come round. It's mere petulance—too ridiculous in a girl that's just gone through the ceremony to be regarded seriously."

"Do please take some refreshments before you go!" sobbed Mrs. Lane.

In ten minutes everybody had cleared out, save Captain Reynolds and his best man Mr. Featherbridge.

Mrs. Lane and these two gentlemen sat staring into vacancy. Said Featherbridge, breaking the silence—

"I have often thought that marriage is like the great sea-serpent: when it's not seen it's believed in, and when it is seen it's not believed in."

"I'll go up and see her," cried Captain Reynolds, starting from his chair.

"No!" exclaimed Mrs. Lane, also starting from her chair. "She has a bottle of poison. She will drink it—I know she will if you attempt force by thrusting against the door or even talk threateningly to her."

"I beg pardon, captain," said Mr. Featherbridge, with something of the deference of an officer to his skipper, "but may I make a suggestion? Suppose you leave Mrs. Reynolds for the day and call to-morrow and see how things are going?"

"It's just what I could wish," exclaimed Mrs. Lane. "It's the advice I would give you, Frank. In the mood she is in nothing can be done, I am sure."

"Well, you may be right," said the unfortunate husband, slowly, and gazing with a little bewilderment round the walls much as he had looked in the vestry. "It's a violent, strange change. Something quite outside any bearings I can take. Could any girl have been more loving? I suppose people can have fits of mind just as they have fits of the body. This seems a fit of the mind, as if it was epilepsy, and she had fallen on the floor with a shriek or two, insensible."

"So much the more reason for giving her time, then, sir," said Featherbridge.

"Just so," said Mrs. Lane. "A night's rest and reflection may work wonders, and I am here to reason with her."

"Is there a hotel in the neighbourhood?" asked the captain.

"Yes, quite close, in Prince's Square," replied Mrs. Lane.

"They've let my diggings or I should return," said Captain Reynolds. "Why," he continued, pulling out his watch, "we ought to be in a cab, going to the station for Scotland. Well, till to-morrow—till to-morrow."

He sighed and frowned, and abruptly left the room, unwilling that his face should be seen.

Mr. Featherbridge shook hands with sympathetic ardency with poor Mrs. Lane, and followed Captain Reynolds out of the house.

Mrs. Lane went to her bedroom to remove her bonnet and cape and put on her cap, and then went upstairs to her daughter.

"Who's there ? "

" Your mother."

" What do you want, mother ? "

"Frank and Mr. Featherbridge have left the house. You can open the door," said Mrs. Lane.

On this the door was unlocked and the mother entered. Scarcely, however, could she command her faculties to address her daughter when the housemaid arrived.

"The waiter wants to know, please, if he's to remain ? "

"Give him this half sovereign and send him away," said Mrs. Lane, pulling out her purse.

Lucretia had removed her hat and jacket, and stood with her hand upon the toilet-table looking at her mother. Her hair seemed to glow as though there was sunshine in the room. It would be absurd to say that her dark eyes shone with the fire of resolution that was like wrath ; because the eyes do not change. It is the eyelids and eyebrows which dramatize those motions of spirit which the eyes themselves are believed to express. If this were not so the actress's face would be a very imperfect representation of the part she takes. There was a certain nobleness and dignity in Lucretia's bearing which was owing to a sense of supernatural triumph of chastity, of a conquest of virtue by something even higher than virtue, as the cold star is more exalted than the lonely peak, moon-like with virgin snow, that points to it at some prodigious mountain altitude.

"Frank has left—— " began Mrs. Lane.

c

" I don't want to hear his name mentioned,"
interrupted Lucretia.

The mother strained her eyes at her daughter's face.
She could find nothing to hint at insanity, not the
dimmest monition of aberration. She was as she had
always been, saving that now she had taken to herself a
stateliness of demeanour, an importance and even pomp
of bearing, lofty and victorious as though her soul was
swelled with exultation over the issue of her extraordinary battle.

" Why did you go through the service, Lucretia ? "
asked the mother, seating herself.

" I felt the change coming over me whilst I was
dressing," answered the young wife. " Mother, it was
agony ! I had not the courage to declare to myself I
would not marry him. I ought to have had the courage.
I can never live with him."

" But you'll wear his ring ? "

" Oh yes. I don't mean to be faithless to myself. I
know what I am, and how I intend to remain."

" How we shall be talked about ! "

" What is the value of the opinion of a few handfuls
of dust in skirts or frock-coats ? I know that I have acted
with sickening stupidity. But that is my concern, I am
still queen of myself, and "—slowly and deliberately—
" I do not mean to live with Captain Reynolds."

A gleam of good sense at this moment irradiated
the darksome cells of Mrs. Lane's brain. What could
be more transparent than that her daughter was in no
mood to be reasoned with ? That the application of
the remedial drug in her condition of mental sickness
was certain to injure her and not benefit her ? She
might be managed with patience, she must be allowed
time for reflection. You may soften a tough steak by

beating it, but you shall not mend a broken leg with a mustard leaf.

Mrs. Lane, influenced by good sense, quitted her daughter and went downstairs to find that five pounds' worth of refreshments had been left on her hands untasted by, God help her! the wedding guests.

CHAPTER II

THE MEDICAL CERTIFICATE

NEXT day, shortly after twelve, Captain Reynolds called at Chepstow Place. He was shown into the parlour, and Mrs. Lane speedily arrived. She was pale and agitated. When this poor woman's spirits were fluttered she could not keep her seat, but flitted about the table, lifting a pinch of her dress and pinning it to the table's side, so to speak, as though she would fasten herself securely.

"Well," said Captain Reynolds, with profound anxiety, "what does Creeshie say?"

" I am sorry to answer that she is as obstinate this morning as she was yesterday. Indeed she is firmer and harder. She will not listen to me. She declares, in the most imperious way, that she will not live with you."

Reynolds' face darkened as though to a sudden scowl of the sky. He held a stick in his right hand. He raised it to his left hand and broke it with an unconscious and obviously involuntary effort, looked at the pieces, and threw them into the grate. The strength of the stick, the ease with which it had been broken, the mood the action expressed, frightened Mrs. Lane, who pinned her pinch of gown to the edge of the table half a dozen times in as many seconds.

" Can you, as her mother, give me any idea why she will not live with me?" said Captain Reynolds.

"None—none whatever," answered Mrs. Lane, shaking her head.

"Has she explained her reasons for refusing?"

"No. She told me that the change came over her whilst she was dressing for the marriage. It worked in agony in her, but failed to give her resolution enough to decide not to go to church. All the rest of her words may be summed up in her one determined remark, 'I do not mean to live with him.'"

He put his hand in his pocket and pulled out an envelope containing perhaps half a dozen letters. He replaced the envelope without looking at its contents.

"I was reading them," he said, "last night. They are a few that I like to carry about with me. She calls me her darling, and tells me that she is mine. One letter, not a fortnight old"—he pressed his hand upon the pocket containing the envelope as though his heart, that beat close under, was paining him—"is full of love, of everything that a man could wish to read in a letter from a woman he is shortly to marry. What have I done to deserve this treatment? What have I been guilty of that she should take her love and her marriage vows away from me? Is she at home?"

"Oh yes; but do not attempt to see her," cried the mother.

"But why not? Why mightn't the very sight of me induce a change in her, and bring about what *you* must wish, surely?"

Again his brow was dark, as though his face was shadowed by a thunder squall in the sweep of the wind over a heaving deck at sea.

"She knows you were coming. Had she wished to see you she would have said so. Her threat to poison herself haunts me like a nightmare. I know she is in that state of mind when she could commit some frightful, heart-breaking act if you attempted by roughness, or command, or any other manner you might adopt to bend her mind, which is now as rigid as that poker."

The little woman spoke with unusual energy. Conviction of the truth of her views compacted her reasoning faculties and supplied ideas and words to her tongue.

"Will you go and tell her that I am here, that I wish to see her if only for five minutes," said Captain Reynolds.

"Oh yes; but I know what her answer will be," answered Mrs. Lane, moving to the door as though she was weary, and she went upstairs, whilst Captain Reynolds stood at the window, with his arms folded and his lips set, as though his teeth were clenched behind them.

Mrs. Lane was at least a quarter of an hour absent, and at every sound Captain Reynolds started, and looked, and listened. When at last the old lady returned, he stared beyond her, but she was alone. She began to pin her dress to the table as rapidly as her fingers could work, whilst she exclaimed—

"I knew how it would be. She went to her bedroom and locked me up with her, and then turned me out and locked herself in again; and she swears that the thought of living with you is dreadful to her. She would rather die, and as I am sure she has poison hidden in her bedroom, she will kill herself if you persist."

She burst into tears.

"Good-bye, Mrs. Lane. I don't know when we shall meet again," said Captain Reynolds; and, taking his hat from a chair, he walked out of the house.

He repaired to the hotel at which he had slept, and

wrote a letter of six pages to his wife. The letter was lighted with flashes of sentiment. It was moving with impassioned appeal. It teemed with memories of kisses and endearments, of promises, vows, and hopes; he described his life of loneliness on board ship, and asked her why she had abandoned him; why she refused to know him as her husband, when in a few weeks his ship would be sailing; when in a few weeks the solitude and the desolation of the ocean would be his, without the light and love of her spirit to brighten the hours of the solitary watch on deck, to set up a beacon of home upon which he could keep his eyes fixed, which should be as a star to him to bring him round the world of waters to his love.

He posted this letter, though it was written within a few minutes' walk of Chepstow Place; and making his way to a cabstand, got into a hansom, and told the man to drive to Mr. Turnover, solicitor, in a street out of Holborn. Mr. Turnover had acted for Captain Reynolds in a lawsuit which arose through a collision at sea. He was a bald, bland, little old man, with streaks of faded yellow whisker, gold-framed spectacles, dressed in the rusty black that Charles Lamb loved; and had he worn shoes with bows you would have thought him shod in keeping. They shook hands, and Captain Reynolds, sitting down, told his story.

" It is certainly a very singular case," said Mr. Turnover. " There is one celebrated case of the sort, but it differs from yours because the parties had, apparently, agreed to separate at the church door. The husband, if I remember aright, left the country, and on his return after some years, claimed his wife, who refused to live with him; on which he kidnapped her and locked her up."

Reynolds frowned and looked at Mr. Turnover steadfastly.

"Her friends obtained access to her; her case was brought before the Courts, who decided that by the law of England a man has no right to detain his wife against her will."

"Is that so?" said Captain Reynolds.

"Quite so," responded Mr. Turnover. "The husband must not use force. If he does the law will punish him."

"But is not there such a thing as restitution of conjugal rights?" inquired Captain Reynolds.

"Yes; but in your case, as in the other, no rights were ever established by co-habitation; there is therefore no infraction upon which to base an appeal for restitution."

"Good God, what extraordinary laws we have in this country!" exclaimed Captain Reynolds.

"But I am quite sure, rights or no rights," said Mr· Turnover, "that you would never get a judge to sanction the detention of your wife by force and against her will."

"What would you call force?"

"Imprisoning her in her home and setting a guard over her."

"What do you advise me to do, Mr. Turnover? I am in love with my wife. I was, as I have told you, yesterday married to her in the presence of her mother and others. I am legally entitled to possess her."

"Yes, but even in post-nuptial arrangements there must be two to a contract," said Mr. Turnover, blandly. "It seems to be a case of perversity—a mood, let us hope, that will pass. I once said to Mrs. Turnover, I compare man and wife to a mill and stream: the mill turns one way and the stream runs the other. But betwixt them both the grain is ground."

"Not in my case," said Captain Reynolds, grimly.

"Are you leaving the country?"

"Yes."

"Shortly?" asked Mr. Turnover.

"I sail in command of a ship on October 8 next."

"Your wife may come round between this and then," said Mr. Turnover. "Her mother, I presume, is well disposed to you?"

"Oh yes. She is bitterly cut up by her daughter's conduct."

"I am pleased to hear that," said Mr. Turnover. "Often in these matrimonial troubles the mother-in-law is as the snake that lies coiled round the stem of the flower that hides it. Some mothers do not like to part with their daughters. They are unwholesomely and unnaturally jealous of the husbands, especially if the marriage was in opposition to their wishes, or ambitions, or, I regret to say, interests. If I were you I would trust your mother-in-law to help you with her influence, and leave the rest to the good sense of your wife."

Captain Reynolds paid the lawyer his fee and left the office, having got as much value for his money out of the Law as most men commonly receive who deal with it.

Who was Captain Reynolds? And who was Mr. Featherbridge? One of these men fills an important part in this sea drama, and whilst the captain sits over a chop and half a pint of sherry in an old inn in Holborn, thinking of how, by rights, he should be enjoying life with a handsome young wife in Scotland, and what he must do to get hold of her, we will expend a few minutes in some account of him and the other.

Reynolds was the son of a gentleman farmer, who

fared ill on the goodly fruits of the earth in Essex. He received a middling education to the age of fourteen, when he was sent to sea as an apprentice in a sailing-ship in the English Merchant Service—vulgarly called the Mercantile Marine. He rose to command several tramps in sail and steam and two mail steamers; but having run into a ship in a fog he lost his berth in the company he served, though he saved his certificate and was glad to accept the command of a sailing vessel called the *Flying Spur* of one thousand tons, owned by Mr. George Blaney of Leadenhall Street. She was bound to Poposa, a port in Chili, some distance north of Valparaiso, and her very commonplace cargo would consist of bricks, coke, and coal, and of nitrate of soda on her return voyage.

Reynolds had saved a few hundred pounds, but he would have found (if questioned) no justification in his occupation or prospects for marrying: which was doubt-less his reason as a sailor for getting married. He had hoped on his return from this next trip to take his wife to sea with him on a voyage, then establish her in a little home in some district where rent was cheap and where her mother might live with her during his absence. But what are the expectations of man? He certainly never, amidst his most gilded and expanded dreams of the future, could have conceived himself sitting, on the day following his marriage, over a chop and half a pint of sherry in Holborn, a more lonesome man than Daniel at his pulse, or Crusoe over a kid steak.

Mr. Featherbridge was the son of a schoolmaster, and learning had been applied to him when a boy at more ends of his person than one. He had been caned by the paternal hand into a considerable knowledge of Latin, which was irremediably lost on his first voyage when beating down the English Channel, and a liberal equipment of mathematics, which he preserved, and which helped him in after years in passing his sundry examinations. He, too, like Reynolds, had been sent to sea as an apprentice, and they had been shipmates on several occasions ; indeed Réynolds had a warm liking for Mr. Featherbridge, and when his friend served under him as second mate he dropped the dignity and importance of command though he was extremely reserved to the mate, and walked the deck with Featherbridge in his watch and talked to him with the pleasantness and candour of a brother. Thus it happened, when he obtained command of the *Flying Spur* he sent a line to Featherbridge offering the berth of mate of the ship, and we now understand why it should have been that Mr. Featherbridge was Captain Reynolds' best man at his marriage.

It will be supposed that Captain Reynolds was careful that his wife should know his address. He received no answer to his letter dated at the hotel in Bayswater. He took a lodging near the Millwall Docks, where his ship was loading, and made a second impassioned appeal to his wife, and he also wrote to Mrs. Lane, entreating her to help him by using her influence with her daughter, and telling her that his heart was aching for Lucretia, and that it must break with grief at sea if she made no sign before he departed, as he would be able to think of nothing but his wife.

Mrs. Lane answered in a letter expressed in affectionate language, but could give him no hope. Lucretia was as chilling and determined as ever she had been, and reddened with impatience and temper if her mother hazarded the subject of her husband. Mrs. Lane thought that the extraordinary mood which possessed

Lucretia had not had time to be modified by thought, by recurrence of emotion which could not have perished, by the sense of dutifulness and loyalty which might visit her when she reflected upon her marriage vows. She strongly advised Frank not to dream of calling, as another visit could only end in a deeper degree of obduracy, and, personally, such a visit as he had last paid was so trying that she felt she had neither the strength nor the nerve to confront such another experience.

So Captain Frank Reynolds found himself completely blocked out from the avenue at the extremity of which, on the pedestal of sentiment, irradiated by the rosy light of his passion, stood the cold, chaste statue upon whose finger he had passed the ring which made her his, though there was no piece of sculpture in England at that time, though there was no picture of a beautiful woman hanging upon any wall in the country, more distant and hopeless to the yearning of love, to fruition of desire, than the wife whose parrot cry was, " I will not live with Captain Reynolds ! "

On Tuesday, October 7, Mrs. Lane and Lucretia were at table in Chepstow Place finishing lunch. It was about half-past one, the day very bright and the air fresh, but the hearth trappings of the summer still decorated the grate in that little parlour. Lucretia was dressed in grey cloth that closely fitted her figure, and expressed its ripeness and beauties : her hair was dressed high in the Greek style, and it shone upon her brow in a neglect of red-gold threads, the effect of which no artist in hair-dressing could have produced. She was somewhat pale, and her looks were cold, but her fine eyes were alight with the strong spirit that was her husband's despair, and you witnessed the nerve-character of the woman in the long white fingers with which she dismounted a beautiful Persian cat from her right shoulder, on to which it had sprung without eliciting a scream or causing a start.

The house bell rang and the knocker clattered. It was natural that Mrs. Lane should exclaim, "Who can that be, I wonder?" and turn her head to look out of window, though of course the person at the hall door would be invisible to her.

The servant came in, and said to Mrs. Lane, "Mr. Featherbridge would like to see you, m'am."

". Where is he?" hissed Lucretia.

The servant slung her head sideways to intimate that he was in the passage.

"In the drawing-room!" hissed Lucretia, screwing her thumb up at the ceiling.

"What can he want?" inquired Mrs. Lane, as though she addressed a ghost.

"Go to him, mother!" said Lucretia, "I shall be in my bedroom." She paused to add, "But make him clearly understand that my mind as regards living with Frank is absolutely made up. It is impossible." And with something that resembled a shudder of disgust in an instant's convulsion of her form she went from the room, a very Hermione of a figure.

Mrs. Lane, with an expression on her face that reflected the prophetic promise of her soul to her of trouble, mounted the staircase and entered the drawing-room. Mr. Featherbridge stood at the round table in the middle of the apartment, bearded, slow eyed, yet with alertness in the suggestion of his legs. He bowed to the old lady with the funeral solemnity of an undertaker, and indeed had he been receiving pounds a week for the talent of his face, he could not have looked more solemn and afflicted.

"I am sorry to be the bearer of ill news," he said, on which Mrs. Lane laid her hand upon her heart. "Indeed, I wish I could call it ill news." He gazed at her wistfully. "Your son-in-law, Captain Reynolds, has met with a terrible—a *frightful* accident! Yesterday he fell through the main hatch into the hold of his ship, and is so injured that he is dying, and may be dead before I can return to him!"

"Oh, goodness me, how shocking!" cried Mrs. Lane, breathing quickly. "Dying, do you say?"

"He may be dead as I talk to you," answered Mr. Featherbridge. "Look at this!" he added; and he drew out a letter, which he gave to Mrs. Lane, who immediately groped behind her for her spectacle case, and put on her glasses with hands which shook as though she had been running down a hill. The letter went thus—

"Hours of Consultation—　　　"20, Gloucester Road, Gravesend,
　10 a.m. to 1 p.m.　　　　　　　　　　*October* 7, 1890.

"I have examined Captain Francis Reynolds, and find him suffering from a compound fracture of the left leg, from fracture of the skull, and also from fracture of three or four ribs on the left side. He is severely collapsed, and this points to some internal hemorrhage, probably from rupture of the liver or kidney, but he is too ill to stand more minute examination, so I cannot state definitely which is the injured organ. It is quite impossible to remove him to hospital, and I fear that he will not live for more than about ten or twelve hours.

"H. PAGET-SYMES, F.R.C.S."

"Poor fellow, oh poor fellow!" whined Mrs. Lane. "Who is seeing to him?"

"I got a professional nurse last night from Gravesend," answered Mr. Featherbridge, receiving the letter,
and viewing Mrs. Lane with his slow melancholy stare.
"He is sensible, and his dying request is that he must
see his wife, and I have come to ask her to accompany
me to the ship to say good-bye for ever, and to give
him that one kiss which will send the poor fellow to his
rest with a smile upon his face."

"Oh, she ought to go! She will go, I am sure," cried
the widow. "It must be her atonement. Oh, how
shocked she will be! Give me that letter!"

And with a respiration full of sobs, due rather to
nerves than to the mind, for consciousness had scarcely
yet time to absorb the full horror of the report, she
went to her daughter's bedroom. She broke into it
rather than walked in.

"What has he come to say?" asked Lucretia.

"Read that!" answered Mrs. Lane, handing the
certificate to her daughter.

Lucretia's cheeks paled into the aspect of white wax
as she read.

"How horrible! How awful!" she exclaimed, as
the surgeon's certificate sank in her hand to her side.
"Where is he?"

"Why, at Gravesend," sobbed Mrs. Lane. "No, on
board his ship, I suppose. You see, the man says he
couldn't be moved. He may be dead whilst I am
talking to you."

"Was he conscious when Mr. Featherbridge left
him?" asked Lucretia, with an incomparable expression
of horror and fear in her face.

"I suppose he was," blubbered Mrs. Lane; "because
he sent Mr. Featherbridge to ask you to come and see him
to say good-bye—for ever—good-bye. It is most awful!"

The sentiment that had induced Lucretia to accept
Frank's hand, to sweeten into a smile under the pressure
of his lips, nay to impel her to the altar with him,
faithless in fidelity, an egoistic loyalty that was ignobly
treacherous to her lover and husband, this sentiment
was stirring in her as she held the letter listening to
her mother.

"Come down and see Mr. Featherbridge!" said
Mrs. Lane.

She left the room, and Lucretia followed. Mr.
Featherbridge slightly bowed.

"Do you think there is no hope?" exclaimed
Lucretia.

"Absolutely none," said Mr. Featherbridge. "You
have read that letter?" he added, sending a glance at
the certificate in her hand.

"Is he sensible?" asked the wife.

"At intervals," was the answer. "He sent the nurse
to me this morning, and asked me to go to you and
bring you to him to say farewell. I hope you will
come. It is a sudden and shocking end, and I trust,
Mrs. Reynolds, that you will not make this event more
heart-breaking than it is by refusing his dying request."

"You must go—you must indeed, Lucretia," cried
Mrs. Lane. "I'll go with you. If people should get to
hear that your husband was dying and you refused to
go and see him, what would they think? What would
be said? I should not be able to show my face. I
should be ashamed to meet my friends, and oh, what an
awful memory for life for you! I'll go and put on my
bonnet."

"I do not think your presence would be advisable,
Mrs. Lane," said Mr. Featherbridge, in his slow way.
"The meeting would be sacred. He loves you, I know,

but it is not you that he wants. Such a meeting might be overwhelming if you made one, and how—and how——"
He looked in a formative sort of way at Lucretia, "I mean," he went on, "that something might be said which could not, and therefore would not, be said if witnesses—even if you, Mrs. Lane, were present."

"Well, will you go and get ready, Lucretia?" said Mrs. Lane.

"How long is it to Gravesend?" inquired Lucretia, glancing at the clock, but always preserving her marble-white face of horror and fear, in which there was now subtly mingled an expression which told of the woman's heart beating a little in love and much in pain.

Mr. Featherbridge drew out a railway guide from his pocket.

"A train leaves Charing Cross at a quarter to three," he said. "We can catch that, if you'll kindly not delay. A train leaves Gravesend at 6.40. You can easily be home again by nine or half-past, and I will do myself the honour to see you to this house."

"I shall be ready in five minutes," said Lucretia, and quitted the drawing-room.

"The poor fellow has felt Mrs. Reynolds' abandonment dreadfully," said Mr. Featherbridge. "God forbid that I should do him an injustice, but this fall in the hold seems strange; the ship lies motionless at a buoy. Nothing struck him to throw him forward. . . ."

"You don't say so?" whispered Mrs. Lane, in a voice of awe.

"I only hope he may be alive when we reach the ship," said Mr. Featherbridge. "I shall have done my duty by a man who has always treated me as a brother, whose character is as beautiful, loyal, and true as any I have ever heard of in a sailor. Why would not she live

D

with him ? She loved him—she must have loved him to consent to be his wife. It was not as though he could give her a title and a great estate, as though there was something outside the mere poor man himself which she was willing to wed."

"Oh, Mr. Featherbridge, you wring my heart!" sobbed the widow ; and she began to pin her gown to the edge of the drawing-room table.

In five minutes Lucretia appeared in a hat and jacket, and with an umbrella.

" Have you got any change, mother ? " she asked.

Mrs. Lane gave her two sovereigns.

" I am ready, Mr. Featherbridge," said Lucretia.

"Give him a fond kiss and my dearest love," said Mrs. Lane, "and tell him—oh, Lucretia, tell him all that you feel and know I would say if I were at his side."

Lucretia went downstairs. Mr. Featherbridge opened the hall door for her ; they passed on to the pavement, and Mr. Featherbridge hailed a hansom cab that was passing. They got in and were driven to Charing Cross, which Mr. Featherbridge considered a safer and surer way of reaching their destination in time than if they took the underground railway. Whilst they drove to the station Lucretia asked a few questions about her husband, about his accident, if he suffered much pain, if he had the comforts he required, if there was the least hope of his living. She was very pale ; her quivering lip denoted much turbulency of heart. Her eyes were tearless, but they were dull with saddening emotions.

On their arrival at Gravesend they immediately made for the water-side, and Featherbridge hailed a boat. The afternoon was fine, a dead calm ; a light cerulean mist floated in the atmosphere, and through it the sun darted his beams in tarnished silver sparkles upon the glass-smooth waters. It was the stream of ebb, and the ships at anchor pointed their bowsprits up river. A large and brilliant mail steamer lay in mid-stream waiting for something, with a black man holding a flag perched on the awning astern. The tremors of the stream thrilled in harp-like lines through the shadow she |floated on and defaced the beauty of that piece of mirroring. The breast of river bore its familiar burden of ships coming, of ships going: all sorts of ships, lofty steamers, lofty square rigs in tow, and the water was a mosaic of tints with the reflection of divers coloured canvas hanging at yard or gaff from one shape or another, straining at anchor or buoy, and all looking one way.

"That's the ship!" said Mr. Featherbridge, as the waterman dipped his oars.

He pointed to the *Flying Spur*. The marine eye easily perceived that she was something old-fashioned : a composite ship, metal ribs and timber frame with a handsome cutwater and old-fashioned figure-head, and elliptical stern, and a white band running round her, broken by painted ports. Her masts were lofty and well stayed—that is, her long topgallant masts had that faint curve forwards from the slight slant aft of the lower masts and topmasts which was admired as a beauty in the old frigates. She was ready for sea ; sails furled on the yards, all running rigging rove : a stout comely ship on the whole, one that had done good service to other owners in her time, and was then bought cheap, as she lay capable of shifting without ballast in the West India Docks, by one George Blaney of Leadenhall Street. The boat arrived alongside : steps dangled from the gangway.

"I can mount by myself, thanks, if you will hold my umbrella," said Lucretia ; and Mr. Featherbridge, remaining in the boat, could not but admire Mrs. Reynolds' fine figure as she lay hold of the ladder and ascended.

She put her foot on the gangway and stepped on to the deck, and Mr. Featherbridge, bidding the waterman wait, was immediately at her side. He had grown pale on a sudden, and an expression of nervousness was visible in his face. No doubt he was dreading the effect upon the wife's mind of the dreadful wreck her husband presented : bandaged, stained, broken, dying, or dead ! He gave her the umbrella, and led the road to the companion-way, for this was a ship with under-deck accommodation. Some of the crew were at work about the deck. Some looked to be loafing on the forecastle head, gazing gregariously at the shore. There is nothing more loafing or lounging than a sailor's posture when he leans over the headrail sucking a pipe.

The mate, Mr. Featherbridge, conducted Lucretia down the companion-steps into a tolerably well-lighted interior : a sufficiently roomy cabin containing five berths, of which one on the starboard side was the pantry, a table and chairs, a swing tray or two, and that was about all. A young man, evidently the cabin servant, was polishing some glasses. The mate peremptorily ordered him to drop the job and go on deck. Lucretia was trembling. This was a new world to her, a singular unimaginable scene, a strange atmosphere with its old marine smells and the giant shaft of mizzen-mast piercing the upper and then piercing the lower deck, the coffee-coloured bulkheads, the light troubled in the skylight by the glass's protection of brass wire, the tell-tale compass in the ceiling over the head of the table : all this was penetrated by the presence or knowledge of anguish if dying, of horror and misery if dead.

Mr. Featherbridge went to the door of a cabin which was clearly the largest, and filled nearly the whole of the space aft, and opening it just a little way, enough to admit of the passage of a human figure, he asked Lucretia to step in : then instantly closed the door, softening to his own ear the shriek which followed the wife's entrance.

CHAPTER III

TRAPPED

LUCRETIA was trapped! Instead of seeing her husband lying in a bunk, broken, hollow, bandaged, stained, dying, or dead, watched by a nurse, what did she behold? Her husband indeed, and only her husband; erect at a little square table, as healthy in aspect as ever he had shown, a fine figure of a man, amongst the last, one should say, to excite repulsion in a woman who had once owned she loved him, and who had been made one with him in the most sacred of human bonds.

She shrieked; she swallowed, almost choking, a sob of terror and dire astonishment. The unexpectedness of this apparition as she viewed it, the abrupt astounding transmutation of the illusion that had filled her mind as a fact into the fact that confronted her, seemed, after she had screamed, to shock the life out of her limbs, to root her to the deck, to paralyze every function. Then, with the instinct of escape, she turned her head, and her husband sprang to the door.

"No, dear," said he, not without a note of sternness in his voice, not without a shadow of austerity in his gravity; "you belong to me. The law has given you to me. You gave your hand to me before God, who is my witness. You are mine, and shall remain mine, and why not? What has happened to me that this change should have happened to you? Why have you refused to see me ?. Have I grown loathsome in appearance and manner since we met at the church ? Have I by any single deed warranted your contempt and aversion ? I love you as I have ever loved you. I am adoring you, my darling, even as I seem to address you in heat. Come to your own, you will find him true ! "

He extended his arms to her, and smiled with such a commingling of pathos in the expression as softened the look almost into the tenderness of tears.

"Open the door and let me pass ! " she answered. "You are a coward and a villain to have betrayed me as you have, sending a lying rascal to me to represent you as dying, and making me——" her voice broke. She swelled her breast, and cried, "Let me pass ! I want to go home."

"You shall return home with me," said he, "but in my own good time."

"You dare not imprison me ! " she almost screamed.

"You are here, and here you remain," he replied. "We will not call it imprisonment. When a wife lives with her husband, whether at sea or ashore, she is not his prisoner. She is his companion, and in my case his love."

"Are you really in earnest in keeping me here and taking me away to sea ? " she asked, with the very spirit of tragedy firing her fine eyes, and making extraordinarily dramatic the forward-leaning, imperiously inquisitorial posture of her figure.

"I certainly am," he answered bluntly.

She looked at him for a few seconds, and speculation passed from her glowing balls of vision. Her eyes swooned in their upward rolling under the descending lids, and the scarlet of wrath died out of her cheeks into their first pallor of virgin wax. She reeled, and would have fallen; but he caught her, and laid her tenderly in the one bunk of that cabin, supporting her head to remove her hat that he might pillow her, liberating her throat, now kissing, now fanning her, and brooding over her with the passion of a man whose love has been consecrated.

Meanwhile Mr. Featherbridge, who had received his instructions, was executing them. He hailed the waterman to bring his boat alongside, got in, and was rowed ashore, and making his way to the telegraph office he stamped two forms already filled up and handed them to the clerk. The first ran thus—

"To Mrs. Lane, Chepstow Place, Bayswater, London.
"Shall remain to nurse Frank. Please send my clothes at once to care of Station Master, Falmouth.
"LUCRETIA, *Flying Spur*, off Gravesend."

The other telegram was this—

"To Station Master, Falmouth.
"Please receive and hold boxes addressed to my wife to your care.
"FRANCIS REYNOLDS,
"Master *Flying Spur*, Gravesend."

This was a plot artfully planned and diligently prosecuted. It is not for the chronicler to pronounce upon its morality. His business is to relate, and to leave the reader to judge. But that certificate? Was a third "party" in this scheme in the form of a medical man? No; Mr. Featherbridge, instructed by Captain Reynolds, had called upon a medical practitioner in Gloucester Road and complained of pains in the bowels and general malaise. He protruded a tongue as red as a powder flag; the doctor felt his pulse, which yielded the rhythm of the hammered anvil. The doctor took pen in hand to prescribe, and whilst he cast his eyes upon the ceiling in search of drugs Featherbridge asked him for a sheet of headed paper, on which he feigned to scribble a note with a pencil. This blank sheet he folded once, ready for its square envelope, and pocketed it, and on this sheet in the cabin of the *Flying Spur* he wrote to the dictation of Captain Reynolds the remarkable and telling certificate which had lured Lucretia to Gravesend and into captivity.

He was rowed aboard, having been absent a little over an hour. It was about five o'clock. At six the tug *Deerstalker* would be alongside to take the *Flying Spur* in tow for the Channel. The air was amazingly tranquil. The delicate colour of the October sun sinking low gave the picture of smooth river, and restful ships, and houses ashore, and the melancholy flatness of the Tilbury plains, a hue of warmth that made a summer scene of it. Every flag hung up and down like a streak of paint from the gaff or mast-head of vessels rooted to their buoy or anchor; but the colours fluttered at the staff or gaff of the steamer, mail, or tramp, noble in bulk, or humped in bow, or hogged amidships, or sagged aft where the leaning funnel threatened the demolition of that extremity of the ship. And these filled the horizon of the eye with the motions of life and the colours of commerce.

Mr. Featherbridge climbed the side, and at the gangway found Mr. Vincent Ralland the second mate, a rather fat, warm-coloured, yellow-haired man, in a round coat that made his figure resemble a cup and ball, with a smile of natal origin which might have passed as satirical or cynical had his utterances justified such an assumption.

" The captain's been asking for you, sir," said this man.

"Where is he?" inquired Mr. Featherbridge.

" In the cabin, I think, sir."

"See all ready for the tug! I shall be on deck shortly;" and Mr. Featherbridge went below.

As he entered the cabin Captain Reynolds came out of a berth on the port side. It was not the compartment into which Featherbridge had introduced Lucretia. The door of that berth was closed and locked, and Reynolds had the key of it in his pocket, and it would remain locked until the ship was fairly under way in tow of the tug.

"Did you send the wires?"

"Yes, sir."

"Featherbridge," said the captain, extending his hand, "I am extremely obliged to you for your part in this unhappy business. I am the more obliged because I know that much that you have undertaken on my behalf is in conflict with your views."

"I am glad to have served such a friend as you have been to me, Captain Reynolds," said Mr. Featherbridge. " But Mrs. Reynolds will hate me like poison, and I shall be ashamed to meet her. And yet, what more proper than that a wife should live with her husband?"

"She fainted," said Captain Reynolds, "and was so long in coming to that I was alarmed. She cries silently, which goes to my heart, for God knows it is not in me to give her cause for a single tear. She shall not have reason to complain of my honour, though I have proved treacherous in my effort to possess that which I lawfully own and loyally love. She shall be as a virgin to her husband, but under his protection and within the embrace of his eyes, which must suffice until the woman's heart breaks through the woman's perversity, and the higher form of chastity asserts itself in union."

These may seem flowery thoughts and shining words in the mouth of a captain in the Merchant Service; but we shall see, as we progress, that Reynolds was a man of reflection and reading; one who had spent a great portion of his leisure in studies outside those to which he was courted by his profession. He had read well into the poets, and had followed science in some of the most eloquent of its exponents, such as Faraday, Tyndall, and Kelvin, was not without some knowledge (for conversation) of sculpture, painting, and music. He was mainly self-educated, and therefore well-grounded, and indeed he had made but a small impression on Lucretia if his fascinations had been limited to his person.

Meanwhile in the captain's cabin sat or stood the captive Lucretia. The husband's hand was visible in the furniture of this sea apartment. The bunk—the one bunk—was cosy with eiderdown quilt, soft pillow, new hair mattress. A row of pegs supplied the absence of a wardrobe for the storage of skirts, jackets and the like. A toilet-table under the round scuttle with which this bedroom was illuminated bore fiddles for the preservation of a powder-box, bottles of rosewater, eau-de-Cologne, and other dressing delicates. On the table were ivory hair-brushes and knick-knacks too commonplace to catalogue. Several pots of plants in flower sweetened the atmosphere.

Lucretia had ceased to weep; her face had taken a hard look of rage and alarm. She gazed about her, but entirely missed the symptoms of marital affection through the resentment and indignation she was consumed with. Had the cabin been lighted by a port-hole big enough to run a gun through Lucretia would not have thrown herself into the Thames. She had threatened poison to her trembling mother outside, but she had not had a drop in the room, and she was a conspicuous figure amongst those people of this world who are the very last to lay violent hands upon themselves. No doubt she would have made a brave dash for liberty could she have found an exit: descended a rope-ladder, say, or jumped a fall of fifteen feet into a boat; but she had no idea of destroying herself, and perhaps her husband knew enough of her character to form an opinion under this head. For would he otherwise have allowed a brand-new pair of scissors to repose in a fiddle on the toilet-table? since even a bare bodkin suffices in the hands of those who will not fardels bear, not to mention husbands.

What a honeymoon was this for Lucretia! Her nostrils quivered, her lips worked as she vowed that if ever she was permitted to return she would pursue her treacherous husband and the scoundrel Featherbridge to the uttermost recesses of the law. And still she gathered from the character of her sea bedroom, from the absence of all instruments for purposes of navigation, and of all hints of a masculine presence, that she was to dwell alone, and from this perception her cold, chaste, passionless spirit sucked in a little comfort. What would her mother think when she came to learn the truth? Unfortunately, Lucretia felt secretly convinced that Mrs. Lane would approve on the whole of Frank's stratagem as rescuing both herself and her daughter from a most anomalous and gossip-breeding position. It was not as though Captain Francis Reynolds had kidnapped Lucretia Lane, a disdainful, handsome young woman, a prize not only for beauty, but for money. He had beguiled his own wife into his arms! The fittest of all harbours for her to bring up in, the safest and surest casket in which to deposit the jewel of her life.

This sort of reasoning would occur to Lucretia no doubt, but not in a convincing way. She might have been agitated by such reflections but not persuaded, as a sea-fowl when the waves pass under it is not carried forward, but moves up and down. She had no fear of violence; she very well knew that she was deeply and devotedly loved. But she burnt with wrath when she considered how she had been tricked and trapped. And again she wept, and sometimes wildly stepped the narrow-carpeted space of deck, and sometimes paused to listen, with vulgar surmises occasionally breaking in: such as, would Frank keep her locked up until she consented? Did he mean to keep her throughout the voyage, or did he merely intend to terrify her into the submission of a wife? If so, then persistent obstinacy must result in his sending her ashore before the ship was fairly away from England. Where would she be allowed to take her meals? Would she be permitted to go on deck?

Hark! What noise was that? Merely the sounds of the helm, the scrape of the wheel-chain, the jar of an old-fashioned system of steering.

She looked through the scuttle, and perceived that the ship was in motion. The pilot was in charge, and the captain was at large. Lucretia heard the key turned in her cabin door, and Reynolds entered. He looked at her wistfully and said—

"We have started. The voyage has begun, Creeshie. Though you may not forgive me for a little, I am happy. It is as it should be, as your mother could wish it to be, as you, dearest, will soon admit it ought to be."

"Do you mean to land me?" she exclaimed, with fire in her eyes.

"No."

"Do you intend to carry me all the way to the South American port you are sailing to?"

"Yes, and back again."

"You are a black-hearted wretch!" she exclaimed, working her hands hysterically. "If I live I'll punish you!"

"The voyage will do you good," he said, in an easy voice of good-nature, almost cheerful. "This is a stout little ship, and in her day she was a proud one. You have the figure for a rolling deck, and the eyes for a tropic calm."

"You are no gentleman!" she exclaimed, frowning at him. "Would any gentleman treat a woman as you are treating me?"

"Talk to me as my wife and I will listen to you," he responded. "What good will scolding do? I am not changed. I am as I was when we first met, and as I was when you said "Yes" to me, and we kissed, and you gave me a rose from your breast. You cannot forget such things! I have you, and I will keep you, and you shall thank me yet, Creeshie."

"I demand to be sent on shore!" she exclaimed, lifting her foot and bringing it down with an angry slap on the deck.

"Those whom God hath joined together let no man put asunder," said Captain Reynolds. "Why should I divorce you? We love and we lose, and the poet tells us that it is better to love and lose than never to love at all. I love you, and I don't mean to lose you. No, Crish, that ring has a meaning as deep as your life and mine, which are one."

She passionately seized the wedding-ring on her finger as though she would tear it off. But she did no more than that. In the minute of silence that followed he grew stern, and looked at her gloomily and even forbiddingly, as though he would have her know that he was her lord, and that one of her vows was obedience, which formed the third of the trinity which included love and honour; but if temper had not blinded her she would have seen that this look was but a mask; indeed, the glow of his love coloured the whole man, and rendered her conduct inexplicable; for we recognize the passion of chastity in the vows of the nun, but it is impossible to interpret precisely that quality in the vows of the bride.

"You will understand," said he, "now that the ship is under way that you can come and go, and do what you please. This cabin has been prepared for you, and for you only. You can take your meals alone or with me at the cabin table as you choose."

In all this he was unconsciously answering the questions which had run in her head before he arrived. He proceeded—

"You have but to name a desire, and if it's in the power of the sea-life to gratify it, you shall not be disappointed. You have nothing to fear. If you can find the elements of happiness in you, you shall not miss in me a solid foundation for the erection of your temple."

He viewed her steadfastly whilst her eyes glowed at him with indignation and scorn, and, rounding on his heel, he walked out.

Her mind fell into a hurry of desperate thought. The idea possessed her to write a letter—she gazed about her for writing materials; nothing of the sort was visible. She was very ignorant of the sea, had some

vague fancy of a passing boat, of throwing a letter into
it and begging the people to post it. But to whom
should she write? there was but one—her mother. And
what could her mother do, even if she proved willing to
separate them now that they were together?

Her reflections grew pale with something like despair.
What a base trick to play her! Helplessness added
fuel to wrath. To bring her away, too, without clothes!
How on earth was she to manage with only the things
she had on, when she had understood from Frank—yes,
she called him Frank to herself—that the outward
passage might run into three, or even four months; for
the ship was bound round the Horn, and from the
Thames to Poposa is a long navigation for an old-
fashioned, composite sailing ship, hedged about by
those conditions of calms and head winds, and long
heaving-to's, with the arrest of ice and other familiar
causes of delay which take no part in the voyage of the
steamer.

She determined to go on deck. Her cabin had been
a prison, and was an exasperation to her. And now she
resolved, even before she quitted her sleeping-room, to
adopt and express a posture of mind that should prove
a death-blow to her husband's expectations. We shall
presently see what she meant to do.

The cabin was lighted; a broad flame of oil in a
glass globe swung pulses of radiance through the atmosphere to the bulkheads, and the sheen rippled in bright
wood, in cutlery, and crockery, and glass. Stars of the
evening trembled in the skylight. It was hard upon
seven o'clock. The cloth was spread for a meal in the
cabin. The servant, who no doubt had received instructions from the captain, stepped up to Lucretia with a
mighty fine air of respect, and asked if he should serve

tea to her. Yes ; her throat was a little dry with tears
and constriction and angry words, and she waited, not
seated, standing beside the table, whilst the cabin
servant went forward to the galley. Occasionally sounds
broke from the interior, noises of straining like to the
groans delivered by old furniture at midnight. This
was a very new scene of life to the lady, and she looked
about her with petulant disgust, with a ceaseless com-
plaining of heart that she should have been betrayed by
a most ignoble trick into a captivity that was really
worse than gaol, as the sage pointed out, for in a ship
you are not only locked up, but you stand to be
drowned.

Whilst she waited for a cup of tea, Mr. Featherbridge
came down the companion-steps on his way to his
berth. He started at sight of her, and averted his face
as he passed. She followed him with a gaze of withering intensity and dislike. She looked a handsome
figure in her hat and jacket ; the oil flame glorified her
hair ; it gave a delicacy to her extreme pallor ; it
accentuated the dark depth of her eyes, and lighted a
little star of beauty in each. Why on earth could not
this woman be commonly human, and take her husband
for better or for worse ? It was Fontenelle who proposed the erection of statues to beautiful women. He
would have gone further ; built an immense hall, in
which figures in wax of the beautiful women of the
country apparelled in the fashion, would be collected.
In such a vast and engaging museum Lucretia would
have made no inconsiderable show.

The servant arrived with the tea-pot and milk, and
placed some thin bread and butter and cake on the
table. She filled a cup, and sipped it, standing. As she
sipped, her husband came out of his cabin.

E

" I am glad to see you are taking some refreshment," said he, looking at her with an appearance of moving affection.

She held her eyes off him, and curled her lip, and kept silence.

"Oh, I forgot to tell you," he continued briskly, as though he would have his good-humour shear, as the cutwater of a ship the wrathful billow, through her rage and resentment, "that I sent a wire to your mother to forward your clothes to Falmouth, where we shall call for them."

Her answer, without looking at him, was a sneer, and she turned her back upon him and drank her tea. It was pretty clear now that she had made up her mind not to speak to him, to be to him a shape without a spirit, a statue without a soul, a lighthouse without a lantern, a moon without glory—a something of which the absence would be a blessing in comparison with the discomfort of its presence.

He told the servant to light the lamp in Mrs. Reynolds' cabin, and passed on deck. In a few minutes she put down the cup and went up the steps. Land and river were clothed in the early October night. The ship was floating restfully in the wake of the tug, whose shape was a shadow, and whose line of smoke as it rose almost perpendicular from the funnel was often full of the spangles of the furnace. There was majesty in the figure of the ship, in the solemn lifting of her masts crossed with yards symmetrically braced, each glimmering with its length of pale canvas ; there was poetry in the lonely figure of the helmsman at the wheel, the incarnation of that spirit of sentience which to the meditative eye is visible in the motions of the compass. Gleams of light, falling one knew not whence, swarmed capriciously in the water; yellow sparks dotted the dark shores, and here and there a lighted house touched the gloom with a misty dash of radiance, like phosphor in brine; visionary forms of ships passed; the coloured signals of the sea in red and green and white shone in the gloom, or hovered over the dark breast of river like lights about a swamp, or the tremulous meteors of the highway, which affright the clown, and hurry him along in sweat to report a lie, namely, a ghost.

Lucretia moved warily about the deck, giving her husband a wide berth. He stood in conversation with the pilot, but whilst she continued above he held her in the tail of his eye. There was a sheen of lamplight and starlight in the atmosphere, and if the expression of the face could not be read the behaviour of the eyes could be followed. Captain Reynolds observed the pilot watching Lucretia.

" She is my wife," he said.

" Oh yes. I thought as much," answered the Trinity House man, whose square trunk, compact of coat and shawl, lightly swayed on rounded legs under skirts that half concealed them. And to himself he added, " She may be his wife, but she don't seem much of a companion."

The evening was perfectly tranquil; the river glass-smooth. A large star or two that went in the water with the ship, hung like a prism of white light, but the movement of the vessel made a little wind, and the threads of hair on Lucretia's brow danced to it as though they were Coleridge's summer leaf in an entranced night on a topmost bough, and she felt a bit chilly. She stepped from the side at which she had been looking at the shore and occasionally glancing at the man who conversed with her husband, and going to the sailor at the wheel asked who that person was who was with the captain.

"The pilot, mum," answered the fellow.

"Does he remain in the ship?" inquired Lucretia.

"No, mum. I expect he'll go ashore at Deal."

She said, "Thanks," and walked to the ship's side again, where she debated whether she should appeal to the pilot to help her to return home. But the sense of the absurd flavoured her anger; she was not without a good and even a strong understanding, and the ridiculous was inevitably the inherent condition of every emotion. For mind, like matter, has the power of selecting its colour, and not the most tempestuous mood could be hers without its taking the hue of the imbecility of the position in which she had partly placed herself and partly been placed. It was not conceivable that the pilot would meddle with what he might regard as a twopenny quarrel betwixt husband and wife, some jibbing perhaps on her part in jealousy. At all events, she reflected that it would be impossible for her to explain to a rough seaman, such as a pilot, her reasons for declining to live with Captain Reynolds whom she would be bound to admit was her husband. Nor was Lucretia a person to court discomfiture. So, with a shudder, contrived partly by the temperature, partly by disgust and a sense of helplessness, she returned to her cabin and closed the door.

Reynolds' appeal to her through the medium of the cabin furniture lay in other directions than that of the toilet-table. Against a bulkhead were ranged some hanging book-shelves, and had she condescended to examine their burden she would have found the volumes by her favourite authors, and those which were new to her were such as she would have chosen. This alone proved that Reynolds' scheme to kidnap her had been long preconcerted, and that he regarded the sequel as a certain triumph to him. She sat in an armchair as comfortable as the one in which Miss Ford had been seated whilst Lucretia dressed for her marriage, but remained clothed as for the deck or shore. In about half an hour some one knocked on the door.

She cried quickly, "Who's that?"

"I'm John, mum."

"What do you want, I say?"

On this he opened the door and told her that the captain had sent him to inquire what she would like for supper. She was again thirsty, but answered—

"I want nothing."

He stared at her with a mind that lagged heavily in the rear of his eyes, and said—

"There's chicken and cold lamb and cold boiled beef, and claret and sherry—what will it please you to take?"

"Have you got any soda-water?"

"Yes, mum."

"Bring me some claret and soda-water!"

"Yes, mum. And what to eat?"

"Cut a couple of thin ham sandwiches!"

He went out, and the moment he was gone she fell into a rage and began to cry. It was evident that she was the only woman in the ship. There was no stewardess. To think of being waited on and perhaps nursed if she should be sea-sick by a tarry young Jack in a sleeved waistcoat, who breathed Spanish onions, and who was so awed by the sight of her that, like people who cannot work and talk at the same time, he neglected his business in viewing her! The position was to be summed up in the old Frenchman's saying concerning a religious drama, "C'est une chose assez risible, mais il manque des rieurs."

When the sandwiches had been brought to her, she locked the door. Her husband, however, did not trouble her. There was no motion as yet in the ship: the cabin deck seemed as fixed a platform as the land. Sometimes she heard the voices of men talking as they ate at table. The tiller chains overhead occasionally strained, and a voice of lamentation sometimes proceeded from some timber weary of its obligation of cohesion, or from the cargo underfoot. Presently she looked at the time and found the hour half-past nine. She wound up her watch, and feeling extravagantly exhausted, what with her journey, what with the amazing passions her betrayal had lighted in her, and what with the tears she had shed, idle and most unworthy tears, she resolved upon taking some rest; so she removed her hat and jacket and got into the bunk, otherwise fully apparelled, and covered herself with the light eider-down quilt. It was a coffin of a bedstead, something very removed from all her experiences of going to rest at night; but novelty was not to negative the commands of Nature, and in ten minutes she was sleeping peacefully.

All through the night the ship was towed down the river into the opening breast of ocean, where the land to starboard rounds into the Channel; but when, next day, a little forest of masts which shadowed the horizon abreast of Deal in delicate pencils, was hove into view, a south-west breeze sprang up and a small swell came rolling along under it, and the *Flying Spur* began to drop curtseys to the mother whose child she was. A south-west wind tarnishes the brightness of the sky and is often a wet breeze. It may lock a sailing-ship up in the Downs when she is outward bound, and the tug that was pulling the *Flying Spur* was hailed, and her master informed by Mr. Featherbridge, who shouted to him from the starboard cathead, that the ship would bring up. Which she did in due course, abreast of Deal Castle, and the pilot went ashore.

Now, at the hour of breakfast, John had knocked on Lucretia's door and found her up. He had received her orders, and taken a tray to her. She was indeed pale, but looked the fresher and the better for many hours of profound oblivion. The sea was then smooth, and the ship floated steadily after the tug. The anchor had been let go shortly before one o'clock, and the tide had canted the vessel somewhat athwart the swell. She rolled as well as pitched, not, it is true, heavily, but with a behaviour that could have been hardly deemed *nursing* by a sensitive stomach. It was breezing pleasantly for homeward bounders, and tacks-and-sheetsmen of all rigs blew with the old moaning of the sea in their lifting white breasts through the Gulls, past anchored ships looking withered as winter pines, with here and there a gaunt steam tramp yearning through wide nostrils at the swell, now breaking into a wet flash of red light as she rolled, now soaring with balloon-round bows, now immodestly kicking up her heels in her *can-can* of the water, to the shameless revelation of the blades of her propeller. Dirty clouds, like smoke, were scattering up from France, and at times slapped a shower into the eye.

"If it was in the east," said Captain Reynolds to the mate, "I should consider this berth good for six weeks. If Mrs. Reynolds comes on deck and sees that town close aboard, there'll be trouble."

His reference was to Deal, which lay abreast, with the foam of the breaker snaked along the base of the slope of grey shingle like a mighty hawser of silver wire. The church spire stretched its vane to the flash of the noon : windows sparkled in terraces : in the foreground were shapes of boats on the pebbly acclivity, and the green land soared to the giant Foreland, with its tower of splendour by night, and its majesty of austere white rampart by day.

It was the dinner hour, and the meal was served below, and the captain and Mr. Featherbridge repaired to the table, leaving the second mate to watch the ship, and John went to Lucretia's door to knock and inquire what she would be pleased to have for dinner.

CHAPTER IV

A CHANGE OF MIND

THE cabin servant, as we have seen, knocked upon the door of Lucretia's berth, but obtained no reply. He applied his knuckles more boisterously, and Captain Reynolds turned in his chair at the head of the table to look and listen.

" Doesn't she answer ? " he exclaimed, springing up.

He tried the handle, and strained the door with his shoulder ; the key was turned in the lock. Reynolds smote the door four or five times with his fist, crying, " We must force this door if you will not unlock it." And this he shouted in a strong stern note of command. His face changed when the silence continued beyond a few seconds. He cried, with the swiftness of alarm—

" Go forward, and tell the bo'sun to lay aft at once with tools to force this door ! "

John sprang up the companion-steps as though driven by a bayonet. The ship's pitching and tossing filled the interior with all sorts of noises, and though Reynolds bent his ear in such passion of attention as rose to pain, no sounds that he could attribute to the lips of Lucretia reached him.

" I hope to God nothing has come to her ! " said he to Mr. Featherbridge, who had risen from his meal, and was standing beside his captain and friend.

" She has not been seen all the morning, sir."

"She has not come on deck," said the Captain. "She breakfasted, and John reported her to me as all right."

But whilst he spoke Lucretia's threat to her mother to poison herself if her husband attempted force or broke through the door, recurred to him, and before the boatswain arrived the man's heart was wild with anxiety and apprehension.

The daylight in the companion-way was eclipsed by the intervention of a figure, and down came the boatswain, who was also the ship's carpenter—a sturdy seaman named Martin Webb—whose eagle nose stood out like a flying-jib betwixt a pair of whiskers standing from his cheeks like the frill of an enraged hen going open-beaked at another.

"As quick as you can, Webb!" said the captain.

And after a few sounds resembling the hammering of the old-fashioned carpenter before the old-fashioned anchor falls from the old-fashioned cathead, and fills the hollow forecastle with the roaring of iron links in an iron eye, the door flew open, and Reynolds rushed in.

What did he, what did the others who stood in the doorway, behold? Merely a woman with dark red hair, and a face of the pallor of virgin wax, lying in a bunk under an eider-down quilt with half-closed eyes, motionless in the prostration of that dire distemper, sea-sickness. The wash-basin was on the deck beside her bunk. One arm overhung the bunk-board, and the hand, with its long, nervous fingers, was suspended just above the deck, and looked as though shaped from the petals of the moon-lily.

Reynolds knelt by her side. She was not dead, but she was scarcely conscious, and the whites of her eyes visible past the lashes of the half-sealed lids, made of

her face such a counterfeit presentment of death as
might have misled a skilled medical inspection. The
husband felt the pale, cold, hanging wrist, and found a
thin pulse in it. Then, lifting the hand, and placing it
upon the eider-down, he turned his head, and asked
Featherbridge for a wine-glass of brandy and water,
which was immediately procured and given to him.
Nodding at the fiddles on the toilet-table, he told
Featherbridge to bring him that bottle of eau-de-
Cologne. He put his arm, with a wonderful tenderness
of love and sympathy, under his wife's head, and succeeded in draining some brandy and water through her
lips, and extending his handkerchief to Featherbridge,
he bade him soak it with eau-de-Cologne, and this he
put to his wife's forehead, kneeling beside her, watching,
and now waiting.

"My poor sweet," he thought, "alone, and so ill;
almost dying! Oh, why, dearest, do you wish to abandon
me?"

He told Featherbridge to finish his meal and close
the door upon him, to relieve the second mate, and to
instantly report if a shift of wind happened, as he would
get under way forthwith. And he was left alone with
his wife, whose lips he kissed, whose hair he smoothed,
whose hand he caressed, until, in about half an hour, she
exhibited some signs of returning animation. The
white lids lifted, and the rich brown irises rolled down,
but fireless, though with a little life of wonder in them
when the shape of her husband filled their horizon.

Throughout that afternoon he hung over his wife,
never suffering the tenderness of his ministering to be
affected by her silence—that silence which is more
irritating than a sneer—as an expression of the aversion
she sought to render as manifest as nausea would permit,

of the wounding and inflaming nature of her resolution to release herself from him and preserve the severe chastity of the beautiful, passionless, faithless, and cruel Ego which she doted on, and whose deliciousness was not likely to cloy *her*. No, the sweet idea of her purity was not to sicken *her* soon, if ever; and there was his deception to resent, and his outrage on her liberty to punish.

Never once would she answer him, though his few appeals to her to be his wife were most affecting with his pity for her sufferings, and eloquent with his love for her, and sweet with his contrition for the trick which had betrayed her to her honourable place by his side.

She did not know where the ship was. She would naturally bring the ignorance of a schoolgirl to the sea. What could she have told you about the English Channel? Had she been informed that the town of Deal, which she had visited when spending a fortnight at Ramsgate, was within a twenty minutes' pull, she would not have been too seasick to have demanded her release—to have raged in her request to be put ashore. But the vessel was rolling and pitching, and Lucretia was convinced that the *Flying Spur* was miles out of sight of land upon the ocean, sailing on a voyage of which the contemplation was like that of eternity.

Towards sundown Captain Reynolds sent for some tea, cake, and thin bread and butter, and placed the tray by her side. She would not look at him; she would not speak to him. No corpse could have been more mute under the grief-stricken gaze of the mourner. He went to the door with a dark face, and, removing the key from the lock, turned to her, and said—

"I would not advise you to bolt yourself in. At sea tragic surprises come in a moment. If we should be run into, so that the ship might easily founder in five minutes, how are you to be rescued if you shoot this bolt or turn this key, and are too ill to leave your bunk, or lie in ignorance of what is happening ? "

He paused to hear if she would answer. Her response was a sneer and a diligently averted gaze. With a heavy sigh and a hot heart he walked out and went on deck.

This man had dreamt of a long honeymoon on the ocean. He and Lucretia would have watched the sunset together. He would have explained to her the heraldry of the sky—talked of eyeless fish in water three miles deep. She would have viewed with him the moon-like bleakness and desolation and lifelessness of the iceberg. He would have instructed her in the causes of the colours of the ocean—why it is green, or grey, or blue, or black. In his handsome young wife he knew that he could, and she had been willing, have found a companion whose intellect was capable of translating the pictures she viewed into a wide poetic and romantic meaning. Such behaviour as hers, such a disappointment as his, might well clothe the manliest and most cheerful spirit in crape, and deeply black-edge the remaining pages in the story of his life.

He paced the deck alone, lost in thought. The beacons of the sea were here and there leaping into the dusk from the lightships off that yellow serpent of shoal called the Goodwins, ashore from the windy headland whence streamed a far-reaching splendour ; from the fore-stays of moored ships, and the familiar red eye of the port lantern went sliding up Channel, dimming yet the shadow that conveyed it ; and the familiar green eye stole glimmering down, wan and elusive as a glow-worm on a summer evening misty with dew. It was still blowing a fresh moist breeze from the westward of south-west, and a starless night was at hand. The waters ran in flickers of froth, and broke into sounds of sobbing along the bends, and the tall masts waved in stately measures, growing spectral under the translating wand of the dusk.

Featherbridge stood in the waist, leaning upon the rail, gazing shorewards. A riding-light shone on the stay forward, and shapes of men were on the forecastle, but you heard nothing but the noise of the wind aloft and of streaming waters, and a dreary clattering of booms ill-secured. After many turns Reynolds went to the side of the mate and said—

"Featherbridge, she is making me the unhappiest man under God. Shall I persevere? Shall I send her ashore? I have her, and I tell you that the idea of parting with her is hell to me."

"Well, sir," answered Featherbridge, after a little thinking, "as I ventured to tell you, when this scheme came into your head, it seemed to me, and I still think, that had you taken this voyage and left her to her mother, you would have found her all you could wish on your return. It is a state of mind that wants time, and I fancy that violence will harden it."

Captain Reynolds looked during a considerable interval at the lights ashore, and then, with a stamp of the foot and a slap of his thigh, he burst out vehemently—

"No, by God! It has given me great trouble to get her. She is with me, and so far as *that* goes, things are as they ought to be. I'll not part with her. If time is to operate ashore, why not here? Here there is at least the constant appeal of the sight of me, of the knowledge of my presence in the ship. But she

ashore and I away, why—this craze might induce her
to take some extraordinary step. Her mother has no
control over her; she might enter a convent."

" Not as a married woman, sir, I think," said the
mate, with a slow shake of his head.

"A married woman!" exclaimed the captain, with
bitter scorn. "Is it the wedding-ring, is it the words
uttered by the priest, that make a woman married to
a man? No; I've got her, and I'll keep her."

The wind shifted at daybreak. It had slipped well
into the eastward of south, and was a clear steady
breeze. The boatswain summoned the crew of the
Flying Spur to get the ship under way. The windlass
was manned, and the castanets of the pawls timed the
chorus which accompanied the entrance, link by link,
of the cable through the hawse-pipe. The date was
the 10th of October. The morning broke fair, with a
fine high sky of feather-shaped clouds. The sea was
a magazine of colours and floating life in motion,
for all the outward-bound vessels were getting their
anchors, and the sun poured a delicate pink light upon
mounting canvas and leaning shafts of cloths, the dark
red sail of the coaster and the white wings of the yacht.
Old Deal stretched salt and sweet as a fresh mackerel
with its wool-white line of surf and its greenish sparkle
of window to the risen day-beam. On the *Flying Spur*
sail by sail was set until the ship was clothed in breasts
of cloth, narrowing at each summit, three pyramids
with curves of canvas like the sea-gull's wings between,
and glowing with the soft purity of untrodden snow in
that autumn morning sunshine.

When breakfast was on the table John knocked on
Lucretia's door. He was told to enter, whence it
appears that the door was not bolted, whilst it could

not have been locked, as Reynolds had withdrawn the key. The captain was eating some breakfast, and the mate had charge of the ship. The cabin servant, coming out of Lucretia's berth, stepped to Reynolds' side, and said—

"The lady asks for some tea and dry toast, sir."

"Is she dressed?"

"Yes, sir, the same as yesterday. She is lying in her bunk."

"How does she seem?"

"She looks nicely," answered John.

"Get her whatever she wants," said Reynolds.

His brow was heavy with thought as he sat alone eating. It was not difficult to see that some consideration, which had suddenly visited him, had sunk deep and was perplexing him. There was in his glances from his plate to the bulkheads about him, and up through the skylight, that imperious vivacity of eye which tells of a soul in storm and conflict. The lightning of the mind was in his regard. He closed his knife and fork, left his seat, and tapped on his wife's door.

"Who's that?" she asked.

"I—your husband—Frank."

She did not answer. He turned the handle and walked in. She was seated in the armchair, very pale; but sleep and time had discharged the sunk and hollow look of nausea, and the very neglect that her hair discovered rendered her the more admirable and pleading to his sight.

When he entered she looked down and stared with riveted eyes upon her lap as though she was in some hypnotic sleep, and the lashes of the lids were impenetrable veils of dark red golden hair. But he observed that she had formed her mouth into a sneer, and there was scorn and wrath in the dishonouring facial expression. It was as though he was a spider or a frog.

"Won't you speak to me, Lucretia?" he said.

She held her eyes steadily fixed upon her lap, nor did her sneer change by so much as an effect produced by a single touch of the pencil.

"Won't you even look at me?" he said again.

Marry come up, not she! He stood viewing her for a little with a frown; but, as she would not look at him nor speak to him, he left the cabin, feeling mortally humiliated. Here was conduct that was darting lances into his *amour-propre*, and his spirit writhed with the pain of the wounds. The old poet says—

> "Sweet are the kisses, the endearments sweet
> When like desires and like affections meet."

Where was he to find sweetness in this union if she held on as she was? Was he not her husband? Was he not a gentleman? It is true he had brought her into the ship by a stratagem, but surely the love that lay at the root of his action should woo and win forgiveness for a greater offence than that. "On pardonne tant que l'on aime," says the French cynic; and Lucretia's inexorable resentment, vital even in the prostration of nausea, was an augury he could not misinterpret. He had used her with a chivalry which the majority of husbands would have held her unworthy of. Moreover, her behaviour was belittling him in the eyes of his officers, and the gossip of this strange affair would reach the forecastle, and he understood the character of sailors well enough to imagine that what might be said

F

in that hollow humming sea-parlour with much expectoration and a vast variety of oaths, would not contribute greatly to the dignity of command and the requirements of discipline.

Once the swelling bosoms of the sails had taken impulse and life from the wind, the *Flying Spur* proved herself nimble of heel. She sloped her masts and slanted her cutwater, and bit with a keen fore-tooth into the gleaming curves, filling the air round about her bows with beauties and miracles: the lightning of foam, the rainbow of the prism, the emerald-green and diamond-white of gems. At noon the wind headed the ship and she broke off three points with her yards braced well forwards. Dinner was served to Lucretia in her cabin, but in the afternoon, about half-past three, when her husband was on deck, she made her appearance and stood in the companion-way, holding by the hand that wore her wedding-ring, and stared about her. A very fine form, as Jack at the wheel thought, her eyes dark and glowing like the heavens at night, her lips slightly parted as though in relish of the sweetness of the wind that swept betwixt them. She stepped out and crossed over to Mr. Ralland, the fat, warm-coloured, yellow-haired second mate, and addressed him as though her husband had been left ashore, or was dead.

" In what part of the sea is this ship ? " she asked.

" In the English Channel, madam."

" Are we far from England ? "

" There is England yonder, madam," answered Mr. Ralland, with a smile that seemed satirical but was not, pointing to some blue films hovering over the sea-line on the starboard quarter.

" Have we left Falmouth ? "

" No, madam ; we are making for Falmouth."

" When are we likely to get there ? "

" Why," answered Mr. Ralland, looking aloft, " the wind's drawn ahead, and we're off our course, and shall have to go about unless the breeze shifts again. So that," said he, with a rather nervous look in the direction of the captain, whose interpretation of this conversation with his wife he did not like to think of, " I don't expect we shall reach Falmouth much before late on the thirteenth or it may be the four-teenth."

She looked at the films of land with a hard, pale face of resolution, and it was impossible even for Mr. Ralland to miss observing that she had arrived at a determination to take a step, and that this time she meant to score.

Captain Reynolds was pacing the weather-side of the quarterdeck when she arrived. She went to lee-ward to the gangway, so as to remove herself as far from him as possible without invading the precincts of the sailors' quarters, and she stood with her arms resting upon the bulwark-rail, looking at the horizon or at the forming or dissolving mounds of water, or at two or three colliers and a screw tramp with raised bows in the outline of a cow lying down. Two sailors were working side by side forward. That they were British and not foreign seamen may be judged by the following sentences that passed between them.

" Fine young party that ! What's called a piece of all-right."

" She's the old man's wife," answered Bill, meaning by " old man " Captain Reynolds.

" Ow d'yer know ? " says Jim.

" Aint she a-treatin' of him as if she was ? If she

worn't his wife——" and Bill, with a wink, nudges Jim in the ribs.

"What's she doin' here if they don't get on?" said Jim.

"Think 'e's goin' to leave the likes of her ashore?" answered Bill. "He'll wait upon yer! Where'd she be when he tarned up? A wife may be like a bad thick 'un; sights better than the real thing to look at, but yer dars'nt spend 'un. Ye've got to keep carryin' of it about. Yon's a thick 'un without much ring in her, you lay."

"Not even the weddin'-ring, p'raps," said Jim.

"Oh, I allow you'll find that all right. He'd live in fear of us men."

"'Ow's a man goin' to command a ship that can't command a woman?" asked Jim.

"If a woman won't answer her 'ellum," replied Bill, "what are ye going to do? You bet the old man's tried it hard-a-port, and hard-a-starboard, and what luffin' 'ud do, or if 'ellum's a-lee would mix nicely in the biling. I think myself," said he, very gravely, "that some women is best left alone. If they prove onmanageable, then turn to and secure the 'ellum, and you'll find the party'll take up her own position and ride comfortable."

It will be judged from this fragment of conversation that Captain Reynolds had not erred in the anticipation of his forecastle's comments.

As eight bells (four o'clock) were being struck, Lucretia left the rail at which she had been standing, and walked up to Mr. Ralland, who was in the gangway abreast of her. Captain Reynolds continued to stump his lonely principality of quarterdeck, betwixt the wheel and the skylight.

"Of course," exclaimed Lucretia, haughtily, "you know that I am the captain's wife."

Mr. Ralland, staring at her, stuttered "Yes," and instantly looked ill at ease. He was waiting for Mr. Featherbridge to relieve him, and disliked this being talked to by Mrs. Reynolds in the presence of the commander of the ship, whose despotic importance was great enough to ruin him, and the whole estate of this fat involuntary cynic lay in his calling.

"I was brought to this ship by a base stratagem," said Lucretia, "and I am imprisoned in her, as you are easily able to see. I desire to return home to my mother. Will you tell your captain that if he does not allow me to leave the ship at Falmouth, I will ask the sailors to help me to free myself? I will appeal to those men who will not allow a woman to be ill-treated. I have always heard that sailors are warm-hearted, and I beg you to tell Captain Reynolds, that unless he liberates me I will go right amongst his crew there, and tell them my story."

So saying, she slightly inclined her head, and went towards the companion-hatch as Mr. Featherbridge stepped out of it. She darted at him the lightning of her eyes, under the shadow of her frown, and sank down the hatchway out of sight.

Mr. Ralland, with a mind slightly muddled, was about to go below to compose himself over a pipe and a book in his bunk, throughout the first dog-watch, should there not come a call for "All hands!" Captain Reynolds called him.

"Mrs. Reynolds has been asking you questions, I think?"

The second mate coloured up, and answered that she had.

"What does she want to know?"

"Where we are, sir."

"Yes?"

"And how long it will take us to fetch Falmouth."

"Yes?"

The fat and purple young man hung in the wind, and after a cough or two said—

"She asked me to tell you——" and he quoted Lucretia's threat, word for word.

"Is that all?" inquired Reynolds, whose expression of face was stern but calm in rigidity.

"That's all, sir."

"Thanks."

Mr. Ralland slunk to his quarters. The captain took a few turns; then, catching Featherbridge's eye, he invited him to his side by a toss of the head.

"She'll do at this for another hour," said he. He looked aloft and to windward. "Featherbridge, I have formed my resolution. I have made up my mind to send Mrs. Reynolds home when we arrive at Falmouth."

"I am sure I think you will be acting wisely if you do, sir," answered Featherbridge.

"She is not to be conquered. She is not to be got at. I could not have believed that her heart was so hard. I make every allowance for her indignation at being trapped, but is there no love in her to help me? Nothing left of the old feeling which induced her to take me?"

The captain's voice trembled slightly, but his face continued stern and tranquil with the tranquillity of the marble face whose expression is that of deep resentment and a heart on fire. And, in truth, it was quite possible the slow-souled Mr. Featherbridge to suspect in

Captain Reynolds a languid motion of mind that must presently harden into aversion, for the elasticity of even such a love as this man bore this woman has its limitations : the tissues crack, the passion sinks shapeless; it takes another name, and a feeling that may threaten the wreck of two lives, replaces the ruined sentiment.

"I did what I thought it was right I should do," continued Captain Reynolds, "and I find that I was mistaken. My blunder arose from an imperfect knowledge of the nature I was dealing with. Could I foresee that the change that has come to her would prove as fixed as though it had been inherent ?—which it never was, for, so help me God, no woman could have been more tender, more sweet, and docile in the privileges she permitted. Many will tell me that I have not acted the part of a gentleman ; but I am a man, and I feel as a man, and she has not treated me as I deserve to be treated by her. Featherbridge, you will continue your kindness to the end. I will ask you to see her ashore. No doubt her luggage will have been received at the station before our arrival."

He broke off. He could not bring himself to say more. He was unmanned, and went to his cabin to collect himself.

Throughout that night the ship was a frequent scene of disturbance. The wind headed her off her course, and to prevent her from running now into the coast of France, or now into the coast of England, the captain put her about—an evolution in merchantmen that is commonly attended with great uproar. Men howl upon ropes as they drag at them. The captain shouts, the mates bawl; the ship plunges, staggers, stops, and reels; the wind roars in the shrouds; the fingers of

the gale sweep the canvas into a slatting like a volleying
of stones from a quay side into a hold; and there is
much confusion below of nimble crockery and sliding
commodities. When it comes to, "Let go and haul!"
the fore-topsail-yard swings, the jib-sheets leap the
stays, the ship leans, and, after a pause of thought,
lets drive her keen tooth into the surge, which parts in
slinging and singing masses of giddy splendour, and
she is again off and away, with her sailors coiling
the ropes over the pins, and the captain and mates
staring aloft to observe the lay of the yards and the
set of the canvas. The scene is one of inextricable
complexity to a landsman's eye on a fine day and in
summer waters. But in the darkness of an autumn
Channel moonless night, when a strong head sea is
running, and the work is to be discharged by two only
of the five fallible mortal senses—namely, touch and
hearing—the scene, or at least as much of it as is
visible, takes for the landsman an element of fear,
and passengers have been known to go to prayers
on their own account when the ship was in the
agonies of "mainsail haul" on a dark night blowing hard, the captain suspecting that the white water
on the horizon was breakers, and that he was several
leagues out of his reckoning, and the mate convinced that if she hung another minute she would
be in irons, and they would have to wear ship, shoal or
no shoal.

When the *Flying Spur* was put about a little before
nine on the night of this day we are dealing with, the
noise on the deck was so great that Lucretia in her
cabin believed the vessel was sinking. The ship, as the
helm was put down, met the seas and pitched heavily;
the rudder jarred; the tramp of feet overhead was as

though all hands were fighting for their lives to get into the boats. Lucretia heard shouts and loud, hoarse bawlings, and, white with fear, with a heart beating quickly—for she could not but remember what her husband had told her about the ship being run into and sunk in five minutes—she opened the door of her berth ; but nobody was in the cabin. It was "all hands" on deck, and John was amongst them.

She stood waiting and hearkening in the doorway until she grew reassured by the comparative silence on deck and the steady floating motions of the ship, and then John's legs appeared on the ladder, and the man descended.

"What is the matter ? " cried Lucretia.

"We've been putting the ship about, mum," answered John.

"What do you mean by that ? "

"Laying her on the port tack for another board, mum."

Had he answered her in Chinese he would have been equally intelligible.

"Is there any danger ? " she asked.

"Lord love me, no, mum ! "

On which she closed the cabin door upon herself, not choosing that her husband should descend and behold her. And then she sat down and cried with rage and other emotions, and detested Frank for bringing her into such a situation, and vowing, whilst she mopped her fine eyes with her pocket-handkerchief, that if he did not release her at Falmouth, she would go amongst the crew, plead to them to help her to free herself, and gain her end, or render her husband's situation as captain of the ship impossible.

The night passed ; a night, as has been said, of

commotion and going about. At the breakfast-table,
Captain Reynolds asked Mr. Featherbridge to visit
his wife and acquaint her with her husband's intention
to send her ashore at Falmouth. There had come a
shift of wind in the morning watch, and the breeze was
so blowing as to allow the ship to look up for her
port. The morning sunshine clothed the glass of the
skylight with silver brightness. The sea ran with a
cradling motion ; through the scuttles you caught a
glimpse of the sparkling azure of it. Mr. Featherbridge did not relish his mission ; but he faced it like
a man, and, ascertaining from John, after Reynolds
had left the table, that Mrs. Reynolds had finished
her breakfast, he walked to the cabin door of the lady,
and knocked.

Who was that, she wanted to know.

"Mr. Featherbridge. I have come with a message
from the captain. May I enter?"

She immediately concluded that his errand was in
the interests of peace and conjugal felicity.

"I decline to meet you, and beg that you will not
come in," she cried.

"I believe the news I bring is what you will be glad
to hear," said Mr. Featherbridge.

After a pause, during which she thought of the
doctor's certificate and the livery of trouble Featherbridge had cunningly worn during his interview with
her mother at Chepstow Place, she said—

"You can come in."

He entered, bowed, and said, "I have been asked
by Captain Reynolds to inform you that you will be
put ashore at Falmouth, according to your request."

She stood holding by the table, swaying her fine
figure with the motions of the deck. Her face slightly

lightened as though to a sudden brightness of heart, but the expression soon faded.

"It is about time that Captain Reynolds acted like a man," she said coldly and haughtily.

Mr. Featherbridge secretly wondered what o'clock it would be when Mrs. Reynolds should think it time to act like a woman.

"The captain expects," says the mate, "that your luggage will be at the station, and I shall do myself the pleasure to attend to that and see you off."

She curled her lips at him before answering, and said—

"I shall not want to be seen off, thanks. I am quite capable of looking after myself. I shall require some money to pay my fare. I had but two sovereigns, which you saw me borrow from my mother."

"Captain Reynolds will see to that," said Mr. Featherbridge, who thought to himself, "If you were the only young woman in England, damme if I'd have you."

She turned to the scuttle or little window, in token that the interview was ended, and, after a slow look at her, Featherbridge walked out. He went to the captain, who was on deck.

"She is very willing to go, sir; but she won't allow me to escort her. She wishes to go alone."

"She shall have her way," answered Captain Reynolds, in a hard voice. " How does she seem?"

"Quite well, I think, sir."

"A stubborn soul, a very stubborn soul to bend," said Captain Reynolds, as though thinking aloud. "Such spirits need but a very little bending to break. I never could have believed it of her or in her. How does she look, do you say?"

"Why, very well, sir."

"What a fine creature to love and lose; to have, and not to be able to hold!" continued Reynolds, still talking as though he was thinking aloud. " I suppose she and I will never meet again."

"I wouldn't think such a thing, sir."

"Oh, my God, look at the chances against our meeting!" cried the captain, with a little storm of passion coming into his voice out of his heart. "It's not the risks only of our lives at sea; there's her nature, which will hold her aloof, and the longer she remains divorced from me the severer will grow the quality that keeps her divorced. A child—oh, a little child—something to humanize her, something to look with my eyes into hers"—he stepped to the rail, and stared away to sea. Featherbridge stood still. The captain returned.

"I suppose her reception of you was cold, perhaps insulting?" said he.

The mate answered, " No-oo, sir ; she says she wants some money. I saw her borrow two pounds from her mother, and she changed one when she insisted on paying for her ticket at Gravesend."

"I'll see to it," said Reynolds.

Half an hour later, he went below. He had lingered on deck trusting his wife would appear, for he loved to look at her. He entered his cabin, and opening a locker, took out a desk, which he unlocked, and from a corner of it picked up a small roll of Bank of England notes. He took two five-pound notes and placed them in a blank envelope, then stood hanging over the desk for a little while, musing; for a small parcel of his wife's letters lay there, and they set him thinking. He replaced the desk in the locker,

and, putting his head out, called to John, and told
him to give that envelope to Mrs. Reynolds. He
then got into his bunk to take some rest, for the night
had been full of business for him, and his whole being
felt strained.

CHAPTER V

THE WRECK

THE *Flying Spur* anchored in Falmouth Bay on the noon of October 13, 1890. She had no business at that port. When Mr. Blaney of Leadenhall Street, her owner, read the report in the shipping news of her having touched at Falmouth, he would probably assume that the crew had given trouble; a Dutchman, perhaps, had stabbed an Englishman, and the captain had been forced to put into Falmouth to supply the deficiencies caused by the knife, and to hand over the prisoner.

As a matter of fact, Reynolds was here to fetch his wife's clothes, and the owner's demands on him as a skipper must yield to that skipper's claims upon himself as a newly married man. And now his wife was going ashore to fetch her clothes herself, and take them home with her, and leave him.

The ship brought up with only her lighter canvas furled, for she was to sail again as soon as might be. It was noon; sweet and calm were the waters of this lovely harbour, glorious the land in the mantle of October, pleasant and fair to see the ships floating upon the mirror, whose margin reflected the burning leaf of autumn. Lucretia was in her cabin when the anchor was let go. She felt the thrill of the chain cable as it thundered through the hawse-pipe, but did

78

not know what it meant. Came a knock upon her
door. The inevitable, "Who is there?" followed.

"Mr. Ralland."

"Oh, walk in!"

The second mate entered, purple and shiny, cuplike
in form, very nervous in demeanour.

"If you are ready to go ashore, madam," said he,
"the boat is ready alongside, and I will steer you to
the landing-place."

She started, not until then realizing the arrival of
the ship. Into the pallor of her face passed a subtler
shade of whiteness, if one may so speak, indicating the
presence of the heart.

"I shall be on deck in five minutes," she answered;
and Mr. Ralland left her.

In five minutes she was attired in hat and jacket, and
with her went the umbrella which she had brought from
Chepstow Place. She passed through the companion-
way into an atmosphere quivering with brilliance, and,
without intention, met the eyes of her husband, who was
seated upon the grating abaft the wheel, in a place to
command a view of the deck and the departure of the
boat. She instantly looked away: no flush of cheek
indicated emotion, no dulness of eye, the sudden gush
of sadness from the springs of the soul. She saw Mr.
Ralland waiting at the open gangway, and went to him.
Mr. Featherbridge was doing some business of the ship
on the forecastle; but all the sailors on the deck, idling
or working, took a look at that fine figure as it passed
to the side, and, could their secret thoughts have been
interpreted, literature would be the richer by several
pages of original ideas.

The port quarter-boat had been lowered and manned,
and lay under the gangway ladder. Without looking

aft, where her husband was, without a glance around
her at the ship she was deserting, Lucretia put her foot
upon the steps and descended, and took her place in the
stern-sheets, where she was joined by Mr. Ralland, who,
catching hold of the yoke-lines, sang out, "Shove off!"
The oars dipped, and Lucretia was going home.

Reynolds, with his arms folded, watched the shape
of the receding boat, watched the diminishing form of
his wife, and his manhood broke from him in a great
sigh and a little hysterical shake of the head, as though
he was wrenched by an inward agony, and, but for his
being in full view of the sailors, he would have covered
his face and vented himself in the convulsed dry sob of
his sex, to whom the tears of women who make men
weep in their way, are denied.

She was gone. He rose and slowly went below, not
unmarked by some of the men, who, rough seamen as
they were, could, in their crude, uninstructed fashion,
enter into his thoughts. He walked into the cabin which
had been occupied by his wife, and gazed around him. He
looked at the trifling comforts, at the toilet fal-lals which
he had provided, he looked at the pots of flowers. It is
true, as Tennyson sings after Dante :

"That a sorrow's crown of sorrow is remembering happier
    things."

But the ship must start afresh. At sea, says Dana,
there is no time for sentiment. The lily-white hand
may be waved ashore, the dark eyes of sweet Susan,
reclining on a rock, may be full of tears, but Jack on
board ship must heave and pawl, must heave and raise
the dead, must sheet home with a hoarse yeo-yeo, which
slants tremorless to the mate's ear, unfaltering, though
the heart-strings be cracking, gay as the leap of the sea

at the bow, though the sailor's sweetheart is transformed into the pickled horse of the harness cask and the pressure of her ruby lips into the benisons of the quarterdeck.

Within three hours of the arrival of the *Flying Spur* in Falmouth Bay, the quarter-boat, in which Lucretia had been rowed ashore,|was again hanging in its place at the ship's davits, and the crew were, for the second time since leaving London, breaking out the anchor to the melody of their voices and the clanking of the revolved windlass. The upper topsail-yards were mast-headed, topgallant-sails and royals loosed and set, and the sinking sun shone upon that fair and still visible picture of the sea, a full-rigged ship under all sail standing out from the land, her bowsprit pointing to the violet line of water in the south, every rope gleaming as though threaded by a hair of gold, every cloth coloured as though touched with a brush dipped in gilt varnish ; every piece of brass-work burning with an eye that was like a little scarlet sun ; a thin racing of beaded bubbles marked the pro-gress of the keel, and the song of the sea, when the heavens are bright and the waters restful, and the breeze a pleasant impulse for the canvas, was chanted under the bows as the vessel slowly sailed out into the English Channel, out into the enfolding pinions of the evening, out into the star-studded raven darkness of the night on her long voyage to a port on the west coast of South America.

The reader is to be spared an account of this voyage of a sailing-ship whose lading was bricks, coke, and coal. Not but that the true romance of the deep is to be found in such vessels : for if it dwell not in them you shall seek it in vain in those steamers which, of all floating structures, are most familiar to readers of novels. The

G

marine Muse shrinks from the giant edifice whose walls
might have been designed for the storage of gas, whose
saloon is the coffee-room of the huge hotel, whose
engine-room is indeed a noble submission of human
genius, but on whose sliding rods and rotating cranks
the fairy foot of Poesy finds no platform.

We pass to the month of February in the year 1891,
and the date was the second. The *Flying Spur* was off
the coast of Chili. Her voyage down to this period had
been absolutely uneventful. Three days earlier—that is,
on the morning of January 31, a man had come running aft to Mr. Featherbridge to report that smoke was
rising from the forehatch. The covers were lifted, and
the cargo of coal in the fore and main holds was found
to be on fire. Drenching volumes of water by the ton
were poured in by hose, by bucket, through holes cut in
the deck. In vain. The stench of sulphureous gases
drove the men out of the forecastle, and the captain and
mates from their quarters in the cabin. The Island of
Santo Cristo then bore a few leagues distant about west-
north-west. On the first of February, the day following
the discovery of the fire which continued to burn with
fury, rendering the decks too hot for the naked foot to
endure, though no flames had as yet leapt up, it came
on to blow from the south-west. It was first a fresh
breeze in the tail of a heavy running swell, which it
wrinkled with snappish little seas. But in the afternoon
the wind had stormed up into half a gale, and the burning ship, with coils of black smoke streaming from her
hatchways, flying low over the lee bulwarks, was hove to
under her lower main-topsail.

A gale of wind and a ship on fire! It is difficult to
conceive a more horrible combination of peril. A ship
hove to and on fire, and an iron beach of an island close

aboard, out there throughout the blackness of the night, throughout the leaden morn that howled in fury as it came and stayed without brightening. The high seas were a sallow green, and poured cataracts of foam into the valleys at their feet. The fore-topgallant-mast had carried away, some sails had been blown out of their gaskets and were streaming in rags from the yards. The ship, labouring furiously, swung her spars in maddened sheerings under the rushing soot of the storm, and the picture was ghastly and wild, not by reason only of the flashing of torn canvas flogging as it was swept, shrieking as it was carried like a pennant at a rolling masthead, nor by the shattering of water falling like the avalanche self-hurled from the mountain brow; but by the leaping of flames through the fore hatch, tongues of scarlet fire which soared like the furnace-wings of the smoke, shrivelling shroud and stay, blackening and cracking and cinder-colouring every mast and spar.

In the morning Featherbridge had been talking with Captain Reynolds in a consultation as to what should be done. If the weather moderated the boats might live; if the weather held, and the fire grew as it was growing, what must follow?

"It is well," said Reynolds, "that my wife is not here."

These were the last words that he ever addressed to his friend, for when the captain had spoken, Featherbridge went forward. The vessel at that moment plunged as though she was going over the edge of the falls of Niagara: before she could lift her bow a huge green sea came with the roaring of a hundred thunderbolts aboard, and Featherbridge was seen no more. No one knew how he had perished, nor was he immediately missed. The mountain-leap of that sea, and then the sudden, volcanic uprush of flame, paralyzed the men with consternation; the three tremendous forces of Nature were let loose upon, and in, that frail and labouring, and lamenting, and brutally used example of human handiwork. The wind and the sea had united with fire, and were a trinity of raging, giant demons to whom the sailors they were strangling and calcining could oppose nothing but the beating hearts of men.

The hour of panic must come. It came when the decks blew up between the fore and main-masts and liberated a belching hell of white fire, blinding as the sunbeam and roasting as the furnace. The seamen rushed to the boats. The second mate and a little crowd were lowered, but it was the act of men driven mad by fire and fright. In a moment the boat went to pieces under them, and they were battling in the water. The senses of a sailor suddenly left him, and he jumped overboard, flinging into the wind as he hurled himself from the rail, a wilder cry than any made by the gale.

Reynolds had no orders to give—no counsels to deliver. To stay was to be broiled—to go was to be drowned. What instructions, then, could he convey at a moment in which the alternative that nearly every crisis supplies, and that enables the vigorous will to form its resolution, had been slaughtered by the wrath of the sea on the one hand and the rage of the fire on the other? But, faithful to the traditions of the British captain, he was the last to leave the ship. He pulled a lifebelt over his head, and got it under his arms, and standing on the leeside of the taffrail watched for the lift of the sea that his fall might not be far, and plunged.

The ship roared herself out in flames and explosions and much mighty hissing. The evening came. The night came. The dawn glimmered wan and sad along the eastern sea-line; the sun soared into a blue sky along which sailed a thousand little clouds like old men-of-war, and poured his glory upon an island glittering with dew, sparkling with cascades, radiant with fore-shore of coral strand, green with tall grass and little trees and bushes, standing in the heart of a shoreless sea like a many-faceted gem that flashes the green and yellow and red of the spectrum. It was the island of Santo Cristo in latitude 40° 16 min. S. and longitude 80° 39 min. W. It is about one mile long, and three-quarters of a mile wide. Two small cascades fall from a hill, and unite in a little horseshoe river on the southern side, prettily fringed with trees. Around the island, to the mouth of the horseshoe river at the easternmost extremity of this little sea-garden, runs a beach of brilliant sand. In parts the ground is covered with brushwood, and some of the growths resemble, or per-haps are, casuarina trees. The grass is long and coarse, and amongst it may be found ferns, and mosses, and mushrooms. Even in gentle weather the seas break in thunder on the coast betwixt the east and south of the island. The huge blue swell, even though uncreased by the cat's-paw, slides with the weight of countless tons, and bursts into the magnificence of foam as it recoils from the blow it delivers. There is a ceaseless play of white water on the north side, where a ledge of rock or coral comes within a foot or two of the surface and troubles the peace of the deep even in its most tranquil mood.

The sun had been risen an hour when the figure of a man, lying on the white sand on the south-west side, stirred and presently sat up. He was in a lifebelt. He was Captain Francis Reynolds, apparently sole survivor of the ship *Flying Spur*. No bodies of men were to be

seen upon the white sand, no sparkle of wet spar, no
blot of blackened beam, invited the eye to the sea. The
ship was absolutely vanished, and with her, her people,
and nothing remained to denote that such a creation
had ever had being, or that a few hours earlier a ship
of a thousand tons was on fire and struggling with half
a hurricane, save that lonely figure in a lifebelt sitting
on the coral sand.

Trying to move his arms, he found them encumbered
by the lifebelt. He languidly passed the thing over his
head, but seemed to get no ideas from the ship's name
that was painted upon it. He was sensible of a smart-
ing pain about his left eye, and at the right-hand junction
of the lips in the cheek, and, touching those parts, he
found that he had been badly hurt and was bleeding.
Had he viewed himself in a mirror he would surely not
have known who he was. He had been flung by the
breach of the sea against a rock which had cut deep
into the flesh and bone about the eye and ripped the
end of the mouth. As likely as not he would lose the
sight of that eye, and perhaps the other would perish in
sympathy.

His senses began to come to him, and he felt his
legs, and moved himself to try his ribs, and then got up
and stood, and found that his bones were unbroken.
He gazed somewhat vacantly about him; first staring
at the sea and then round upon the land, and again he
cast his eyes upon his legs, and looked at his arms and
pressed his hand against his head from which his cap
had been washed. His catching a sight of one of the
sweet and sparkling cascades made him feel as though
his throat was of hot brass, whilst his tongue stung
behind his teeth. He walked very slowly towards the
foot of the falls, where they sang in a glory of froth and

went away in a horseshoe-shaped river. He knelt, and
fashioning his hands into a cup, drank ; and then he
bathed his face. By which time his five wits were once
more vigorous, and he clearly understood that he was
Frank Reynolds, and that he had been cast ashore on
the little empty island of Santo Cristo, and that, so far
as he could judge—for the view of parts of the island
were intercepted by rises and little downs—he was the
sole survivor of the crew of the ship.

When his thirst was assuaged he felt hungry, and
sent a look at certain birds which were wheeling about
the island—petrels, gulls, whale-birds, and penguins.
They were not many, but they gave a vitality to the
air, and enriched its brilliance with the grace of their
flight and the soft hues of their plumage. But they were
not to be come at for a meal.

Reynolds' eye fell upon a creek, about one hundred
fathoms long, in the bight of which was a flat rock.
The water had sunk, and this rock was covered with
coloured oysters, limpets, and mussels. He was an old
hand ; he had sought oysters at Sydney and elsewhere,
and knew what to do. He looked about him for a
hammer, and found what he wanted in a heavy cucumber-
shaped stone, which was undoubtedly a meteorite.
Armed with this stone he slowly made his way to the
creek, and stepping on to the rock which was black and
gleaming, salt-smelling and hairy with weed, he knocked
off a meal of oysters, which he opened with a strong
clasped knife he had carried about with him at sea for
years past. Here was a very good repast. When he
had eaten as much as he needed—and whilst he ate he
took notice of certain large fish, of a rock-cod sort,
floating deep in the crystal water betwixt the rock and
the shore—he stepped from the rock on to the land,

which was scarcely at the distance of a jump, and going to where the grass was growing, he seated himself under a tree with his back against the trunk, and as quickly as a man dies whose heart fails him, he fell asleep.

He slept for three hours, and if his good angel stood beside him and watched him as he slumbered, her heart would have been melted by pity, for never did ocean reject the life of a more forlorn figure than this broken and wounded man, scarce recognizable as the comely, somewhat military looking Captain Reynolds who had commanded the *Flying Spur*. The whole spirit of the mighty desolation round about was incarnate in him.

When he awoke he stared about him as before, with a wondering eye, but was soon as sensible as ever he had been. He knew where he was, and that the coast of Chili lay at a distance of about two hundred and fifty miles. What were his chances of escape? He must keep throughout the day a sharp look-out for ships, and prepare and hold in readiness a big heap of rubbish to make a thick, black, tall smoke with when a sail should shine upon the horizon. How was he to make fire? He might rub two sticks together for years and scarcely warm them. This getting fire by friction is a trick which one must be a savage to have the art of. Fortunately for Reynolds he carried in his waistcoat pocket a burning-glass, a piece of crystal with which at sea he used under a high sun to light his pipe or cigar for love of the purity of the flame. So, whilst the sun shone, he could never lack fire, and whilst those oysters clung to the rock he could not starve, and the cascades of fresh water were as sweet to the palate as they were lovely in their glancings and flashings to the eye.

Still sitting at the foot of the tree under which he had slept, he thought of his wife. Had he forced her to

accompany him, she must have perished in the shipwreck. He knew, when he recalled with shudders those
days of horror, of tempest, of fire, that when the crisis
came he could not have saved her life, unless God's
hand had brought her ashore as he had been; but this
salvation of her would not have been of his working.

What had he lost by the shipwreck? He had
brought with him one hundred and fifty pounds, of which
he had given ten to his wife, and this money had gone
down; likewise all his clothes, charts, chronometers,
nautical instruments. Should ever he be rescued, he
would have to begin life afresh. Would life, any form
of life, be worth the effort of its maintenance, deserted
as he was by his wife, ruined as he was by the sea?
Never was any man more bankrupt in heart and estate
than this poor lonely fellow, who had been guilty of the
great blunder of loving not wisely but too well.

After looking at the brilliant beach, or as much of it
as his vision compassed, as it swept from rock and soil
into the tall feathering wash of the sea—for in every
breaker that rolled upon that little island dwelt the
power of the mighty Pacific—an idea visited him, and
he walked down to the coral stretch. He looked along
it to the north, where it terminated at the margin of a
little bay whose low face of cliff was abrupt. Here and
there were rocks, lumps of large grey stone, but no
corpse, and no signs of a living man. He sighed, and a
sense of solitude oppressing him, he clenched his hands,
thinking, as he turned round to look along the beach
towards the west, "I am alone." The thought of the
extinction of the sailors he had commanded—for he had
been the last to leave the ship, and since no man had
saved his life by this island he knew that it was inevitable
that all had perished—this thought and the memory of

Featherbridge, a shipmate he had loved, the comrade of many a quiet watch, overwhelmed him, and he wept.

He continued to walk slowly, and a speculation which seemed somewhat out of place in a maimed and hopeless castaway troubled his poor brains. He said to himself, as life is a property of vital matter, and as we are taught that nothing is destructible, what becomes of life at death? What has become of the life that enabled Featherbridge to talk to me? I can conceive, perhaps explain, the passage of heat and all forms of energy from the human body at death into other states, but what becomes of that property called life which is in me now whilst I reflect, and which, as, like heat and all other things, it is indestructible, cannot cease to exist because it has quitted my body? Perhaps, he mused, still thinking of Featherbridge and his drowned sailors, the belief in the human soul may be based upon our knowledge of the indestructibility of all created things. No, he argued to himself, belief in the soul existed long before it was known that matter and all the conditions of matter cannot be destroyed, can only be changed. The hope of the soul is based upon the innate and inborn desire of every man to project his life beyond the grave.

These were strange speculations to trouble him in such a place and under such circumstances; but the mind is not responsible for the ideas which spring in it. There is a frequent impertinence in thought, as, for instance, when you find yourself humming some tune of which you are heartily sick, but which teases you with irritating iteration, be your mood what it will; for a man will hum such an air within himself at the grave side, or when occupied in business which should utterly remove him from the vexing ghost of melody.

He walked along by the beach around the western
extremity of the island, until he was within sight of the
mouth of the little horse-shoe shaped river, and constantly as he walked he looked up at the slope or frown
of the land with a dumb and throbbing yearning, like a
pain in his heart, for the sight of a human figure. The
sun was rolling low down the sky, and the west was
gorgeous with colours, and in this beautiful light the
two waterfalls or cascades, leaping midway from an
altitude of about three hundred feet, shone like ropes of
fine pale amber, and the picture was made exquisite by
the fern-like delicacy of the boughs of trees defining
their foliage and their branches upon the tender depths
of the eastern blue. He climbed a green slope and
gained the higher parts of the island, and looked about
him for a spot in which he might shelter himself for the
night. Hard by was a little dell covered with mosses
and other growths, and he observed on one side of it a
horizontal fissure about six feet deep, whilst the gap
was about five feet. He gazed carefully about him in
search of snakes or other dangerous reptiles, but saw
nothing of the kind. That fissure, he judged, would
provide him with a bed-place. So he walked towards a
tract of tall grass, like guinea grass, and, pulling out his
knife, cut down a quantity, enough to make a little
bundle to serve as a pillow. This bundle he compacted
by binding it with grass which he knitted into withes,
for this man was a sailor who could lay up sennit, or
weave grass into a hat.

He put his pillow into the crevice and went across
the island to the beach again to get his supper off the
rock. How sad were the splendid colours of the west,
how heart-subduing the vastness of the solitude! The
voice of the spirit of desolation was heard in the sound

of the wind in the trees, in the organ-roll of crushed and seething swell, in the troubled rustling on the shoal, in whispers of running waters coming from afar. He got upon the rock armed with his meteorite. It was but a long stride from the edge of the land to the rock. The oysters were large and sweet, and provided him with an excellent meal. It was a calm evening; the swell came rolling from the sun in liquid gold; the sea-fowl were fishing diligently, and some of them, whose plumage gave resilience to the western light, wheeled in shapes of brass and ivory through the air.

Reynolds regained the shore, and ascending the slope behind which was the dell that was to shelter him from the night, sat down and watched the sun set and the sumptuous pageantry fade, watched the sea-line that perished in the evening shadow which was trembling with stars. He wondered how long he would be forced to remain on this island, and if it was his destiny to die upon it, and his imagination grew morbid, and he pictured his dead body supine, and the decay of it, till a shudder compacted his mind, and the tone of it grew more manly. Oh, for a companion, he thought, but one —but one to speak to! He tried to recollect the people who had been in his situation, and could recall but two, Peter Serano and Alexander Selkirk. It brightened him for the moment to recollect that both were delivered from the horrors of an island's loneliness. Peter, he remembered, was covered with hair when he was suc-coured, and looked like some furry imagination of Pagan mythology, and was frightful to see.

A shooting star caught his eye. He followed the brilliant track of it, and then his chin sank, and he put up a short prayer to God for mercy.

Though never religious, Reynolds was always a

devout man. He had read and reasoned himself into a full conviction as to the being of a Creator. It is ridiculous, he would argue, to talk of chance, when you witness design everywhere. If the theory of chance is right, then creation is nothing but a dice-box, the issue of every throw unforeseen. He held that in nothing is design more visible than in evolution, with its enduring elements of prevision and provision. If evolution were merely chance, Creation would be chaos. He had once said to Lucretia, "What the learned call chance, I, who am not learned, call intention. Look at this little daisy: consider its colour, its form, the hand that grasps the petals, the airy beauty of the orange throne in the heart of it on which the viewless shape of the queen of the fairies sits on moonlighted nights, and let the Darwins of the age call this miracle of the meadow *chance*, if they can or dare!" Once, in taking a ramble in some fine scenery in New Zealand, he watched two birds, called huia birds, and was struck by the intention in form which their procedure explained. The male had a short, stout bill; the female a long, curved bill. He observed that they earned their living in company thus: the male, hopping or flying to a tree, with his strong bill knocked off the bark and exposed the grub, and the female, with her long curved bill, took the grub out, and between them they made a meal.

Thus it will be seen that when this man prayed to God, his heart spoke with conviction that he was addressing a Spirit who would give him heed though He made no sign.

It was lonesome sitting there with nothing but the voice of the sea to hear, and nothing but the sparkling suns of the sky to behold, for the island sank into ink on a moonless night; he rose, and made his way to the dell, and got into the cleft and laid his broken face and weary head upon his grass pillow.

He fell asleep, and dreamed that his wife stood by his side. A cold star glittered on her forehead, and its radiations struck lances of ice into his heart. He awoke, and looked for his wife, and saw nothing but the stars shining at the edge of the fissure above the dell. But she had been with him, and with him in that same repellent spirit of chastity that had sundered them. Why should we deal lightly with, or speak in scorn of our dreams. Half our lives are formed of dreams, whether the visions shape themselves to the slumberer, or dwell in the stare of the waking abstracted eye. The boy dreams of the sea and of fairy lands forlorn; the maiden of that ideal man whom she shall not meet this side of the grave; the politician of power, and the philosopher of the undiscovered bourne; the king of a people's love, and the beggar of a copper ere noon. Rob the mind of dreams, sleeping or waking, and you extinguish one-third of the solid joys of life and two-thirds of its solid troubles.

Reynolds fell asleep again, but his wife did not return.

CHAPTER VI

THE FISHERMAN

WHEN Reynolds again opened his eyes the day was broad, brilliant, and noisy. He got out of the fissure which had supplied him with a sheltered moss-coated couch, and immediately made his way to a rise of ground to obtain a view of the sea. He swept the horizon with the practiced gaze of a sailor, observing in his wounded eye a little dimness of vision. Nothing that could be named a ship was in sight. Large dark clouds were sailing with the wind, but above them was a ceiling of mother-of-pearl that was settling slowly westwards. A fresh breeze was blowing. The sea was alive and leaping. On the shoal the water was the glaring whiteness of wrestling waves. The blow of the surge on the south-east side boomed with the deep note of heavy guns through the wind. The trees sang and the surf bellowed, and the full and spacious scene, from dome to liquid floor, throbbed and shouted and danced and roared with the spirit of ocean liberty.

Reynolds walked towards the foam-heap at the foot of the cataract and drank, then, stripping himself, plunged into the bright water of the little river, which was as sweet as honey for the distance of half a cable, with the force of the current that was rushed through the foam-mound by those water-falls, when it grew brackish and rapidly passed into salt water. He was

95

much refreshed by his bath, and ran to and fro to dry himself, and when he had put on his clothes he walked to the sand and got upon the rock to breakfast.

He ate heartily, for these were very fat and choice oysters though big. And for condiment they needed neither vinegar nor pepper, but the contents of the best of all cruet-stands (which he had)—that is, appetite.

Whilst he was thus occupied he saw swimming deep in the green crystal space of water betwixt the rock and the shore, where the creek began to widen, a number of big fish, of which he had before taken notice. He judged by their bulk that they would weigh from eight to thirty pounds. If they were not rock-cod they resembled that fish, but some were of a different species, and they were gay with colours and shaped like perch. Reynolds saw abundance of food beneath him, but how was he to get it? He was without hook or line, though there was plenty of bait in the thousands of limpets which adhered to this and other rocks. He recollected that a naval officer who was in a surveying ship off Patagonia had told him that the 'long-shore natives of that country took fish in this way. They fashioned lines out of tendrils of shrubbery; to the end of a line they attached a limpet; this they dropped over the edge of their canoe. The fish gorged the limpet, and was warily drawn to the surface by the fisherman, who then dexterously passed his hand under the fish and tossed it out of water into the boat.

This memory determined Reynolds to try his hand; he was a sailor, and the possessor of a knife and a burning glass. And thus equipped he could not be at a loss. But as he never could be in want of food whilst oysters and other shell-fish abounded, he resolved first to explore the island and to climb its highest point, which was a hill several hundred feet high, that hill from whose steeps the cataracts "blew their trumpets." It must be his business to prepare the means of making a smoke should a sail heave into view.

He wished to catch a sight of himself to judge of the extent of the injuries to his face, but there was no pool of water that was not blurred by the hurrying fingers of the wind. He got upon the shore and set out upon his adventures. This little principality was but a mile long, as you have heard, and three-quarters of a mile wide, and it was to be compassed and examined without much fatigue of walking. He climbed the hill and gained the summit, and the island lay below him in green and brown and grey, tender with verdure and splendid with its mighty dazzle of foam on the south-east side, and the brilliant cream of the surf that roared upon its coral strand from the north to right around by west to south. It blew fresh up there where he was, and the salt song shrilled past his ears as though he was aloft in a squall on a top-gallant-yard. There was a hollow a short distance down, and in that hollow he determined to collect the materials for a fire; but he was compelled to make many journeys before his heap for burning was collected and sufficient. There was no wood fit for his purpose on the hill. He cut and hacked with his knife, and painfully ascended with his arms full, but he did not cease in his toil until his work was ended, and then he sat down on the top of the hill to rest and muse and survey the sea-line.

He asked himself, "What is my chance of escape?" The island was far out of the track of steamers bound north or south; nothing was likely to come that way

H

but a ship blown out of her course, or a whaler to whom
this island might be known for the purity and value of
its fresh water. He had again and again looked at his
chart before the shipwreck, and memory submitted a
clear map of his situation to him. He understood, with
a sense of dismay that grew into consternation as he
realized the magnitude of his ocean loneliness, that
weeks, that months, nay, that even years might pass
and find him, if alive, a captive on this shore. The
weight of a reflection so enormous was crushing, and he
said to himself, "Oh, my great God, it may happen as
I fear!" and again his heart was rent by an insupportable pang of yearning for one—but for *one* companion
only to speak to.

This passionate desire caused him to scrutinize the
coast and foreshore, of which he commanded the whole
extent from where he sat, but he could not perceive the
least signs of wreckage or anything resembling a
stranded human body. His spirits were so sunk that
he found no heart to make grass lines for fishing that
day, and until he laid himself down in the cleft in the
side of the dell, he rambled aimlessly here and there,
often sending a forlorn gaze seawards, sometimes sitting
with his head bowed upon his folded arms, sometimes
going to the river for a drink of water, twice to his rock
for oysters. He looked at the trees for fruit, but saw
none. Here on this island was vegetation that he had
met with in other parts of the world; some flowers, one
of which he plucked, but it was without smell, though he
afterwards discovered that this flower blew a very sweet
perfume at nightfall and through the darkness, and likewise when the moon whitened the scene. The several
growths were more or less familiar to him, for in his
time Reynolds had visited many different parts of the

globe, but in respect of knowledge he was like the boy who, in speaking of the letters of the alphabet, told the schoolmaster that "he knew them by their fyaces but not by their nyames."

Next morning, which was another windy, sparkling, singing day much like that which was gone, he fell to his task of making fishing-lines after he had bathed and breakfasted. He cut some long grass and plaited it, but found that when it was in six or even eight strands it broke easily. He strolled to some of the trees, conceiving he might meet with some withe-like tendrils; and sure enough he discovered, coiled round the trunks of several dwarf trees in a little bit of a wood near the dell, a parasitic growth of the thickness of the thong of a coach whip and as strong. He cut away one and uncoiled its embrace, and found himself equipped with a supple fishing-line between eight and ten feet long strong enough to have hanged him with.

He was pondering how he should attach a limpet to the end of this creeper, when his eye was taken by a little collection of bush, in the midst of which he seemed to see a sort of darkness. He approached the bushes and found himself looking into the mouth of a cave. The aperture was scarcely obstructed by the growth which stood thick on either hand, leaving the mouth a sort of blackness when viewed from a distance. The entrance was a little more than the height of a man. Though a natural formation, the roof of the opening stood out from the slope of the land as though the invention of human labour.

Reynolds went close and peered in, and as he stared a large sea-bird came sailing out. It looked like a ghost as it grew out of its own glimmering, and it hit Reynolds over the face with its wing. It would have knocked his cap off had he been covered. He started back in terror; the apparition was sudden and unexpected, and at the instant frightful to the man whose nerves were very low. But when, following the thing with his eye, he perceived that it was a very large kind of sea-gull, white and grey in feathers, seemingly sick, for its flight was languid, and it sank upon the ground after a short excursion, his spirits rallied, and again he peered into the cave.

He entered by several paces, and then stood stock still, awaiting the passage of another sea-bird, for this might be a kind of hospital for decayed ocean-fowl; and then, his eyes growing used to the shadow, he found himself in a natural cavern running back from its mouth about twenty feet, sloping low at the extremity so as to oblige one who went there to crouch, but in the middle part tall enough to stand under, the walls about eight feet apart. As his vision grew educated to the gloom, objects shaped themselves within its horizon, and he judged that this in its day had been the haunt of one man, or more. The floor was hard and sandy, with a little dim sheen in it as though it was bestrewn with grit which possessed a property of shining. On the left-hand side stood an old-fashioned sea-chest. Close against it, resting against the wall, was a shovel of a very elderly pattern; upon the ground were a musket and a carpenter's axe.

Reynolds went to the chest and found it locked. He picked up the axe, and forcing the sharp corner of the cutting part betwixt the lid and the side, he prized the lid open. Indeed, it was something rotten, and not only did the wood split and yield very easily, but the metal of the lock and the screws and nails about it showed like old teeth, grinning and rusty. The chest was furnished with a shelf, in which he found a brass tobacco-box, some clay pipes, three spade guineas, and a few five-shilling pieces and some shillings, about three pounds of leaf tobacco bound in canvas and twine, a coil of copper wire, a roll of yellowing paper, and a flat pencil. In the chest were two pairs of cloth knee-breeches, several pairs of coarse grey stockings, two pairs of buckle shoes, two waistcoats, one coat, and a cloak with a chain to connect it at the throat. He judged the date of this apparel to be about eighteen hundred. On the lid of the chest were chiselled deep two letters, " L. B."

He looked about him for the remains of a man in the shape of human bones. Nothing in that way was to be seen. It was clear, from the state of the chest, that the cave had not been entered since the departure of the man or men who had used it. He conjectured that the furniture illustrated a story of shipwreck. Some men had come ashore from a foundered craft, bringing with them the sea-chest, the shovel, axe, and musket. Whether they had been taken off, or whether they had perished or rotted out of being on this island, was not to be gathered from their dumb memorials. And yet it warmed Reynolds with a little heat of cheerfulness to reflect that others had been here before him. The sense of previous life, though charged as that life might have been with dire suffering and a miserable ending, humanized the island. He again scrutinized this interior for signs of human remains, and then stepped out into the daylight, bearing with him the creeper he had cut from the tree.

It is difficult to imagine any scene of human life more interesting than the spectacle of a man suddenly flung, by some such stress of destiny as shipwreck, from all the resources of civilization into the obligation of living as though he was something primordial, dwelling in a time that knew not the plough nor the blacksmith, nor the shop which calls itself "Stores." A man is cast almost naked upon an island coast. He is alone—a Crusoe, a Selkirk. How shall he feed, and clothe, and shelter himself? His needs must fire his ingenuity. The mongrel dog knows as well as the two-legged customer the butchers of the town, and lives by snatching. A hungry, half-stripped man deals with nature as the mongrel with the butcher ; he scrutinizes her, not in admiration of her divine skill, but for what he can steal from her to eat. Whether a princely noble-man would, as a castaway, suffer equally with a sweep in a like situation might depend upon the state of his health. It would be true, perhaps, if it be said that we should take more interest in the struggles of his grace to find a breakfast on a rock, or a supper in a tree, than in the labours of a man to whom a bloater and a potato are a banquet.

Outside the cave Reynolds fell to considering his fishing-line, and how he was to bait it with a limpet. And whilst he reflected he constantly sent looks at the horizon, for at any moment the white star of a sail, or the stain of a steamer's smoke, might break the con-tinuity of that everlasting girdle. Suddenly it entered his head to use the copper wire in the sea-chest. He re-entered the cave and took the wire from its shelf, brought a guinea to the cavern's mouth to examine it, went back and picked up some of the clothes and carried them out into the light. They were perhaps a hundred years old, and almost rotten, save the cloak, which, being made of some strong ribbed material like corduroy, seemed as stout and promised to be as useful as though it was fresh from the sign of the board and shears. He left the clothes on the ground as worthless to him, and by help of the axe he struck a nail from the ripped lock of the sea-chest, and hammered it into the side of the cave and hung up the cloak.

He brought the little parcel of tobacco to the light and cut it open, but the leaves within crumbled to powder when he touched them, and he threw the stuff away. Now drawing forth the copper wire, he cut off a piece and passed it through the end of the creeper, turning it up into the shape of a hook, and thus armed he made his way to the rock.

This business occupied his mind, and kept him a little away from melancholy. He took his meteorite, which lay on the shore near the rock, and struck at some limpets. These creatures adhere with so much tenacity that to detach one you must strike with a force of sixty-two pounds, that is to say, close upon two thousand times its own weight. He baited his strange fishing-line and dropped it into the water. In a few moments a fish of about ten pounds floated up and swallowed the bait, and then Reynolds perceived that he had calculated amiss. He brought the fish to the surface, but when he tried to land it he drew the bait out of the creature's throat, and perceived, unless, Patagonian-wise, he could pass his hand or something else under the fish, his angling would be little more than a tickling. He must make a net stout enough to lift the fish on to the rock.

He regained the island, leaving his line and the cucumber-shaped stone on the shore opposite the rock, and walked inland, with many a glance at the horizon. He easily understood what to do. He selected two boughs and curved them into a hoop, binding them with strong fibres of creepers. He then cut another bough for a handle, and this he skilfully secured to the hoop by cleaving one end of the stick and fitting the hoop into it, and securely binding it. He chose fibres of creepers for a mesh, and, cutting as much as he needed, sat down in the shadow of a tree and began to weave.

It was now past noon; the sun was high, and shone with great splendour upon the sea, which was full of the life of the fresh breeze. The booming of the surf was like the roaring of a city heard from a church-top. The sea-birds slanted and curved in lovely flight, and the waterfalls sparkled like quicksilver into the glory of foam at their foot. From time to time he would remit the diligent plying of his fingers to look seawards, and then around him. It was a kind of toil that suffered plenty of room for thought. His fancies flowed to his wife, and he said to himself—

"Supposing she had consented to stay with me, and she had been saved with me only, and we two had found ourselves alone upon this island—how strange it would have been! how would I have cherished her! what delight should I have found in this imprisonment in providing for her wants! So that hereafter, should it have ever come to our being rescued, we should both recall this island as a happy garden—an ocean's gift of a dwelling for us whilst our honeymoon ran."

He sighed, and his hands sank, and for some minutes he sat motionless with his eyes fixed upon the grass. The tree overhead sang and shivered and scintillated with little suns, and the taller shrubs and bushes were gay with "nods and becks and wreathed smiles," as though there were a minstrelsy in the breeze which made them dance.

A great quantity of mushrooms flourished in this island. Reynolds had peered at the trees for fruit, but it had not occurred to him to look upon the earth for food. His eye lighting on some mushrooms, it struck him that they would be good to eat and supply the absence of bread, and going to them he picked one, and knew enough of the vegetable world to distinguish at once the eatable fungus from the toad-stool. He skinned some and eat them with relish.

His work of weaving was not half ended when the dusk came. He had often dropped the job to climb a height and scan the sea, to walk to the river to drink, and twice to the rock for oysters. In that part of the world it was the season that corresponds with our July, and extremely warm ; indeed, the sun bit with a fang of fire, but the shadows cast by the trees were deliciously fanned by the fresh wind. Another night had come. He had no mind to occupy the cave. He was a sailor, accustomed to the wide freedom of the sea, and the idea of the natural bed in the dell, over which sparkled the firmament, pleased him better than the thought of the cave, which was a sort of sepulchre to his imagination, with its mute memorials of human life which had passed. He, however, entered it to fetch the cloak, which he spread on the floor of the fissure, and it made him, with the moss beneath, a softer couch than many he had dreamed deeply on at sea.

Next morning, after bathing and breakfasting as before, he went to work again upon his landing-net, which he completed in the early afternoon. Already the spirit of solitude was doing its work in him. His beard and moustache had sprouted, and accentuated a melancholy shadow in the hollows under his cheek bones. He was bareheaded, and his hair lay wild. The wounds at the corner of his mouth and eye had healed. He was sensible that the sight of his left eye was affected, but he could not have imagined how great was the structural change in his face in consequence of the injuries. To be sure, when his moustache grew the disfigurement at the corner of the mouth would be concealed, but the real transformation lay in the left side of his face, owing to distortion of the eyebrow and to a new expression of the eye, drawn by the pencils of the healed flesh. He had looked into some pools of water here and there, but in no silent surface even could he find an adequate portrait. The misery of his situation had already wrought in him, and was strangely visible in the infixed sadness of his looks. But it was not only his shipwreck, his being a lamentable castaway, his being so alone that, if he had been that last man described by the poet Campbell, he could not have been lonelier; there was memory to yellow and skeletonize what had otherwise been the green leaves of his mind. Even as he sat making his landing-net he would think of his wife, and wonder why she had forsaken him; whether through some perversion of brain she had, when standing before the altar, conceived something in him—a quality of mind, a characteristic of person—that had suddenly excited in her a deep and abiding loathing. Then, too, he mourned the death of his friend Featherbridge, and the shocking tragical extinction of the whole of the ship's company, for men who are cooped up for many long weeks together in a ship will take that colouring of sentiment which the sailor feels when he speaks of a messmate and a shipmate. All those men whom he had commanded; who had sprang readily to his order; who had proved dutiful and an excellent crew—for he was a sailor who knew how to treat sailors—were as clean gone out of life as the cloud that sailed two hours before across the sky.   Here were thoughts to put a pang into every heart-beat, a sigh into every respiration.

His fish-lifter was a basket rather than a net. He carried it to the rock and baited his line. The fish, unused to the sight of the human figure, and ignorant of the human character, exhibited a tameness that would have been as shocking to Reynolds as Cowper thought a like sort of indifference must have proved to Selkirk, had he heeded it. They floated in various-sized green and silver shapes beneath him, and scarce was the limpet under water when a fine fish gorged it. Reynolds softly brought his prey to the surface, and then, quickly putting his basket under it, whipped the noble fish on to the rock, a prize of fifteen pounds weight, where it sprang and gasped.

This was a clever achievement, and Reynolds was sensible of a little heat of triumph. Whilst he watched his victim he considered how he should cook him. His first idea had been to dig a pit for a furnace, which was now quite easy, as there was a shovel in the cave. Over this pit he proposed to arch a stout bough, and hang by grass a steak of fish over the fire. He foresaw trouble, first because only the lower part of the fish would be baked, and next because the fire was certain to burn the grass lanyard and let the fish fall into the flames. But it now occurred to him to use the shovel for a frying-pan ; so, full of this business, he took up the fish and carried it on to the mainland, and walked with it to the cave, where he placed it for safety, as he had no mind, after his labours, to be robbed by those insatiate gentry of the air who were wheeling and curving over the sea, by the shore, and sometimes over the land.

He laid hold of the shovel, and saw that it would

serve very well indeed as a frying-pan after it had dug him an oven. He pulled off his coat and waistcoat and placed them in the cave, and began to dig outside, and dug with such diligence as though he was a Trappist intent on his own grave, that in a very short time he had made a considerable square hole. He took care that it should be well in the sun, as he needed the fire of that luminary for his burning-glass. He then collected a quantity of fuel, and set fire, with his burning-glass, to some grass as dry as hay, and the fire burnt merrily. With the axe which was in the cave he cut wood into little logs, and presently the hole was glowing, and a delicate blue smoke was soaring and arching over, when the wind took it, like a feather.

He thoroughly cleaned the inside of the shovel, then stepped into the cave and gutted his fish and cut it into steaks, two or three of which he lay in the shovel along with the creature's liver and some slices of mushroom. Next, going to the fire with his shovel thus furnished, he placed his queer frying-pan upon the furnace, contriving that it should rest without his support, and with his knife he turned the slices of fish about, until one of the goodliest smells he had smelt for a long time past arose: for here was a fish wonderfully fresh and sweet from its native brine, resembling a cod, though the flesh looked like turbot. It was a real treat to the poor fellow, whose nature loneliness was colouring with a childlike simplicity, insomuch that presently he would be finding a joy in very little things, and a keen distress in trifles, as a prisoner long confined gets to love a spider and tears his hair when it dies, or as a sailor after a long voyage takes delight or finds trouble in things whose triviality excites the wonder of the people he steps ashore amongst.

A number of sea-birds flew in circles over his head whilst he cooked. When the meal was prepared he plucked a large leaf for a tablecloth and set a fried steak and mushrooms upon it and fell to, scarcely missing salt. Maybe the sweat of his toil supplied that seasoning for his appetite. Never had he banquetted more sumptuously, and when he had drank from the river he felt strongly the force and truth of the line, "Man wants but little here below," even if he should want that little long.

This day passed and the next, and the hours moving into weeks swelled into a month, which was like to prove a twelve-month, and perhaps a lifetime, for all this man could tell; for never once, though he was ever on the watch, did he catch sight of a sail or the shadow of smoke. Constantly he would ascend the hill from the hollow where he had assembled the materials for a fire, and strain his sight until the balls of vision ached. He was now bearded and his mouth concealed by hair; although no more than a month had passed he looked as wild, pale, and ragged as any wretched pauper that one meets on a highway with his skirts in ribbons, and limping in old boots, of which you shall presently meet one left in the middle of the road, discarded for ever, an object very fit to muse upon.

This brought him into the month of March. One night he had put himself away in his cleft, which he continued to occupy, as his first aversion to sleeping in the cave had now, by the strain of melancholy that was in his mind, been changed into a sort of superstition, and as a lonesome man he was afraid to rest in that place. The moon was up, and her light shone in a fine silver haze in the dell. The night was still; the trees slumbered. The little white cloud on high lingered as though for love of the glorious glowing star that gemmed its skirt. But old ocean, perturbed by memories of wreck and ruin, tossed in her dreams and shouted as she drove her liquid shoulders at the island's step, and muttered moodily and hissed her own thoughts on the coral strand. The whiteness and coolness and calmness of the night brought Lucretia into Reynolds' mind, and he remembered his dream when she appeared to him with a light on her brow that froze his heart with lances of ice. He thought of her. Her eyes were a clear, liquid dusk, within whose tender horizons admiration witnessed the passions, the sensibilities, the tastes it desired for so fine a figure of a woman. What was the truth? Her eyes were altars on which her spirit had placed the cold white lamps of chastity; lights which like the remote stars revealed themselves only and warmed and illuminated nothing.

He lay thinking of his wife with his eyes upon the moon, which, with a considerable circle of sky over the dell, was visible to him in the position he occupied on that natural shelf. The moon stands as a symbol of purity. Such beautiful women as Lucretia should be viewed by the moonlight only. The moon stands as a symbol of desolation, and the words which Tennyson makes Lucretius use in his reference to the seat of the gods, are strangely applicable to our satellite—

> "Where never creeps a cloud or moves a wind,
> Nor ever falls the least white star of snow,
> Nor ever lowest roll of thunder mourns,
> Nor sound of human sorrow mounts to mar
> *Its* sacred everlasting calm."

He fell asleep for about two hours, then opened his eyes, waking suddenly. The dell was still bathed in the moonshine, and he saw the figure of a man who was walking very slowly. Every bush cast its ebony shadow, but the figure of this man was shadowless. He was dressed in a long coat with side skirts of the old-fashioned sort, knee-breeches and shoes, and held his hat in his hand. His face in the moonlight was pale and full, and it was without hair. He was bald, with flowing hair falling from the semicircle it made at the back of his head between his ears.

Reynolds' heart beat hard. He stared, and if that which was perceptible to him had been visible to an onlooker, it would have been difficult for him to decide which was the stranger sight, the face of the living man in that cleft, or the apparition he watched. He took notice again that it was shadowless, whilst at the foot of every bush slept its ebon ghost.

He threw his legs over and got out and stood looking at the shape as it walked; approached a step with his heart thundering, like the swell against the cliff, in his ear, stood still and looked, and found he was alone. Slowly he turned his eyes round the dell. The vision of the brain had vanished.

He was awed and terrified. He perfectly understood that what he had beheld was an illusion, and he conceived that it was a sign he was losing his reason. Or could it be that he had dreamt vividly that he had seen a ghost and had left the ledge to watch it, and it had disappeared because he awoke, having quitted his bed in his sleep with the dream working in his head? He was without superstition, he had never believed in ghosts; he knew that what had stalked in the dell was an imagination, a deceit, a coinage of some brain-cell that had mutinied and irresponsibly acted. But for the rest of the night he could not sleep, nor for many days afterwards could he shake off the horror that that vision of the dell was a premonition of madness.

Wherein he proved that not then, at all events, was he mad: for he was unwittingly following the logic of Coleridge, who said, " If I see a figure enter a room and know that it is unreal, I am not mad: but if I start and believe it real and behave, whether by accost or by other conduct, as though it were an actual entity, I am mad." The poet's reasoning ran to this effect, not quite in these words. It was certainly very strange that the shape should have been attired in the costume in the sea-chest in the cave. Yet it might easily have been that the irresponsible brain-cell, in indulging in this freak, would select the garb and figure a presentment of one who was perhaps the last man who had lived on this island.

The months rolled on, and Reynolds remained alone.

CHAPTER VII

THE BOAT'S CREW

CAME September 14, 1891, a bright cool morning, making it seven months and rather more since Captain Francis Reynolds was flung ashore, bruised, bleeding, and insensible, on the uninhabited island of Santo Cristos, there to languish. During which time he had never once set eyes on the sails of a ship or the smoke of a steamer by day, whatever may have passed in the night. He knew not the day nor the month. In seven months he had not spoken: no, there was not even a dog nor a parrot for him to address. Sometimes in the beginning he would speak aloud to himself, fearful lest his voice should perish by disuse. But he neglected this custom later on, and never broke the silence, not even when he put up a prayer for mercy and for deliverance.

He was now presenting the most grotesque and uncouth appearance that could be imagined. His hair had turned grey, and streamed far down his back, like that of the Welsh bards of yore. A considerable beard had grown, and his cheeks and his mouth and the half of his breast were concealed by hair. His left eye was dim and stained, and its vision was so weak that when he looked through it alone, closing the other eye, he could barely distinguish the outline of a tree fifty feet distant. And all about that side of his head, was the puckered flesh and distorted bone of the defacing wound. He was much burnt by exposure to the sun, but the mahogany was not the healthy brown of the sky-and-sea-blistered sailor; there was mixed with it a sort of ashiness which produced a complexion impossible to convey in words. His clothes and boots were sadly broken. Unhappily the shoes in the sea-chest were too small for him. He presented indeed a most melancholy, shocking figure, stooped, suggesting by attitude and motion a perpetual hopelessness at heart that would have moved the most soulless to witness.

On the morning named, he left the fissure which he had continued to occupy, having outlived the trouble of the ghost who had never again appeared, and made his way slowly to the horse-shoe river, where he drank and washed, and then came back to the cave, where lying in the shovel were some cutlets of cooked fish. He took one, and sat down outside the cave and began to eat.

Whilst he was eating he chanced to cast his eyes up at the slope above the dell, and beheld a man. The man stood looking at him. He wore a fur cap, and sleeved-waistcoat, and pilot-cloth breeches. The arm with which Reynolds was feeding himself, was blasted as though struck by lightning. The whole man was turned into an inimitable effigy of stone. The morning, as has been said, was bright and cool : the splendour of the sun was far searching, the life of the earth, of the ocean, of the heavens, was in the bending and swaying of plants, in the movement of the boughs of the trees, in the sparkling fall of the cataracts, in the resounding organ-note of the sea, in the speeding of clouds. Yonder, then, surely was no ghost.

"Hallo!" shouted the man. "Who are you down there?"

Then, turning, he bawled with the sharp of his hand at his mouth—

"I say, mates, there's a man down here, eatin' his breakfast and lookin' as though he belonged to the island." Then, again addressing himself to Reynolds, he cried, "Are you English? How long have you been here?" And with that he stepped out to approach him.

Even as he walked the forms of several other men appeared on the rise which he had quitted. Reynolds rose; the piece of fish he was eating fell; he was trembling violently; his features worked as though in convulsions. As the man approached him, a wild smile irradiated his face as though a beam of electric light had been passed over it, and he dropped upon the ground in a fit.

The men who collected about him were seven in number. Six were manifestly sailors. The seventh was a strange and striking-looking personage: about six feet tall, broad, and so stout about the chest that he seemed to be padded. He was bearded, and looked about fifty years of age. He had a large, full, mild face, rather protruding eyes, bland, like a cow's, with intellect and thought in their residual expression.

"Has he dropped dead for joy at sight of us?" said one of the sailors. "I've heard of such things."

"How long has he been 'ere, I wonder?" said another.

"Turn him over!" exclaimed the tall man, pronouncing these few words with great deliberation and a slight Irish accent. "Poor fellow!" he exclaimed, looking at Reynolds, whose face, though calm in the oblivion of the brain, was pregnant with pathos in the appealing expression the spirit of solitude had chiselled upon it.

"Is he dead, sir, d'ye think?" said a man.

The tall personage stooped and felt Reynolds' wrist, and said—

"No. I guess by his appearance that he's been here many weeks."

"Why, ain't that a cave?" said a man.

"There's the pit he uses for cooking," exclaimed another.

Three or four of the sailors left Reynolds to the tall man and two who stayed, and entered the cave. They peered in warily, then entered. They blinked a bit before they could fairly see; and then one said—

"See that there shovel? Gord's life, that's how he's cooked his food! See the bits of fish in it, bullies?"

"A regular castaway, and no blooming mistake," said another.

"Here's his old chest," cried one, "with his letters cut on it. Why, whoever sees a chest like this nowadays? How old's he? Why, this old chest's all a hundred years old, you lay."

He opened the lid. As we know, Reynolds had removed the clothes.

"Why, see 'ere," continued the man, taking up one of the buckle shoes; "this is what they wear when they dresses up for old men in stage plays. Shoes of this pattern ha'nt been wore for o'er a century."

"And look at his old gun lying down there!" exclaimed another. "My grandfather had a piece like that, and it belonged to his grandfather. So how old is that gun, I should like to know?"

"Ain't there a yarn," said a man, "about a Dutchman who fell asleep upon the top of a mountain when
he was young, and came down bald, with a long beard,
and found everybody he had known dead and gone
years and years ; there wasn't even anybody as he
might have owed money to alive to ask him for it ? "

A man lifted the lid of the shelf. " What's this ? "
said he, picking up a guinea.

It was examined by the others, whilst the first man
scrutinized the silver.

" It's good money," said a man. " More here than a
month's pay, by a long chalk. The dating of it'ull tell
you how old he is. What's the latest numberin' ? "

" 'Ere's a bit marked h'eighteen-one," exclaimed a
sailor, talking in the better light at the mouth of the
cave.

" Poor old man ! " said one of the others.

They replaced the money, and went out. Reynolds
was just then coming to. He was fetching his breath
with difficulty, and opening and shutting his eyes.

" There's h'evidence in that cave, Mr. Good'art," said
the sailor in the sleeved-waistcoat and fur cap, " that
this man can't be less than a hundred and thirty years
old."

" What d'ye mean ? " asked one of the men who had
stayed.

" Go and look for yourself," was the answer. " There's
a musket that's over a hundred years old. His sea
chest's just as ancient. The youngest of his money is
marked eighteen hundred and one."

Reynolds opened his eyes, gave two or three gasps,
made an effort to sit up, was helped by the man who
had been called Mr. Goodhart, into a sitting posture,
rolled his eyes with tokens of astonishment and of a

spirit kindling into transport, tried to speak, muttered "Water!" and then continued to stare around upon the men.

"Where's fresh water to be got?" asked the man in the waistcoat.

Reynolds pointed to the cascades.

"What's it to be brought in?" continued the man.

It did not seem that Reynolds could speak until he had drank. One went to the cave, and came back, saying there was nothing that would hold water in it.

"Run down to the boat for the soup and bullie can, one of you," said Mr. Goodhart.

A man procured this can, went to the river, and returned. During his absence the sailors who thought Reynolds a hundred and thirty years old, gazed at him with the emotions of a boy who views a mummy. The man who brought the water exclaimed—

"Oyster shells has been used for drinking with down at that river. A blamed sweet river. It begins up there," said he, pointing at the cascades, "and it's like watching fire-engines a-playing. Go and taste it. Nicest drop of water I ever swallowed."

Whilst this was being said, Reynolds drank and the draught liberated his voice. He strained his sight at the only piece of sea that was visible from the place they occupied, and said—

"Where's your ship?"

"At the bottom of the sea," answered Goodhart. And then, with a singularly cordial manner, very gentle and charming with kindness, he said, "Pray, what might be your name?"

"Francis Reynolds."

"How long have you been here?"

Reynolds struggled with his memory, and replied, "I have lost all tally of weeks."

"To-day," said Goodhart, "is September 14, 1891."

"My ship," answered Reynolds, "was lost, and I was cast ashore here on February 2, 1891."

Swiftly and secretly computing, he was overwhelmed by the magnitude of his time of loneliness, and looked most woefully and wistfully at Goodhart as though for commiseration.

"What was your ship?"

"The *Flying Spur*."

"A steamer?"

"No."

"Were you a passenger?"

"I was her master."

At this the sailors stared at him with an attention which was tinctured with a visible colour of respect.

"Her master!" exclaimed Goodhart. "Are you the only survivor?"

"The only survivor."

Life was brisker in him now, and memory quickened, and he began to talk. There had been times when he believed he should, by long enforced silence, lose the power of articulation. He spoke well, with fluency, for this man, through reading and reflection, was master of an ample vocabulary. The sailors knew that they were in the presence of a gentleman and an educated man, and they ceased to think him a hundred and thirty years old. Goodhart followed the narrative with sympathy and earnest attention.

"The lifebelt I came ashore in is somewhere about," said Reynolds. "My ship's name is on it. What's your story?"

"I'm going for a drink of fresh water," said a sailor.

"What's there good to eat on this island?" asked the man in the sleeved-waistcoat.

"Plenty of fish and oysters. No fruit nor vegetables saving mushrooms," answered Reynolds. "What's your story, sir?"

The men went roaming off in ones and twos, and Goodhart sat down beside Reynolds.

"We've not been arrived above an hour," said he. "I was a passenger in the ship—the only passenger. She was the barque *Esmond*, of nine hundred tons, bound from Sydney to Valparaiso, and thence to San Francisco. Her captain was a man named Mordaunt, and his wife and child were on board. But I was the only passenger in the sense of paying for a cabin. I was at sea when a boy. My health needed a successive change of climates; so, knowing Mordaunt, who was a very good fellow, I hired a cabin in the *Esmond*, intending to make my way from San Francisco to New York, and so to England. Three days ago we were in collision with a large steel sailing-ship, which cut us down on the starboard bow, and made off in the gloom of the evening and vanished. The water gained upon us, but we held on till yesterday evening, when the ship was within half an hour of foundering. This gave us time to lower the boats, and stock them. The captain went with his wife and child, and a little crowd; there was another boat; and ours. The man who fetched the water for you was the boatswain. We lost sight of the other boats in the night, and this island shone out upon us this morning when the sun rose. You have been seven months here," he added, looking slowly around him. "Am I to believe that no ship has ever come within sight of this island in all that time?"

"I vow to God," answered Reynolds, "that I have not once caught sight of a sail or smoke."

"But, surely," said Goodhart, "an island almost directly in the way of the course shaped by vessels bound from Australia to South Chilian ports must often be passed by ships."

"Never have I seen one," cried Reynolds. "Though conceive—conceive the sort of look-out a man in my situation would keep."

Goodhart looked very pensive.

Reynolds cried rapturously in a sudden hurry of joy, "How often have I exclaimed to myself, if I had but one—but *one* to speak to!" And, laying hold of Goodhart's hand, he bowed his head.

Goodhart viewed the poor fellow with a most noble and touching expression of pity that seemed to lie upon his face like a sort of holy light, as though there was something divine in the spirit within him, and that shone in his face as one could conceive of a saint, or of the Redeemer—not to speak profanely—when He addressed soothing words. Reynolds released his hand, and Goodhart, looking towards the cave, asked—

"Do you sleep there?"

"No; my bed is yonder, in a crack in the embankment of that dell. This island has been occupied. I found some old relics of human habitation in that cave."

"How have you lived?"

"I have taken fish and drank that water," answered Reynolds, directing his eyes at the cascades. "When do you mean to start?"

"I shall not trust my life to an open boat," answered Goodhart. "This is solid land, and I intend to remain to be taken off."

Reynolds looked startled. "You will not surely remain alone here?"

"A thousand times over, sooner than take the risk of an open boat. Consider," said Goodhart, speaking with great deliberation, and with a slight Irish accent; "when we were in the boat we found that she was without mast or sail."

"Ho!" exclaimed Reynolds.

"We hailed the nearest boat to be taken in tow; but I don't think she heard us. The night came along so fast that until the moon shone the sea absorbed the boats like bits of ebony afloat on ink. Next, our breaker holds six gallons only. Now, you are one of us, and think of what a breaker containing six gallons for eight men in a rowing boat, and a great ocean to measure—think what such a thing signifies! But I beg your pardon, sir, you are a sailor."

"I quite agree with you; the risk is enormous," said Reynolds. "But surely it is preferable to this imprisonment."

"No; because I am quite certain that ships do at times come within sight of this island," said Goodhart, mildly, but firmly. "It is a coincidence that nothing should have appeared during your stay here. Probably, within the next few days something may come along, and take us off. My heart is weak. I have suffered for years from that organ, and shall die of it, if nothing else kills me. Exposure, the horrible suffering of thirst, would make haste to do their work with me, and I shrink from the idea of my body being thrown over the gunwale of the boat by those sailors. And I have my reasons for choosing a possible sentence of imprisonment here that may run into months, rather than take my chance in an open sailless boat with seven comrades and a breaker of six gallons; and what to eat to last us if we are not soon picked up, or make the land?"

"We must rig up a mast," said Reynolds.

"Where's the sail to come from?" exclaimed Goodhart.

"The sailors must stitch their shirts together," answered Reynolds.

"Have you got needles and thread here?"

"None."

"Nothing in which fresh water may be stored?"

Reynolds considered, and answered, "Nothing."

"The sight of these waterfalls makes me thirsty," said Goodhart, who rose, and walked with Reynolds to the bank of the river where the bright water foamed.

Here Reynolds had placed several large oyster shells for his own convenience, and these made good saucers for dipping and drinking. The men had drank, and had lounged down to the beach for oysters and shell-fish.

"This is delicious water," exclaimed Goodhart. "It sinks sweet and cold to one's very marrow, like the flavour of a banana after a long voyage."

"Ah, I have found it sweet and good medicine," exclaimed Reynolds. "A few weeks ago I received an ugly visit from an old friend of mine—Mediterranean fever. I might guess my own temperature, about a hundred and four, and a slow pulse—not the pulse of fever—and a weary throbbing headache, and a thirst which scarcely those waterfalls," said he, looking up, "were able to quench."

"And with the chance of that fever recurring at any moment, as its habit is," said Goodhart, "you would trust yourself in a boat without sails, containing eight men, and a breaker of six gallons?"

Reynolds looked down upon the ground thoughtfully. There could be no doubt that his mind had been weakened by solitude and suffering, mental and physical, and he was in a state when he was to be swayed, and not with difficulty. There had been a time—it would have been the same with him now had he been alone—when, could it have been said to him, "There is an open boat in that fishing creek of yours; she is without mast or sail, and in her bow is a little cask that holds six gallons of fresh water," he would have fried fish in his shovel with incomparable despatch, hove into the boat a freight of oysters and of mushrooms, if the season yielded them, and have gone away with a hymning heart, taking his chance by sculling her out to drift into deliverance; taking his chance of the most lonely, the most God-forsaken death a man can die, sooner than remain locked up, a broken, solitary, speechless, and hopeless prisoner in this island solitude.

"I should like to look into that cave," said Goodhart.

And together they went into it.

Goodhart entered, and gazed about him as a man might who inspects a room he has a mind to rent. When the sight was used to the gloom, Goodhart examined the contents of the shelf in the chest, peered at the little bundle of clay pipes, looked at the old musket and the buckle shoes.

"It makes one think of the old buccaneers," said he. "I should say, with you, the date is about eighteen hundred. They did not maroon men then, though it is true that the captain of a man-of-war sent a seaman named Jeffreys ashore to perish as fast as he could. He was rescued, and did well on the merits of his sufferings. Who was the owner of this chest?" said he, viewing the letters on the lid. "I remember at Bath Abbey looking down upon the pavement and seeing a memorial stone, from which the lettering had been totally effaced, saving the single word 'Esq.' Of such is the pomp and importance of man."

"I once saw the owner of this chest walking in the dell by moonlight," said Reynolds. "The bushes made a shadow, but no shadow walked with the man. He never again returned, and I was glad."

"Oh, what can equal loneliness as a vision-breeder!" exclaimed Goodhart. "And yet," he continued, gravely regarding the old sea-chest, "I don't know, Captain Reynolds, why the illusions of the brain should be more unreal than the ideas we receive from our sensations. We are beset with mysteries vaster and more profound than ghosts. They are so familiar that few give them thought. Yet, though we walk in the sunshine, no man knows what brightness is, no man what heat is. We slumber, but no man knows what sleep is. We don't know why the inverted image upon the retina should be accepted right-side up by the brain. We believe that time is a thing measurable by the flight of the heavenly bodies, and that it would cease if the sun stood still; but we do not know what fills the interval, sun or no sun, between our leaving a chair and reaching a door, or quitting Liverpool and arriving at Boston."

This was a form of speculation very much in Reynolds'' way, and he watched the speaker with interest.

"Where do you catch fish?" said Goodhart.

Reynolds replied; and they walked together to the creek. A boat of a whaling pattern lay snug in the

little harbour betwixt the fishing-rock and the shore.
Reynolds started at the sight of her.

"Ah, my God!" he exclaimed softly. "How often
have I dreamt of such a thing."

"The open boat stands next to the raft in my
catalogue of the direst horrors of the deep," exclaimed
Goodhart.

A man was in the boat handing provisions to the
rest of the fellows ashore; one or two of whom were
already seated and eating. These stood up when
Goodhart and Reynolds approached. Presently the
whole company were seated and eating. They had
drunk plentifully, and did not want water. To Reynolds,
after months of oysters and fried fish, the tinned meat
and ship's biscuits were delicious.

"I beg pardon," said the waistcoated man, whom we
shall call boatswain. "Do you catch your fish with
'ooks and lines?"

Reynolds explained how he caught fish, and added
that he would catch some for them presently.

"Please, capt'n, how fur off 's Chili?" inquired a
sober-looking young sailor.

"All three hundred miles," answered Reynolds.

"What are the ports, sir?" asked another; for
Reynolds had been master of a ship, and these seamen
naturally looked up to him as a navigator.

"Santiago, Valdivia, Valparaiso, and some smaller
ports," was the reply.

"Ain't Joan Fernandez knocking about close by
somewheres?" inquired the boatswain.

"It's as distant as the coast of Chili from this island,"
responded Reynolds.

"How are you going to make a port without a sail?"
said Goodhart.

"My answer to Mr. Goodhart was, let the men take their shirts," said Reynolds, "and connect them into a sail with fibres of creepers."

"I'm afraid," said the boatswain, with a slow shake of his head, "that such a sail 'ud blow away from its yard in the first bit of wind like smoke from a baccy pipe."

"Have you got a compass?" asked Reynolds.

"No," answered Goodhart.

"How are you going to find your way along?" inquired Reynolds.

Goodhart shrugged his shoulders.

"By the sun, and by other bodies in the 'eavens, as others have done in their day," said the boatswain.

"I'm for keeping all fast and giving ourselves a chance of a ship passing, and making for her in the boat," said a sailor.

"Yes!" exclaimed Goodhart, with a warm nod of approval.

"But," said the boatswain, "here's Capt'n Reynolds bin seven months and never sighted a wessel, though I reckon you kept a sharp look-out, sir?"

"I've climbed that hill two or three times a day. A look-out! But my sight is not as it was."

"You see," said a sailor, "that we are shipwrecked men. I've lost all but what I'm a-sittin' in, and I want to get ashore and begin again. I don't take on to the notion of turning crab or cockle, and that's what a man becomes who lives without wages, or clothes, or a house in islands of this sort."

Murmurs of approval attended this delivery.

"I'll show you how to catch fish," said Reynolds.

He fetched his fishing-line and landing-basket, which he kept snug in a little hole on the mainland, and

showed the men what they were made of. He took his
meteorite and hammered off the requisite bait. Goodhart and the sailors watched him with profound interest.
This was the product of bitter experience, the reality of
human need and suffering on Nature's own stage: no
delusive coinage of imagination such as a dramatist
might introduce in a sea play. A fish took the bait
readily, and Reynolds landed a twenty pounder of the
cod species in his basket, to the admiration of the
seamen.

"It's bloomed clever," said one of them. "Durned
if I should have thought of it."

"Is it your own idea, captain?" inquired Goodhart.

"The Patagonians fish like this," was the answer.

"A couple of you had better turn to," said the
boatswain, "and cut lines after that pattern, and I'll
make another landing-basket, which 'ull be enough."

Nothing more was said about stopping or going.
The boatswain asked Reynolds if there was a piece of
sailcloth in the cave, or any other stuff in the island
fit to make a sail of. Reynolds told him there was not
a rag, except the old cloak that wrapped him at night
and the clothes they wore. Some now went to work
to make lines; one or two searched the island for anything that might prove useful to them, particularly for
anything in which water might be stored for a boat
voyage. But Reynolds could easily have told them
that this quest must prove worthless.

He and Goodhart went to a green slope under a
tree and sat down. The autumn vegetation clothed the
island with many beautiful and some glowing tints.
The season's growth of mushrooms was plentiful. Wild
flowers, with petals blue and crimson and orange, blew

a small fragrance into the air. Reynolds again took notice of the peculiar bulkiness of Goodhart's figure: it was as though he wore stays or was padded. His attire consisted of a yachting cap, a double-breasted round cloth coat, and dark cloth trousers. He wore a wedding-ring on his little finger, and a large signet-ring on his right forefinger. When he seated himself now, he unbuttoned his coat, and discovered a dark-red waistcoat with gilt buttons; a heavy gold chain lay upon it, and when he drew out his watch Reynolds saw that it was a fine and very valuable gold time-piece.

"I never thought," said Goodhart, "that I should be wrecked on a desolate island. I believe I hankered after something of the sort when I was a boy. You have been sharing the experiences of Robinson Crusoe. To what degree does your practice correspond with Defoe's imagination?"

"I should have been glad," answered Reynolds, "had a ship been stranded within rafting distance full of everything that I wanted. It is easy for writers of romances to oblige their castaways by wrecking ships, not only to feed and clothe, but to put plenty of money in their pockets. Your reckoning makes out that I have been here seven months, and I have never caught sight of even the royals of a ship, and no more smoke than you now see."

"You missed Man Friday," said Goodhart.

"Yes," said Reynolds, with a faint smile. "I could have put up with somebody to fish with, to have made signs to, even if he no speakee."

"Are you married, sir?"

Reynolds slightly bowed.

"Any children, might I ask?"

K

Reynolds gravely shook his head.

"A wife in England, waiting and hoping. Ah," said Goodhart, with a face of abstraction as though he thought aloud, " none but the sufferer knows the pathos, the pang of the heartache, the depth of the human sigh, the bitterness of the human tear contained in that one awful word, *missing*. But, Captain Reynolds, I have faith in the direction of the drift and in the issues of life. It does so happen at the end that things have shaped themselves for our good. If you are spared to look back upon this incident of your career, you will find a circumstance of good in it, a gem set in a crown of thorns and nettles which you could not have done without, and would not have forfeited for twenty-fold more of suffering than you have endured."

"Are you married, Mr. Goodhart?"

"This was her ring," Goodhart answered, taking between his thumb and forefinger the wedding-ring on his little finger. "It was enlarged to fit me. It was her wish that I should wear it and be buried in it. She died in childbed. I am as absolutely alone, captain, in this wide universe of correlations as you were yesterday."

"It's the happiest state of life!" exclaimed Reynolds. "Nobody to work for, nobody whose future must be your bitter business, nobody who by misconduct could disgrace your honourable name, nobody to—to—— " He looked away to the deep ocean recess, into the miles of hollow blue there, and the figure of Lucretia shaped itself before his mental vision. He started and found Goodhart observing him intently.

"Is that an old scar, captain, at your eye?"

"No. When I came to after being flung ashore here, I found my brow cut and bleeding and my mouth injured. The blow has affected the sight of the damaged eye, and it may be—I *hope* it may be—that ships' hull-down, have passed and I have not seen them. I have tried to catch a sight of myself in a pool of water, but never could distinguish such an image as could give me the view I want. Am I much distorted?"

"That could only be answered by one who knew you before you were injured. You have grown a fine length of hair," said Goodhart, with his placid, kindly smile. "I venture to say that you did not give that fathom of locks to the breeze on your quarter-deck."

"Nor this," said Reynolds, grasping his beard. "If you stay here, Time will adorn you too."

"I am not to be disturbed by the idea of hair," said Goodhart. "Nothing shall induce me to venture my life in that boat we arrived in. Good Heavens, look what a mighty surface the ocean is! What a contemptible atom, a microscopic monad, is an open boat—a vibrio of the deep which the passing telescope shall easily miss!"

Now, it is a fact, whether credible or not, that when these two men's conversation had reached this point, it was interrupted by a fellow who was half-way up the hill of cascades bellowing as though for his life, whilst he flourished his hand in ecstasies of gesture in the direction of the south-east horizon.

"Sail ho! sail ho!" he bawled, in a note that fell as clear upon the ear as the song of a lark in the sky.

Reynolds sprang to his feet.

"What's that he says?" he shouted, rounding to look up at the man.

"Sail ho! sail ho!" yelled the fellow.

And some figures of his shipmates went scrambling up to him.

"Go, and judge for yourself, Captain Reynolds," said Goodhart. "My weak heart will not allow me to attempt that hill."

CHAPTER VIII

CONVERSATIONS AND CONFIDENCES

REYNOLDS started to climb the hill, stepping fast. He gained the group of sailors, who all pointed at the sea together, as he came, and exclaimed, nearly in one voice—

"There she is, sir!"

Far out upon the sea hung what might have seemed to a landsman a rising star, pale as the pearl of the moon when she floats in the blue of the day. But the sailors knew that speck of light to be a ship, which way standing they could not then tell. Reynolds looked, but could not see her.

"There she is, sir."

Ah, they might point; but Reynolds failed to perceive her.

"You have no doubt she is a ship?" said he, with a look of a blind man, as he turned his face upon the seamen.

"Oh yes, sir; that's the sail of a ship right enough," answered the boatswain, who had dropped his task of plaiting a mesh to view the ship from the hillside. "Can you see our boat down there, sir?"

"Why, of course, clear enough; and I dare say I should be able to see that ship if she lifted her hull," answered Reynolds.

Again he strove with his eyes at the sea-line, and saw nothing but the junction of heaven and water.

"It may be that vessels have passed within sight, but at a great distance, and I have not seen them," said he.

"She is too far off to be of any good to us," said one of the men, with a nod at the sail. "But it's clear that this island *is* sighted, and, as I was a-saying down below there, I'm for keeping all fast and giving ourselves a chance before we agree to take what is to come by putting to sea without a sail."

"And with a beaker holding six gallons only," said Reynolds.

"Ay," said the boatswain, "it ought to be a vat."

"You'll find plenty of fuel laid ready for a smoke up in that hollow there," said Reynolds, pointing to the place he meant. "Day to day I have seen to that, but never a chance was given me to fire it."

"Where d'ye get fire from, sir?" asked the boatswain.

Reynolds pulled out his burning-glass. "Can you still see her?" he asked.

"Oh yes," answered one of the men. "But she's passing away; she's dying out."

One remained to watch and report. Reynolds rejoined Goodhart.

"I am not surprised that you shouldn't see her," said Goodhart. "You generally find that the vision of one eye sympathizes with that of the other; and how far distant is she, do you think?"

"Why, we should command a view of twenty-five miles up there, and she's just in sight, the men say, and fading," said Reynolds.

"Well," answered Goodhart, "her appearance determines me to stop. I am convinced that an island, situated as this is, must be frequently sighted and occasionally visited. What do you say now to the chance supplied you by a passing ship and a fast boat to get at her, and nothing but that same boat without mast or sail and a six-gallon keg?"

"Oh, Mr. Goodhart, you have not yet had seven months of it," answered Reynolds, with a sort of sick shudder.

"But you're alive, sir, and well, and you need but a barber and a tailor to return to the aspect you have doffed. But an open boat! Figure three weeks, and all the fresh water gone, and the fever has come upon you again——" Mr. Goodhart added blandly, but with a deliberation that made you understand that the teeth of his mind were set, "I stay here. And I hope those men won't be foolhardy enough to quit the island unless to pursue a ship."

They looked up at the hill, and saw the man who had been left to watch coming down, whereby they knew that that distant vision of light had vanished.

The men passed the day in fishing, cooking, preparing the cave with couches and bolsters of grass for the night. The river was just a walk; for this was, as we know, but a little island one mile long and three-quarters wide, and if a man felt thirsty, he could slake his thirst in a few minutes in the sweet cold water that came down the hill in silver hawsers, and foamed in glory where the little river began.

A fine night came along, this the first night of Goodhart's and the men of the *Esmond's* visit. They had some plug tobacco amongst them, and there were pipes of the year 1800 or thereabouts in the old sea-chest. A coat that had been taken from the chest by Reynolds and cast and left upon the floor of the cave proved as good as tinder. They cut off a piece, and Goodhart gave them a wax match out of a silver box, with which they set fire to the piece of old coat. This glowed long enough to enable them to smoke and re-light and smoke again.

Goodhart and Reynolds walked together upon the white beach that streamed before and behind them like ivory in the clear light of the moon. Their shadows marched black at their sides. The sea under the moon quivered with her light. The air was filled with the solemn roar of the bursting surge south-east, and with the cymbals of the cataracts threading with metallic music the delicate orchestra of the wind in the dark vegetation, and with the weary voice of the wheeling breakers rolling into foam upon the sand. As they paced, Goodhart talked of himself.

"My father," said he, "was a clergyman, who had a living in Ireland. Do I call it a living? God help him! We were so poor that unless he caught a hare for dinner we went without a midday meal. Of all forms of poverty the poverty of the poor clergyman is the most distressful, for he cannot lie in hiding as a retired Service man might. He must go about; his linen must be clean; his apparel decent. He must have words of sympathy, and even a trifle in money when, as God knows, he grievously wants these things himself. He had but two children—myself and my sister. She was a girl sweet to the sight as a plum tree in May. But the good die first, said Wordsworth, and she was carried off by a galloping consumption. I did not choose to starve at home, so I made my way to Waterford, and got a berth as cabin boy and cook's mate in a crazy old brig called the *Emerald Isle*. She was a coaster, and the soft tack we got was not half so soft as the hard weather was hard. I afterwards shipped as an ordinary seaman in a barque commanded by a Yankee, who was, without doubt, the greatest outrage upon the image of God that was ever perpetrated by those dangerous confederates against the peace of the world—I mean man and woman. I fled from this scoundrel at Boston, and shipped for Australia, where, in company with nearly the whole of the crew, I ran. I found work, and made a little money and married. Oh, Captain Reynolds, it is hard to love and lose ; to love well, and lose irremediably."

"I have loved and lost, and know what you mean," answered Reynolds.

"But your wife lives ? "

" Tell me your story, Mr. Goodhart."

" It is told. I lingered in Australia, and then made up my mind to return to England and die there. I think I explained why I chose the *Esmond*. Did nothing belonging to your ship, a body, or what the law holds more precious, goods, come ashore ? "

"Nothing. I looked for a corpse. My ship's sole relic is the person who speaks to you."

" Do you lose much by this disaster ? "

"More than I can afford. I am a poor man."

Goodhart halted and looked at the sea.

" It is a mighty cemetery," he said. " There is no foaming head of billow that should prove one too many as a gravestone for the dead in the deep. I can't but think drowning one of the most painful forms of death. The agony may be brief, but——whilst it's with you ! "

" I have sometimes, during my loneliness," said

Reynolds, as they resumed their walk, "tried to disturb my mind by conjecturing whether we suffer pain after death."

Goodhart's head slowly shook in the moonshine.

"A man dies," continued Reynolds, "and a new form of vital activity begins. His body changes into chemicals, gases and the like. Are these changes accompanied by sensation? Sensation can exist without the consciousness of sensation, as we know from the circumstance that sensation occupies an appreciable time to travel from any given part of the body to the brain."

"If there is no consciousness to receive sensation," said Goodhart, "it is not present, so far as we are concerned, and, therefore, when we die pain ends."

"I forget the speed of sensation," said Reynolds.

"Helmholtz," answered Goodhart, "computes it at about seventy feet a second."

"Yes, I remember," exclaimed Reynolds. "So that if you should let fall a paving-stone on the bunnion of a giant seventy feet tall, a second would elapse before his brain received the news, another appreciable interval must be allowed to enable the molecules of the brain to adjust themselves for the reception of the report, and another second must pass whilst the brain is telegraphing to the foot to kick or stamp. Sensation, therefore, in this case, is present without consciousness. Why not in the human corpse that is undergoing all sorts of transmutations?"

"The times have been that when the brains were out the man would die, and there an end," answered Goodhart. "I do not care whether I am to have sensation or not after I am dead. I only desire to understand that I shall not feel."

"You remarked this morning, Mr. Goodhart, that we are beset with mysteries," said Reynolds. "What is more absolutely impenetrable than the mystery of sensation ? We are told that it is merely the translation of the vibration of an object into consciousness in us, but why that consciousness should clothe the vibration with form, colour, music, flavour, fragrance, softness or hardness, heat or cold, and the countless conditions of life, spiritual and physical, is God's secret, and apparently must for ever be so."

"I answer you thus," said Goodhart. "We have five senses, and all the qualities and inherent conditions of the objects we hear, see, and feel, and so on, make individual appeals to us through those senses. The objects are there, and they report themselves as there ; for, if they were not there, what news could vibration vehicle? I have no shadow of a doubt that, outside what we know of objects, such as their perfume, brightness, shape, colour, and so on, are attributes and qualities of which we know nothing, and can know nothing, owing to the limitation of our senses. Could a man err in plucking a flower and saying, 'there is more in this than meets the eye or the touch or the smell'?"

"This is a strange platform for the discussion of such things," said Reynolds.

"I judge as a sailor you have been a student, Captain Reynolds."

"Well, yes, I have read and I have thought. The night-watch at sea finds you leisure for the latter."

"Does it not occur to you," said Goodhart, "that the mere circumstance of the *Esmond* having gone down within a night's pull of this island should convince us that ships must pass within sight ?"

"Yes, and that sail to-day is hopeful," answered

Reynolds; "but I do assure you, keen as my look-out has been, that in seven months I have seen nothing."

After a little more talk of this kind they went to rest for the night—Reynolds to his bed in the dell, and Goodhart to the cave. The men had prepared grass beds for all hands. The moon shone bright, and Goodhart easily found the mouth and entered. It was very black within. He struck a wax match, not knowing where his couch of grass was. Dim outlines of sleeping men were thrown up. By his little taper, Goodhart perceived a vacant couch close at hand. He blew out his light and lay down. A sailor called out in his sleep—

"'Ow's a man to 'ook on if yer don't luff and shake it out of her? Luff, damn you, luff, I say, luff!"

"What buddy old owl is that a-hooting?" exclaimed the boatswain, in a deep voice.

A wave of snores followed, and Goodhart slumbered with the rest.

Reynolds, in his fissure, lay watching the moonshine that bathed the sky over the dell. The glowing stars of those temperate heights trembled in the silver mist. The hysteric hurry of mind, which had been his in the morning lon his discovery of men in the island and a boat, and which had remained his for some hours, was gone. A sober tranquillity and abiding emotion of gratitude and of peace had replaced it. He lay thinking of Goodhart. There was something in the manner, the voice, the looks, the gentle smiles and tender pensiveness of the man, that fascinated Reynolds, and won his heart with the beautiful and irresistible power with which truth, no matter in what it dwells, wins human affection. He impressed him as a man whose character was a harp from whose strings the spirit-fingers of the soul swept music that was always sweet and good. What had passed between them in conversation had expressed them as intimate in sympathy, for it had not needed a day for Reynolds to discover that Goodhart had in his time been a student and a thinker, more particularly in those metaphysical walks which Reynolds loved to tread.

One point Goodhart had made clear : he was determined not to risk his life by a voyage in a little open craft which was without mast or sail, and in which it would be impossible, so barren was the island in this respect, to store water enough for eight men, to last, even on the leanest allowance, for more than two or three days. This was a resolution to give Reynolds pause too. His desire to leave the island, which was consuming when he was alone, was moderated by companionship ; moderated to the extent that he was too old a hand as a sailor to take his chance in an open sailless boat when, by waiting, as the sail that hove into sight that morning promised, his deliverance might be procured with comfort and safety. If a sail could be obtained the hazard of the voyage would be diminished, because even though they should be unable to shape a course for a port, yet by heading due east they were bound to blow into the track of ships steering north or south. But to start in a rowing-boat he easily understood would be suicidal, and think as he might, and think as he did, as he lay straining his mind in the fissure, he could not conceive what the island might yield in the shape of a sail, unless the men put his idea about their shirts into practice, and it did not seem to him, as he reflected, that the manufacture of such a sail would be worth the effort.

For some days the men were patient and watchful.
They dried and smoked a quantity of fish, which they
stocked in the locker of the stern-sheets of the boat.
They were also careful to keep the beaker filled with
fresh water in preparation for the instant emergency.
They seemed to enjoy this lounging life of the island.
They culled nosegays and decorated themselves. They
ate oysters and mussels. They fished diligently and
cooked their takes, and it will be judged that, after the
salt horse and worm-bored sea-bread of the forecastle,
the mushrooms and cod steaks and steaks of other fish,
and the fish they dried and smoked, provided them with
a heavenly banquet. But they had brought with them
but a lenten store of plug tobacco. The pieces soon
gave out, and the want started a spirit of discontent and
restlessness. They hunted for a substitute, but could
find nothing of any sort to replace the black cavendish
of their love. They were without rum, and wanted tea,
cocoa, or coffee for a hot drink. They were sailors, and
a sailor without a grievance is a tool without a handle.
After a few days they began to feel thoroughly shipwrecked, and the gaze they levelled at the sea-line grew
more and more ardent, and more and more rebellious.
It was easily gatherable from their general bearing that
they did not mean to stay long for a ship to appear.

Goodhart and Reynolds were inseparable. They
had contracted such a liking for each other as promised
to become a bond of affectionate friendship. For some
time Reynolds was reserved about his past. One afternoon they were seated on a knoll in the shade where
they commanded a fine view of the dazzle of thunder-
sounding foam on the south-east side, and of the two
lovely cataracts which arched in apparently polished
motionless glass from the rocks, then quivered into

prisms, tinting the immediate air with pallid lights of the spectrum. Goodhart for a few moments watched a bird in silence.

"How wonderful that fellow's wings and body are dyed!" he exclaimed. "Look at his white breast, and the blue edgings to the indigo that stains the feathers of his wings. God works with a purpose in lights and colours."

"Oh yes, undoubtedly," said Reynolds. "I've heard of a little fish whose dorsal spine consists of a long filament arching over the head and mouth, the mouth filled with frightful teeth. At the extremity of the filament there is a brilliant phosphorescent spot. The hideous little monster hangs out this lovely star, and everything small that comes to admire is devoured."

"Yes," said Goodhart, "I have heard of a fish found three miles deep with a phosphorescent eye which it kindles at pleasure, either to scare its enemies or allure its victims."

"Take the ptarmigan," said Reynolds, with a glance at the wheeling sea-bird that had attracted Goodhart. "This bird is almost black in summer. Nature protects it by providing changes of colour with the seasons. If it remained black it would be at the mercy of the hawk or the owl in winter, when the country is white with snow. In summer the country is dark, and the ptarmigan is black. In autumn the country is gray, and the ptarmigan turns gray. In winter the plumage of this bird is white. This is also true of the falcon and the snowy owl. If they were black in a country covered with snow, they would be eluded and starve."

"Some queer stories are told of the cuckoo," said Goodhart. "It is declared that it lays eggs coloured so as to deceive the birds in whose nests they are deposited.

The hedgesparrow is the greatest sufferer at the hands of the cuckoo. I remember reading that a German writer has declared that the cuckoo will sometimes lay perfectly blue eggs. The hoopoes are another illustration of purpose in colour. Their hue is sandy, and by virtue of that they may be known almost certainly to be inhabitants of a sandy region. When this bird sees a hawk it throws itself flat on the sandy ground, turns its wings up, and erects its bill so as to resemble as closely as possible a bit of old rag." He looked seawards and exclaimed, " I would swear that yonder is a ship, if I were not sure that it is a cloud." He pointed.

Reynolds determinedly bent his vision, but what Goodhart saw was invisible to him. His companion viewed him with a gaze tender and touching with commiseration, the sympathy that does not depress like pity, but that exalts by unaffected fellowship of feeling, working like nature from the inside, and not like art from the outside.

" I devoutly hope," said he, " that we shall soon be released, if only for your sake. It is sad to think of your poor wife."

Reynolds fixed his eyes upon the ground.

" Have you been long married ? "

" Long married ! " exclaimed Reynolds. " How long have those waterfalls been married ? They leap together and unite at the foot in a common grave of foam. But if they coexist, they also possess a most consuming divisibility. I'll tell you a queer story of a wedding, Mr. Goodhart. You are a man of deep thought and great humanity. Perhaps you will be able to suggest a key for the lock of a safe in which lies a jewel so absolutely embowelled that no pearl in its oyster at the bottom of the sea is more secret and distant."

Goodhart's face wore an expression of benevolent attention.

"Conceive a man loving a woman as purely, loftily, loyally as it is in the power of male flesh and blood to love that which God wills it to yoke. They were married. The mother of the bride was present. She was the bridegroom's very good friend and well-wisher. The bride on her return home from the church locked herself up in her bedroom and refused to see, or to speak to, or to have anything to do with her husband. No, by old Harry, Mr. Goodhart, she threatened to poison herself if the man ventured so much as to approach her bedroom door. Had the Marriage-Service converted her husband into a hedgehog, or a bat, or a toad, or something which makes women scream and shrink and faint, this wife's loathing could not have been more phenomenally profound. He had his memories of endearments, and was paralyzed by astonishment and dismay, and, indeed, despair. What had come to her? But his letters, his entreaties, her mother's influence, availed nothing. He sailed from Falmouth, leaving her behind him; his ship was burnt, and he was cast ashore on an island, and was seven months alone." After he had pronounced these words his voice failed him.

"It is a strange story," said Mr. Goodhart, regarding the poor fellow with an expression of touching kindness. "When you sailed you were separated?"

"We have never lived together."

"When were you married?"

Reynolds gave him the date.

Goodhart mused, and his face took on a look of judicial gravity.

"It is impossible to consider it as aversion in her,"

L

he said. "Human nature does not change in an hour. If we are to call it aberration, then we shall know what to think. I should regard it as a sudden violent distemper of morality. It is not dislike of you, but love of ego, a disease of self which the physiologist would view as the antithesis of a mania not rare amongst women. If I were you, I should hail this state of shipwreck as an avenue that is to conduct you to her heart."

"How?"

"Already your ship is overdue. She will soon be posted. To the imagination of your wife you are a drowned man. Your appeal of abandonment and of death will prove an eloquence that must find her a heart. Give her that, and when you again meet, as surely as she is human, and as surely as you love her, you will find her yours by virtue of an ordeal that shall make her more triumphantly your own than any other form of conquest could render her."

"The Marriage Service changed her into a statue. Nothing chiselled in marble could be more insensible."

"Depend upon it, Captain Reynolds, that a woman's heart beats under that hard surface, and her conviction of your death and her memory of what preceded your departure will work in her."

"If I return," exclaimed Reynolds, with a little wildness in the look he sent at the sea, "I shall not seek her. To be repulsed again—spat upon—— Time, Mr. Goodhart, time! I have been alone for months, and my thoughts have run as a lonely man's would ; but, despite the carved figure that weeps over the urn, despite the sumptuous memorial window, I must believe, I must hope, that the inscription wears out, that the slate is cleansed by something else than tears, that the flame is often extinguished before the candle is expended." '

" I trust it will happen as shall make best for your happiness," said Goodhart, with emotion. " What is your age ? "

Reynolds replied.

" And your wife's ? "

Reynolds told him. Goodhart smiled gravely.

"You must meet again as sweethearts," he said. " You are proud of her, and fond of her. Indeed, you are rapturously fond of her. The charm that won you is still hers. She is your wife. Nothing but God's hand can keep you apart. Not, indeed, but that chastity so rigid is extremely unamiable and very undesirable. A sister of mercy who nursed me said, 'To prove how bad an opinion God has of us, observe that He is perpetually replacing us and trying others. Generation succeeds generation.' 'And what opinion,' I answered, ' can He have of those who think it improper to help Him ? ' It is an oversight on the part of a person to marry one with whom personal association is, when rather late in the day, considered objectionable. For example, how much trouble would be saved if men made it a rule to choose the right sister to begin with ! The hearts of the bishops would be lighter ; there would be a little less talk in the House of Lords. You will find no difficulty in getting another berth ? "

" I can't say," answered Reynolds. " Captains are very plentiful, and I have not been very fortunate."

" I have a friend in Sydney," said Goodhart, " who is a managing director of a coastwise line of steamers. The pay is good, and the people employed are loyally used. I should be most happy to give you a letter to him."

"You are extremely kind, Mr. Goodhart."

"But you will naturally wish to return to England to follow your profession in that country."

" Why ? "

" Your wife is in England."

Reynolds shook his head. Goodhart smiled.

"We were just now talking of purpose in colour," said he, breaking from a subject that might have easily been made painful by even a *nuance* of insistence. " I have often asked myself, to what degree is colour necessary as a fibre or thread in the woof of matter ? The solar light is formed of coloured rays, visible and invisible, and by and in that light does Creation move and have its being. But is colour essential as a constituent of matter ? For instance, is colour a part of the flower's life, so that in the absence of colour the flower would need something as necessary to its being as any formative condition of its existence ? Or, restricting myself to the flower, is it painted merely to delight ? If so, for whose delight is it coloured ? Is it to be supposed that the sole purpose of colour is to gratify the æsthetic sense in man ? That colour is a created thing, whose existence is independent of human sensation, is too clear to need talking about. If visually we know that colour is a concomitant of state or change, we have a right to infer that colour is an abiding quality in coloured matter, and that the conditions under which it accompanies all mutations render it inseparable from matter ; a property, therefore, indwelling in objects both in darkness and light."

"You mean," said Reynolds, " that if, for example, you carried a red rose into a black room, it would retain its colour ? "

"I mean," answered Goodhart, " that the cause of

the redness remains in the rose in the black room, and what is that cause but colour ? "

" It seems to me," said Reynolds, " that the causes of colour consist of three things ; first, the solar light ; secondly, the selective properties of the coloured objects ; thirdly, the human eye. Extinguish one of these things, and you extinguish colour. In this way, perhaps, it may be shown that colour is as much a property of the object that possesses it as of the light that reveals it or the eye that beholds it."

" I cannot allow your red rose to lose its glory," said Goodhart, "simply because you can't see it. For example, take a glass of port and a glass of sherry into a black cellar. Taste them. You will recognize each one by its flavour. If the flavour is present, why not the colour ? There are certain crystals, forms of fluorspar, which, though they have remained buried for centuries in the earth, have, nevertheless, what has been termed a 'potentiality of light' locked up in them. Do you hold that that potential light is not light until you see it ? "

" You want to corner me," said Reynolds, smiling, " by forcing me to admit that the extent of creation cannot be limited by our knowledge of its existence through our sensations. But what other guides have we ? If I can't see colour or light, it has no being so far as I am concerned."

" But the sun shines, and the rose is red, though the blind man sees neither. Snow is melted by those rays of the sun which are invisible. Those rays may be made visible by a process called calorescence. Do they not exist as a part of the sun's light because you can't see them ? "

" Pardon me, Mr. Goodhart, but isn't there a smack of sophistry in this reasoning ? "

Goodhart smiled. It was evident that he talked rather to divert than to convince his companion.

"You doubtless remember," said he, " Tyndall's noble illustration of the invisibility of light. He took a box like a photographic camera : either side was pierced with a little window. He allowed all the floating particles in the atmosphere contained in the box to be deposited. He then darted a powerful electric beam through the windows. The light streamed in brilliance to one window, passed in blackness through the box, and flashed through the other window with the splendour with which it had entered. Thus that great man proved that light, which renders all things visible, is itself invisible." He added, pleasantly smiling, " We must place but little confidence in our sensations."

Now what should seem stranger than that two ship-wrecked men, one of whom slept in a cave whilst the other took his rest in a fissure in a dell, should be found upon a little island seated on a grassy rise in the shade, discussing abstract problems of science with as much sincerity as if they were going up for an examination, with their chance of deliverance from their awful position so feeble as to entitle them to a habit of mental prostration? But in the human mind there is latent a power of philosophy which almost unconsciously helps it to adapt itself to any state it may chance to be in without violent departure from old habits or forms of thought. Suppose two maids-of-honour flung ashore from the sea, why should not they at intervals talk of drawing-rooms, presentations, the duchess's red face, the blazing fat throat of Lady Throgmorton Street? things it is true of a past more or less recent, but topics of habitual inspiration nevertheless. Two stock-jobbers similarly cast up by the deep might be expected in the pauses between the meal of mussels and the search for something more digestible, to talk of loans and mines, of Goschen's year, and the prospects of Japan. Our two companions loved science, and from time to time, as we see, there was nothing in shipwreck to stop them from talking about it.

But their story, after a brief passage of rest, was to change suddenly into the eventful.

CHAPTER IX

THE CHASE

ON the 2nd October, making it rather more than a fortnight since the arrival of the boat's crew, a man named Lydiart, being the first to awaken, quitted the cave and came into the open, where he yawned and stretched his arms, and then slowly looked around him. It was blowing what sailors would call a royal breeze. Wings of dusky cloud sailed under the sky. The east was a moist purple and the clouds came out of it stained with that tint; but before they gained the central heaven they changed into greys and browns with their skirts gilt by the sun. The stretch of coral sand was noisy with breakers which charged in cannon-shocks and receded sweating, cruelly fingering long black lines of weed as though they were tresses of the land they were seeking to tear off; and the ocean was filled with lighted lines of seas whose edgings of foam ran athwart in parallel archings till the whole surge sank in its own splendour of whiteness. Loud was the organ-thunder rolling from the stern abrupt which the island opposed to the sea south-east. The little piece of land was full of the music of the morning ; and the sea-birds glanced as they wheeled and slanted from dark shapes into bright.

A second man came out of the cave. He was grim with a fortnight's growth of hair on face and head.

" Anything in sight ? " he asked.

" Ain't 'ad time to 'ave a look round."

" I'm growing buddy sick of this," said number two. " I'm for making a start and chancin' it. That there Captain Reynolds ain't fur out, you lay. Seven months, he says, and nothen showin', and 'ere we've bin getting on more'n a buddy fortnight, and what's hove into view good for anybody but a blind man ?"

Here a third sailor came out. He was followed by Goodhart and the other people, whilst Reynolds was to be seen approaching from his crack in the dell. Just on that part of the island where the men stood, only a little piece of the ocean was to be seen.

" Jim ! " said the boatswain. " Run aloft up that 'ill, and see if there's anything to report."

" Good morning, Mr. Goodhart," said Reynolds. " Good morning, men."

" Blamed slow work this, sir," exclaimed the boatswain. " I feel sometimes as if I could have swum the distance. Three hunnerd miles, ain't it ? The English Channel's bin swum."

" Strike me silly," said a sailor, " if I wouldn't rather turn jelly-fish than keep all on 'ere."

" Wait till you've had over seven months of it," said Reynolds.

" That's just what we don't mean to wait for, then," answered the boatswain, who, though he recognized Captain Reynolds' position as a master and gentleman, was heedful to assert himself as commander of his own little company who would take their opinions from him, or at least submit to be advised by him, without allowing that Captain Reynolds, though a shipmaster, had the least authority amongst them.

The man who had gone up the hill to report, having

climbed about a hundred feet, stopped to take a look, and no sooner were his eyes upon the sea than he pointed and yelled—

"There she is, all a-growing and a-blowing! Sail ho! There she spouts!"

On which everybody rushed up to him saving Goodhart, who followed very slowly and with pauses. This time the whole of a ship's sails were in view. A square of white, like a butterfly on the margin of a meadow. She was down away westwards, too far off for the trim of her yards to be discernible, and the hull of her was out of sight behind the sea-line. Everybody but Reynolds saw her. At times he thought he caught sight of her, but his injured vision was betrayed by the white leap of the seas, and had he been alone she would have passed unnoticed.

"Which way is she standin'?" exclaimed the boatswain, panting with his hurry of limbs and excitement of spirits.

"She's on the port tack," said the man who had reported her.

This man had the best sight of any amongst them; in fact it was as good as a little pocket telescope.

"'Ow's the wind?" cried the boatswain.

"East," answered Reynolds.

"If she's on the port tack," cried the boatswain, almost shouting with sensation, "and the wind's east, she'll be heading so as to be liftin' her hull by the time that she's abreast of this island, and I'm for makin' for her and shoving right athwart her as she comes headin' up, so as to bring the north-east point of this rock on her starboard quarter."

This was closely followed and immediately understood by the men.

"I'm ready."

"So am I."

"So am I."

So were the whole six.

"Will you come, Mr. Good'art, and take your chance?" shouted the boatswain to that gentleman, who was painfully and slowly ascending the slope.

"I don't understand you," was the bawled reply.

The boatswain ran down to him.

"There," he cried, in his eagerness catching hold of Goodhart's arm, "there's the ship. D'ye see her, sir?"

"Yes, about ten miles off," answered Goodhart, staring at the vision on the sea.

"We're all for making a dead pull to wind'ard, so as to bring us within sight of her by the hour she's got the north-east point of this island on her starboard quarter. Will you come? There's no time to lose, sir."

"You mean to pull to windward against this sea and breeze?" exclaimed Goodhart, with a lift of eyebrows and a blank stare of wonder.

"Yes."

By this time the others had come down and were gathered round these two.

"What d'ye mean to do?" said Reynolds.

"We're a-going to row within sight of that ship," shouted the boatswain, hoarsely, and with a danger-signal in the tone of his voice.

"I advise you not to try it. Not against that weight of sea and wind," said Reynolds, striving to see the ship.

"We shall lose her if we stand here jawing," cried a man.

"You'll need to pull eight or ten miles to put yourselves within reach of her sight," said Reynolds. "What's her speed? You say she's on a taut luff? Call it seven."

"Come on, all as means to come," roared the boat-swain, smiting down Reynolds' reasoning as you might hit a man on the head with an iron pin, and away he ran in the direction of the creek where the boat lay, bawling, as he sprang along, "If we stop argyfying we lose her."

Instantly the sailors followed, racing and leaping like schoolboys just let loose.

"You'll report that we are left if you come up with her!" shouted Reynolds.

A fellow flung his arm up in token that the request had been heard. Reynolds' heart was in that distant sail, which was now, when he looked, a very dim delicate vision in the horizon of his eye; his soul raved for release from the withering imprisonment of this island. The mere figures of the running men fired him with a passion to run with them. For a minute the inward conflict was a very madness of mental convulsion, a tempestuous lunatic dance of contending feelings.

He was a man, however, habituated by his profession to the forming of the instant resolution. This is the inevitable education of the sailor who is worth his salt. Fog, collision, fire, the sudden tempest, the mighty ice island looming in thunder of bursting surge out of the snow-storm, do not admit of leisurely deliberation. Now he was understanding that vessels might have passed and he had not seen them, and Goodhart's hope and expectation of a comfortable deliverance, therefore, might be shared. Next he witnessed rashness, danger, and disappointment in that long pull against a head sea in a fresh wind. Likewise he perceived that the men's chances of salvation would be Goodhart's and his without their peril, for it could not be doubted that when the captain of the vessel had been informed that two men were left, he would heave his ship to and send for them. And finally, he was impelled by the affectionate regard in which he had already come to hold Goodhart to stop with him and share with him in such fortune as was to befall, be it what it might.

The men gained the boat, and jumped in. She was of the whaler pattern, sharp at both ends, a good boat, pulling five oars, with inboard air-tight boxes under her gunwales. They had taken care to keep her stocked with food and fresh water.

" It's a pity," said Goodhart, who, with his companion, had walked a little distance to obtain a better view of the boat's departure, " that they did not think of cutting down a long bough to attach a shirt to for waving ! "

" I can see the ship now," said Reynolds. " She can't be less than ten miles distant. If the boat heads due east, then, at three miles an hour—and they'll not sweep more out of her—it will be noon before she arrives at the point where she is to come in contact with the ship. And the ship," he continued, making his calculations as he spoke, " will, if she holds on all, have to sail a distance of thirty miles to arrive at the spot aimed at by the boat. She will accomplish this in four hours, and the boat will be one hour away from her—three miles short."

" What headstrong fools ! " exclaimed Goodhart.

But the men were already rowing. The boatswain steered. The oars flashed and sank, flashed and sank as the little fabric was urged over the still waters of the creek ; then she was in the open, and leaping, and Goodheart and his companion saw the figures of the men bending and backing with those motions of energy and determination which signify that the impulse which governs the toiler is the heart's cry of life or death.

The boat sprang bravely, showering crystals, heading right into the glittering lines of light which were rolled by the breeze under the soaring sun, until she faded out, even to the straining gaze of Goodhart, whilst the ship had floated up the horizon to the line of her bulwark rails, lifting jibs and spanker boom, and passing on with the beauty, grace, and dignity which are the gifts of sunshine and the blue breeze and flashing waters to a ship when she is under full sail, leaning the stirless bosoms of her canvas to the spectator, and beheld from afar.

"I shall make a smoke for that ship, but not yet," said Reynolds, who was now seeing her clearly.

"All's ready up there!" exclaimed Goodhart.

"I saw to it yesterday afternoon," Reynolds rejoined. "It will take her two hours to give us a sight of her hull."

"I am going for a drink and a dip," said Goodhart, and he walked leisurely in the direction of the river.

There was not much room for the exhibition of the mysterious in this little island, though an illustration came when the lonely captive had awakened and seen the figure of the owner of the chest walking shadowless in the moonshine, hat in hand ; but two points Reynolds had observed in Goodhart. He was never seen to take off his coat night or day, and though he bathed three or four times a week, he always contrived to take to the water with the strictest privacy, never before saying, as he had just now said, that he was going to the river for a plunge, but mentioning the circumstance to Reynolds afterwards, as the minutest incident came weighted with deepest interest in this dull and dismal routine of

watching the sea and catching and cooking fish. From
these trifles Reynolds inferred that Goodhart's dispro-
portioned bulkiness of trunk was due to some painless
but morbid growth, or that it was a deformity which he
desired with a feminine passion to conceal from the
sight of others.

Reynolds stood for a little while with his eyes fixed
on the ship. His gaze was yearning, his heart ached.
She was scarcely wanted to bring before him the image
of his wife, for not an hour of the day rolled past
but he thought of her. But that floating cloud out
yonder recalled the *Flying Spur;* how she might have
been out there just where that ship was ; how, if Lucretia
had given him her heart again, after he had decoyed her
on board, she might have been with him as though they
were together in that vessel, leaning side by side over
the bulwark-rail and viewing this same little island, with
its silver lightning of cascades and its lace-like trimming
of brilliant breakers, the theatre to him of a most sad
and pitiful drama of shipwreck.

He sighed, and cast his eyes up at the hill where the
fuel lay ready for kindling, and after weighing the
chance afresh of such a smoke as he could make being
seen by that ship which was still very nearly hull down
from the altitude from which he regarded her, he went
to work to build up a little fire in the cookpit, then
entered the cave, where were some fish taken yesterday,
cut off a couple of steaks and put them into the shovel,
which remained the only frying-pan in that island ; all
the while strenuously thinking of the probability of the
boat being seen by the ship, heartily praying for it, and
gravely doubting her chance.

There was nothing to eat but the mushrooms and
the fish. When the little meal was dressed he sat down

to wait for his companion and his friend. He presented
a most ragged figure, and one who had previously known
him might have judged by his face that his nature had
undergone a change. His look was pensive; he wore
an habitual air of melancholy; there was no fire or
spirit in his speech. He suggested a man whose heart
is cowed by thought that is ebon-tinged with memory,
and forlorn almost to hopelessness in anticipation. The
mother of this man would not have known her son. He
had that shaggy look which is often the impress of
toil, and nearly always accompanies privation at sea.
Seven months of solitude and the dismal eternity of the
encircling ocean had so wrought in him that if you had
met him in a crowded street he would have been the
one to seize your gaze and compel you to look after
him, and to proceed in thought about him.

Goodhart came from the river, and sat down beside
him.

"We should be thought vulgar for eating this fish
with our knives," said he, with an easy smile and gentle
voice that might have made you suppose they were
breakfasting comfortably at home.

"One does not learn good manners at sea," answered
Reynolds.

"The best of manners, surely," replied Goodhart.
"When a sailor is a gentleman, a more perfect gentleman you shall not find. I am fond of observing the
contrasts of life. Take our situation; compare a noble-
man in Grosvenor Square at breakfast; take the tramp
who has dossed it under a hedge through the night
breaking his fast on a turnip he has sneaked from a
field after a wary look round. I remember passing a
church where a wedding had just taken place, and the
bells were pealing joyously in the tower, and in the

graveyard stood the marble figure of an angel pointing with one hand to heaven, with the other to the grave, at its feet, of a girl of twenty."

But whilst they talked they kept their eyes upon the ship, for it was impossible to foresee but that at any moment she might shift her helm to obtain a closer view of the island, and Reynolds must be ready to rush up the hill to light the fire.

"I sometimes wondered," said Goodhart, "what form madness would take in a man who should lose his mind in shipwreck on such an island as this."

"I have sometimes thought," exclaimed Reynolds, "that madness is the delirium of a disposition that has lain latent and even unsuspected. For example: I am an ambitious man, but do not know the absurd heights to which my soul secretly aspires until I lose my reason, and then I believe I am a king or god. In my case I believe had I gone mad here I should have imagined I was Brigham Young."

Goodhart was amused, and laughed with gentle enjoyment.

"I have heard of a man," said he, "who believed he was his own father. He had made a will leaving all his property to himself as his only son; but his worry was to know what he should do if he was to happen to die before his father. I have also heard of a lady who believed she was the author of the novels of George Eliot, and was afraid of looking into a mirror for fear of seeing the ghost of George Henry Lewes."

"The only instance of sanity I have heard in madness," said Reynolds, "was the case of a journalist who, whenever he felt the drink fiend taking possession of him, compelled his wife to put him away."

He stood up to look at the ship: Goodhart also

M

rose, and they viewed the distant sail for a while in silence. She was holding stubbornly on. So far it was certain she had not brought the boat within sight, unless she was to give the spectators an illustration of behaviour, which most happily is very rare at sea, by seeing the boat, yet standing on and leaving the tossed men to their fate. The breeze was steady, and gushed in large, liberal folds; the island sent up its patient moan of shaken trees and shrubbery, and the beach its sullen roar of surf, and the south-east cliff its sulky thunder of foaming surge.

They continued to watch and wait, then Reynolds went up the hill to kindle the prepared fuel in the hollow. The stuff made a thick white smoke, but it was blown low at a sharp angle from the hollow in which the wood flamed, and as the ship drew further eastwards, and as the smoke was blowing due west, it was less and less likely that the fore-shortened beacon-trail would catch the eye of any one on board; or, if it did, the white smoke, like one of those country fires which discharge shafts of vapour from dead leaves and rubbish into the autumn atmosphere, might be thought to proceed from a little volcano. But Reynolds was bound to give himself and Goodhart a chance, and for a whole hour he plied his fire, laboriously fetching big armfuls of stuff, and raising a thick smother whilst the ship grew smaller and smaller, as, with something of the slant of the seagull's wing when it wheels in its flight, she vanished in a shadow of mother-of-pearl into the east. Reynolds rejoined Goodhart.

"What time is it?"

Goodhart pulled out his watch and said, "Eleven."

Reynolds glanced at the sun, and judged Goodhart's report to be fairly accurate.

"That ship is not to prove our salvation," said he. "If she is to catch a sight of the boat she should have seen her before this, with a long enough pause to enable us to know that she had hove-to to receive the people, or by a shift of helm which would have changed her shape."

"I shall keep a look-out for the boat," said Goodhart. "If the men are disappointed they must return. What else remains?"

"I don't know," exclaimed Reynolds, with a gloomy shake of his head; "there are some mules amongst them, and the bo'sun is a good leader for people of that sort. They may reason, having left the island and come so far, 'What will be the good of returning? We know what we've got to expect. Much more chance of our being picked up the further we go than keeping all fast aboard that piece of rock.'"

"They are without a compass," said Goodhart. "Suppose they get some thirty miles distant and resolve to come back; this island is small, and without its bearings being known or a compass to help the helms-man, it may easily be missed."

Thus they conversed whilst the hours wore on. Reynolds as a look-out was of no use. Goodhart did the staring part, but never could see anything to report. He was calm, resigned, grateful. He said—

"At all events, Captain Reynolds, we know where we are, but we don't know where the boat is. I am thankful to God I was not tempted to trust myself in her. Figure the weariness of that little skipping structure, the hopeless grinding of the oars compared to which the toil of the galley slave is a joke, for the felon is not threatened every instant with death, the miserable and pitiful look-out—for what? Why, to see only the curling heads of seas, clouds of spray which must keep you baling, the breeze freshening, the night coming on, and a little stock of dried fish, a few tins of meat and six gallons of water for eight souls—for that's how it would have been with us had we gone."

"I believe you are right—I believe you are right," said Reynolds, in a voice that was coloured with the spirit of consolation that he drew from the happy resignation and comfortable philosophy of his companion. "If the boat does not show itself before dark I shall give her up, not necessarily as lost so far as the men are concerned, but as lost for us."

He snapped his fingers to a sudden uncontrollable impulse of vexation.

At one o'clock by Goodhart's watch the ship was out of sight. At six the dusk was gathering, but the watchers saw no signs of the boat. The long runners of the ocean streamed in steady procession out of the east; the clouds, opening as they rose, flew in many windy spectral shapes, a very Chinaman riot of shadowy monsters. The moon floated up and tinged with a delicate silver green the foliage and the waters which she shone upon.

"It is strange," said Goodhart, viewing the satellite as she swept through the phantom rush of wings on high—"it is strange," he said—his habit of moralizing and philosophizing constantly taking form—"that God should have thought fit to hang up in the heavens two wonderful symbols of creation—its life and its death. In the glorious sun Nature lives and moves and has her being. The moon is death, white, silent, cold, awful. In the morning you awaken with life; in the night you go to rest with death."

"I wish to God," cried Reynolds, with a little glow

of passion, "that the moon would reveal the boat. There was good hope whilst that boat remained in the creek. The beggars, in going away in her, stole her from us, and, in my opinion, they are lost men, and we shall be prisoners for months, and perhaps years."

He wrung his hands, unseen in the gloom by his friend, for just then the weight of his months of solitude came down upon his heart in a sensation of almost physical oppression, and in imagination he was alone, with nothing to look at but a desolate breast of ocean, with nothing to hope for but the sight of a ship, with nothing to live for but a burden of being that love had abandoned, and shipwreck rendered crushing.

Goodhart took his hand and pressed it,

"Keep up your heart, Reynolds!" he cried cheerfully. "A ship will come, and we shall be rescued. All will be well. Not very much is needed to make rich the man who has nothing. The coming of a ship is no very mighty affair, no prodigy, nothing that shall have anything of the miraculous in it, and I look forward to being rescued with profound confidence. Did you ever hear of the 'sweet little cherub that sits up aloft' forsaking poor Jack?"

"It was a passing mood," answered Reynolds, softly. "But, remember, that for many months I have heard this noise of the trees, I have watched that moon, I have listened to the sea, I have thought through many bitter waking thoughts, I have prayed to God, alone—always alone."

That night they occupied the cave together. There was plenty of grass in it, and Reynolds easily felt and found a couch near Goodhart's. It was totally black inside, but the silver dimness in the atmosphere lay like tissue-paper stretched over the mouth of the cave.

Twice before one o'clock in the morning Reynolds went out and gained a height and looked about him ; but the boat had not returned. Nothing moved upon the surface of the island, but a quick, though stormy, dance of shadows. It was blowing fresh ; the dwarf trees roared with the surf, and the moon shot through the swift drift. He fell asleep, but was awakened by a loud report.

Goodhart cried out, " What was that ? "

" Was it a cannon shot ? " said Reynolds, standing up.

Another sharp rattle, and the lightning glanced in blue splendour at the mouth of the cave.

" My God ! " cried Reynolds. " What chance will this sort of thing give the boat ? "

" But think," said Goodhart, " that we might be in her."

The sheen of the lightning sank in instant pulses into the cavern's blackness, and the two men in the flashes were revealed to each other. Again Reynolds stepped out. It was not raining on the island. A heavy thunderstorm was playing over the sea about two miles distant, and the moon was sunk into a mere jelly of moist light in the shrouding of the weather that was stretched out over the heavens from the electric vapour.

" Goodhart," cried Reynolds, running to the mouth of the cave to shout, " come and see a wonderful sight !"

What was it ? The lightning was frequent and fierce, and every white or crimson spark that flashed upon the eye its wire-like rill of fire, illuminated two gigantic waterspouts about half a mile distant on the west side ; touching them into stately columns of the aspect of white-hot metal, their foot in foam, their head lifted with inky vapour into the aspect of the cocoanut tree.

"If they are coming this way we shall be deluged," said Goodhart.

But their waltz was to the southward. The two men watched this wonderful, lightning-revealed picture, sublime and awful with its accompaniments of the midnight, of the lightning-dart, of the thunder-shock, and the universal roaring of an angry ocean. They returned to the cave and lay down; but for some time neither could sleep, though one was a sailor and the other had been well salted, owing to the rushing noise made by the rain, which descended in a living sheet, as though it was a great lake coming down from the edge of a mountain, and but for the cave being on a slope, they would have been floated out.

The morning was cool, calm, and bright. Their first act was to scan the sea for the boat, but the ocean was a plain as naked as a looking-glass. The water swang to the shore softly, and melted in caresses of froth.

"Do you see anything like a sail?" said Reynolds.

"Nothing," answered Goodhart, after a long and careful scrutiny of the whole circle of horizon. "But I am not to be depressed. I am perfectly satisfied to think that I am not afloat in that boat."

"It is inconceivable that she was picked up by the vessel," said Reynolds. "As likely as not they were swamped in the night."

Goodhart went to the river and Reynolds to the rock to catch a fish for breakfast. This morning he secured a fish shaped like a salmon, gorgeously dyed, and weighing about eight pounds. He had caught this sort of fish about twice or thrice before, and found it delicious eating. He made his fire and began to cook. Goodhart kept him waiting; indeed, he grew anxious, and was going to seek him when he saw him coming slowly from the direction of the river, holding what resembled a satchel in his hand. He stepped with this satchel-like thing into the cave, and emerged with nothing in his hands.

Reynolds looked at him and instantly observed a diminution of his bulk—that bulk of trunk whose extravagance had often puzzled him. He said nothing, and Goodhart, coming near the cook-hole with his kind and gracious smile, seated himself. Undoubtedly his figure had undergone a change since he had visited the river. He was now a well-proportioned man, without that stuffed look which had excited conjectures in Reynolds. His coat lay open. The massive watch-chain rested upon his waistcoat; his attire was indeed in a state of princely freshness compared with that of his companion; but then he had not been seven months on the island, nor had he been thrown ashore on toothed rocks by the breakers of a gale of wind.

Goodhart's smile vanished as he viewed his friend thoughtfully, with an impressive and inspiriting air of kindness. They had ceased to " captain " and " mister " each other.

" How long will you be able to support this sort of existence ? " said Reynolds.

" I keep my mind tranquil with the fixed assurance of release," answered Goodhart, taking up a slice of fish with a leaf and beginning to eat. " It may be delayed ; but it will come. I do not think of myself as a prisoner. I could be worse off, I *have* been worse off. This fish is excellently tasted. I do not miss liquor ; those cascades are a noble drinking-fountain. I should be glad of a substitute for bread, but whilst our mushrooms flourish I shall not grumble."

"I am sick of it, Goodhart," said Reynolds. "So will you be soon."

"I assure you, Reynolds," replied Goodhart, with a note of cordial cheerfulness, "that your companionship, and my own state, tastes, and habits of life render this imprisonment, as you term it, so little disagreeable to me that if a few comforts could be contrived I should be very well pleased to accept this brief sentence of exile as a pleasant holiday in a delicious climate under circumstances delightfully romantic."

Reynolds smiled and bowed, and said, "You are a true philosopher."

"What are our wants for this holiday until we are taken off? A little cottage, a loaf of bread a day, a joint of fresh meat to vary the eternity of the produce of the creek, tobacco for the pipe, and a few boxes of cigars. We enjoy a royal state, for we do not need money, and the greatest monarch might envy us for that. But weigh against our humble requirements the blessings of our escape from shipwreck, yonder glorious privilege of bright falling waters, the agreeable dishes swimming in that creek, or sticking to the rocks, or growing in the ground. We might go further," he added, looking significantly seaward, evidently thinking of the boat, "and fare worse."

"When you get home—I will not say *if* you get home, in the face of your magnificent spirit of hope—where shall you settle?"

"Not in Ireland."

"You are the sort of man they want there."

"Well, it may come to Great Britain dealing with Ireland as a colony and extirpating the few lingering natives by swamping the country with British emigrants and settlers."

"That would solve the Irish question," said Reynolds.

"I shall settle in London," said Goodhart. "There you can get everything you want, the best and the worst of everything, and with judgment you can make ten shillings do what a sovereign scarcely does in a provincial town."

"I hate London," burst out Reynolds. "Particularly Bayswater."

"But why Bayswater?" laughed Goodhart. "Why not Hackney or Clapham?"

"I was married in Bayswater," answered Reynolds; and, jumping to his feet, he hove a stone at a penguin that was sitting like a robed bishop on a rock.

Goodhart viewed him for a moment or two in thought.

"Do you observe," said he, putting his hands to his sides, "that I have lost weight since bathing?"

"You are certainly thinner."

Goodhart again viewed him as though he had fallen into a fit of profound musing, then, rising, he said—

"Reynolds, come into the cave with me."

CHAPTER X

TWO GRAVES

REYNOLDS, greatly marvelling, followed his companion into the cave. After the necessary pause to accustom the sight to the interior gloom, Goodhart, stepped to the old sea-chest, and, opening the lid, took from the bottom two thin bags united by a pair of shoulder-straps. He carried these bags or satchels to the mouth of the cave. Each bag was formed of a waterproof tissue with a rope handle of silk connected with straps like a man's braces. It was easy to see that these satchels or bags had been made to wear on the back or chest. They were filled with folded documents.

"These," said Goodhart, holding up the satchels, "represent all that I possess in the world outside what I carry in my pockets. They contain the product of thirty-five years of hard labour."

He hung the satchels by their straps over his arm and extracted one of the documents, and opening it, handed it, with his delightful smile, to Reynolds, saying—

"There are eleven of them, and they all carry the same face."

The document in Reynolds' hand was a one-thousand pound Victoria four per cent. bond, the date of whose issue was 1885. It was shorn of the coupons which had matured.

"These bags," continued Goodhart, receiving and returning the bond to its sack, "contain Colonial Government securities amounting to the value of eleven thousand pounds, and you will easily understand why I chose to remain a bloated body whilst the sailors stayed on the island."

"But why do you carry such things about with you?" said Reynolds, who was not very much affected by the sight of the sacks: rather disappointed, indeed, for he had looked for something solemn and deep, and not a commonplace exhibition of Stock Exchange securities, in his friend's invitation to follow him into the cave. "All that money might have gone down in the *Esmond*."

"When it was suggested to me to convert the bonds into inscribed stock, I found the difference in price sufficiently great to determine me to keep what I had got. Besides," said Goodhart, with his mild look and gentle smile, "had these bonds foundered with me, I should have been disproving the general belief that a man cannot take his money with him to the grave."

He was going to the chest to replace the sacks.

"Do you mean to keep them there?" said Reynolds.

"Why not?"

"Suppose such another crew as yours comes ashore —would to God they would!—and we are on the other side of the island, or they catch us napping, and they come to this cave and forthwith open the chest."

"Where shall I put them?" said Goodhart, looking round the gloomy interior.

"Bury them. This is good dry soil."

Reynolds went outside to fetch the shovel, and began to dig a hole in the corner of the cave.

"You are right," said Goodhart, "and we never could forget where we had placed them." And whilst Reynolds dug, his friend proceeded: "Plenty of time was allowed us aboard the *Esmond*. I went below and took off my coat and waistcoat and put these bags on. They bulked me out, but not in such a way as to excite attention, unless in a Customs man, whom I was not afraid of meeting. You noticed probably that I have always bathed in a furtive sort of way. Naturally I did not desire my satchels to be seen by the sailors. Marine tradition has been enriched by some dark stories founded on sums of money much smaller than the amount you are digging a grave for."

"Oh yes," said Reynolds, manfully plying his shovel and scraping rather than digging into the hard dry cavern floor. "I should have felt very uncomfortable of a night, or even of a day, to reflect that you were sleeping or going about bulged out with those bonds, if their existence and the value of them had been known to the men. 'Lead us not into temptation, but deliver us from evil!' I am glad that you did not tell me that you had them upon you. I should have trembled for your safety if by the merest accident the secret had been betrayed to the sailors."

When the hole was made, Reynolds went out and cut a quantity of dry grass, with which he lined the grave. Then, putting in the bags, he covered them up with the stuff he had thrown out.

"There," said he, with a final appreciative pat with the shovel. "No gem could lie more secret fathoms deep in rock."

They walked into the sunshine and down upon the lovely length of coral foreshore, which they paced. The breaker was curling to them out of the blue water. The sea-bird hovered and glanced, glistened and darkened as it winged about; the morning light lay in glory upon the ocean, and the off-shore breeze was scented with the land.

"Eleven thousand pounds is a small sum to represent the savings and labours of thirty-five years," said Goodhart.

"It's more than you would have made as a philosopher," exclaimed Reynolds.

"I don't know," answered Goodhart, "there are some professors who are deucedly well paid. I knew a man who received two thousand a year, and a more bigoted coxcomb, insolent in cocksureness, contemptibly venomous in hostility, never led others astray."

"What are these professors paid for?"

"To lecture, for the most part," answered Goodhart, with his lip taking a slight curl of contempt.

"Well, of all vocations," said Reynolds, "I do hold the sea life to be the most beggarly—I mean the merchant sea life. In the Navy you get a pension. You invest your labours, for which the State pays you, and when it is done with you it sends you a sum annually that may make you easy for life. You shall serve a shipowner for years honestly, anxiously, most dutifully, and when he is done with you you go about your business—to the workhouse for all the employer cares."

"How are you off?"

"Badly."

"No savings ? "

"A few pounds."

"Has your wife money ? "

"A little. But if she had a million what good would
it be to me ? "

"It is difficult to meet a man without a relation of
some sort," said Goodhart. "But that, as I told you,
happens to be my case. Both my parents were only
children. I am the sole survivor of my family. I have
many acquaintances, but no friends ; but I believe I
have found a friend." He looked with a smile at
Reynolds. "Our association," he continued, "has not
been long, but it has given me very great pleasure, and
I trust it may not end with our release. There is
enough for two up there," he continued, inclining his
head in the direction of the cave, "and if I am called
first, to whom but to a sufferer who has taught me to
respect, and admire, and like him, should I wish it
to go ? "

The pale, worn, and scarred face of Reynolds
flushed with emotion, his eyes moistened ; the passion
of gratitude and of that sort of love which is born
of beautiful feeling, cordial kindness, and sincere
sympathy between man and man ran a-trembling
through him.

"It is not your money, Goodhart," he exclaimed in
a low voice, catching his breath with a sharp, hysterical
shake of the head. "It is your goodness."

He was right in that, for surely it is the smile that
sweetens the gift ; it is the impulse of which the deed is
the fruit that endears and is best valued by the heart
whose purest and most exalted emotions it excites.
And it is quite conceivable that two men thrown into

each other's company by the adversity of shipwreck should grow so attached that when their deliverance has come about they have chosen to dwell together as brothers. Let us not doubt that such things have happened, for the story of marine peril runs back deep into time.

"But do not suppose," said Goodhart, with a little pensiveness in the arch look he put on, "that I flatter myself on being sure of you. Your first act on reaching England will be to inquire after your wife."

"To inquire, perhaps, and there an end."

"No, you will learn that she is living somewhere, and you'll write to her and entreat her to grant you an interview."

"I don't think so."

"My dear fellow, the fascination that won you must still be hers, and when you see her the old spell will exert its magic."

"Spells are often broken," said Reynolds, moodily.

Enough had been said on this subject. Goodhart stopped to view the breakers as they curved in caves of liquid blue glass, and broke with summer softness and tropic glory.

"It seems to me," said he, "that Science is a little too willing to overlook the precedent idea in Nature. The ultimate link in the chain of causation is neglected because philosophy is indisposed to discuss the only hook by which it can be hung up. All that we produce in art is the result of antecedent idea—the house, the picture, the statue, the fountain. Without the idea of these things the things could not be engendered. Now, why are we forbidden to witness idea—the Divine idea— in what we behold in Nature—the tree, the flower, the man? Molecules form themselves into shapes of beauty.

I don't claim sentience for these particles of matter, which may be a snow-flake, a fibre of colour in liquor, a red rose ;" he smiled as he spoke. "But I claim these formations as the effect of a law which has been preceded by idea! 'Mind cannot create, it can only perceive,' once wrote Charles Lloyd, a remark which deeply impressed the poet Shelley. We perceive the idea in Nature, and in our way we produce it as Art. As we cannot create, how should we be able to perceive the idea if it were not the antecedent of what we know and study ? I think it is Dr. Alcock who expresses surprise that those whose business it is to create should have generally neglected the wonderful examples and perfect models which abound in Nature. He tells us that all animated Nature is full of hints for perfecting existing mechanical contrivances, and of suggestions for inventions not even thought of. The teredo (or ship-worm) inspired Brunel with the plan of tunneling which was employed by him in the Thames tunnel, and yet Science denies idea, and commits itself to a fatuous theory of chance."

"I have always held the opinion you express," said Reynolds, "and upon it I have based, as rootedly as a lighthouse upon a rock, my faith in the existence of God."

"It is Tyndall that speaks of matter," continued Goodhart, after a pause, whilst he gazed at the arching breakers, "as possessed of a power of shaping itself into forms of beauty. It is a gift. Who or what is the giver ? Mark the beauty in those arching waters ; in the conformation of that rock ; in the spout and fall of those cascades ; in all that meets the eye. When alum crystallizes perfect octahedrons are formed. The crystallization of carbonate of lime results in beautiful

N

rhomboids. By crystallizing silica you get hexagonal prisms, capped at the ends by pyramids, and, of course, you know that when carbon crystallizes you get the diamond. Surely all this loveliness must be the effect of the precedent idea reaching its end by laws which proceed from the creative mind."

"During my stay here," said Reynolds, "I have discovered a flower that smells only by night. It is absolutely scentless when the sun is up. It will not be found at this season. I have wondered what virtue there is in darkness, that puts most things to sleep, to waken life in a flower in the shape of perfume."

"You will probably find the phenomenon explained by the law of vibration," answered Goodhart. "Take, for example, the sensation of hearing. If the sound-vibrations number less than sixteen a second we are conscious only of the separate shocks. If they exceed thirty-eight thousand a second the ear does not receive the sound. The range of the best ear is said to be about eleven octaves. I suppose the sensation of smell may also be computed in octaves. What the range is I can't imagine, but undoubtedly the vibrations of the flower that is scented by night only are so rapid in sunlight as to exceed the power of consciousness in the sense of smell. Now that I come to think of it," he added, "Humboldt, I believe it is, tells us that from a certain position on the Plains of Antures the sound of the great Falls of Orinoco resemble the beating of a surf upon a rocky shore, and is much louder by night than by day. He held this to be due to the sound passing through an atmosphere which frequently changed its density. At night differences of temperature ceased, and sound-waves, travelling through a homogeneous atmosphere, reached the ear undiminished by reflection. As the operations of nature are uniform in their infinite variety, the law that applies to the sound of the great Falls may be the law under which comes the flower that is fragrant only at night. . . . I am a little tired. I wish my heart was stronger."

They walked slowly in the direction of the dell and sat down.

And now, on this the day immediately following the boat's attempt to intercept the ship, it was the destiny of these two men to enter into a spell of waiting and hoping until May 20, 1892, when came a change, for though it is true that matter is indestructible, it is equally true that things as they are do not last for ever.

In this time of expectation, and during the course of their constant conversations, it came to be clearly understood between them that, if it should please God to call Goodhart away whilst he was on the island Reynolds must consider himself his heir, and would take possession of the bonds and the property he would find upon the person of his friend. This, indeed, was obvious and inevitable, because it was not to be supposed that, if Reynolds survived Goodhart and was rescued, he would leave eleven thousand pounds of securities to rot in a grave in a cave, though, had Goodhart owned connections and expressed his wishes, Reynolds was the man to have fulfilled his desires as completely as though Goodhart himself had acted.

A true and honest love for each other had penetrated these men's hearts. There was a kinship of nature between them. They were congenial souls—Goodhart the loftier and the more simple, but Reynolds was liberally endowed with those gifts of character which enable a man to adorn life when his means suffer him to occupy a position for their proper display. He would have done well in the Royal Navy. He would have been a popular officer as president of a gun-room mess, or as a talker or listener at the ward-room table. He was too good for the Merchant Service, as, unhappily, it is in these days in the main represented. Goodhart loved Reynolds for the simplicity of his nature; for his habit of thought; for a bouquet or aroma of character which cannot be conveyed by words. He sympathized with the deep, the apparently irreparable sorrow his wife had caused him, and affection is often in close alliance with sympathy. He liked him as a sailor, himself having used the sea for a living; he compassionated his distress as a castaway whose fortune was broken, whose " hearth was cold." Indeed, Goodhart was a man in whose soul dwelt a quality of greatness, and his character was exalted by the nobility of his manhood and the possession of those virtues which make men blessed in the eyes of God, and Reynolds would have died for him.

In all these dreary, weary, and spirit-quenching weeks they kept a close look-out for ships' sails and the smoke of funnels, and held in readiness a stock of fuel in the hollow on the hill ready for the burning-glass; but never once did Reynolds catch sight of a ship, and Goodhart, in all that while, four times only, three sail and one trail of smoke, all far in the north, two happening in a week and the others in three months, but all at such a distance as to make them of no more good to the poor disconsolate watchers than the sea-fowl that wheeled between. It seemed incredible to Goodhart that no ship should ever approach the island; but for all that he declared again and again that he would sooner take his chance of three, ay, or even of five years' captivity, than have trusted himself in that open boat to intercept a distant ship with oars only and a slender store of food and fresh water, and eight men, as there would have been. And again and again he would say in varying words when sunset flushed a desolate, bare plain of ocean, and they had stood together looking into the liquid distance till they saw a star—

"No matter. It may be but one more night for us to wait. To-morrow may find us on board ship; and how long will it take us to forget this brief detention? How easily we forget the operation we feared we should die under, the quarrel which we thought we should never be able to make up! I am fond of Swift's remark: 'It is always too hot or it is always too cold, but, somehow or other, God Almighty so contrives it that at the end of the year it is all the same.'"

It was fortunate for them that they occupied an island which lies in the temperate latitudes, where there is almost constantly a summer softness in the air, and where even June, which is our December, has no fierceness. The cave was dry and sheltered them well, and the tangle of bushes on either side of the entrance was a good screen when the wind blew into the mouth from the south-west.

As the time wore on, Goodhart would often fall into long fits of abstraction, moods of pensive withdrawal from the visible, a deep sinking into himself, with that inward-turned expression of face which betrays the mind that is wandering through the long corridors of memory lighted by the mystical irradiation which is also memory's. Occasionally he complained of the weakness of his heart, and there was no doubt that

the privations he was enduring could not help him
to fight this organic trouble. If he mounted a rise
for even twenty feet he would pause to breathe with
evident distress, and Reynolds often watched him with
deep solicitude.

Came the 20th of May, 1892, which is our November.
Reynolds awoke and went out of the cave, leaving Goodhart sleeping. The figure of his companion was easily
visible to Reynolds, whose sight, fresh from the seals of
sleep, found a good light reflected from the radiance
outside the cave's mouth. He went about as usual to
prepare the cook-pit, taking a look at the sea, but in a
sort of hopeless way which was a habit and would have
been most moving to a spectator: and the look he
directed was also influenced by the knowledge that
unless a ship was hull up and within two or three miles
she would be invisible to him.

He walked down to the creek to fish. This was an
inexhaustible source of supply; the fish never seemed
to go away: no sooner was the bait sunk than a cod, or
a salmon-shaped fish, or a fish shaped like a turbot but
gloriously adorned, would come up, and Reynolds, as
you may suppose, was now an adroit artist in the use of
his landing-basket. When he returned he found that
Goodhart still remained inside. He cleaned and cut up
his fish and lighted his fire, every minute expecting
Goodhart to appear. He prepared his shovel with a
couple of slices, but before he set his strange pan upon
the fire he thought he would look into the cave. After
the necessary pause, he stooped and peered at the
sleeper. Goodhart's eyes were partially closed. He
was fat in the throat, and when lying, his chin reposed
upon its own layers, and prevented the jaw from
dropping.

Reynolds said softly, "Goodhart!" Then "Goodhart!" more loudly; then cried his name strongly, taking him by the shoulder and shaking him. The corpse, though often entreated, has never yet responded to the human cry. Not one of the millions since the beginning of things has spoken to tell us what it means and what it has found out.

Reynolds took up the dead man's hand. It was as cold as putty and fell like putty when released. A wild and frightful heart-cracking sensation of horror and consternation seized the unhappy, lonely, forsaken man. Again alone, how much lonelier now than when he was alone before he but too surely knew. He reared his figure and gazed at the dead, motionless as a statue. A flood of sorrow overwhelmed his soul. He fell upon his grass couch, and hid his face, and sobbed, and sobbed, and sobbed.

He rose again and looked at Goodhart; then ran out into the sunshine and fell to pacing the ground as though he was gone mad. Nobody to speak to now. Nobody to soothe him with precious and beautiful words of hope. He thinks his heart must break. He will die, and again before his mental vision the picture of his body, supine, a ragged, bearded, rotten, shameless corpse shaped itself, and his long finger-nails dug themselves into the palms of his hands in the agony of his thoughts.

The morning had advanced before the tempest of distress that flashed and groaned in the poor fellow was spent, and then he entered the cave and again looked at Goodhart. Oh yes, he was dead. Death never made a plainer report that It was in possession. He went to the river to drink, and feeling faint with fasting remade his fire and cooked a piece of fish. What his reflections were you shall readily conceive. Never was the enormous solitude of the island so oppressive. Never did the horizon of the sea seem more remote, never the prospect of release more hopeless. He would go mad! Those birds uttering cries like the creaking of strained timber in a sea-way, the melancholy monotonous roar of surf, the eternity of the dwarf trees, of the falling cascades, of those circling winged shapes, of that sliding, burning eye of sun: these things must, by endless iteration, drive the reason out of his skull.

In the afternoon he went about to dig a grave. He was slow because he could not ply the shovel as though it were a spade. He chose the centre of the dell for a resting-place for his friend, as the soil was more easily dug up in this part than elsewhere. It is hard to imagine a more pathetic figure than this poor man made, bearded, pale, and ragged, alone, surveyed now and again by a circling sea-bird, digging a hole in which to screte the remains of a man he had learnt to love.

He had finished his sad task by sunset, but not before. He made his way by the twilight to the river to drink, and came back to eat the remains of his cooked fish, and that night he slept in the old fissure, his bed-place of seven months. He was very low and nervous, distracted by the grief occasioned by his loss, subdued into a sense of dumb, aching suspense which was a sort of hysteria proper to raise a ghost again to pace the dell, and he could not bring himself to lie in the cave with the dead body. He obtained some rest in the night, and after attending to his needs in the morning, he proceeded with the task of burying Goodhart.

Nothing could be more painful to him than the idea of despoiling the body of its property, removing the clothes, and dragging the dead to its burial-place. But all this had to be done. Reynolds possessed the strictest title to all that Goodhart had left. The man who was dead had never named a relative : he had, indeed, stated again and again that he was as much alone in the world as Reynolds on his island ; so that, his being dead, his bonds and belongings were as much Reynolds' as if they had been willed to him, or as if he had preceded Reynolds in his lonely occupation of the island, and left his bonds and property to be taken by the first who was lucky enough to find them.

Reynolds found these things in the dead man's pockets—a very handsome gold watch and chain, to which was attached a spade guinea and a small revolving seal, bearing his wife's initials on one side and his own on the other ; a handsome Russia-leather pocket-book, the contents of which he did not then examine, but which he afterwards found to hold four Bank of England notes of fifty pounds each, eight of ten pounds each, and five of five pounds : also four letters from his wife, one containing a lock of her hair. These he would have buried with the body if he had thought of inspecting the contents of the pocket-book before the interment. But he was too much worried, affected—he was grieving too much over his loss and the sorrowful task imposed upon him, to think of examining the value of his poor friend's pocket possessions. He also found an elaborate knife full of useful blades and tools, a gold pencil-case, a purse containing some sovereigns and silver, a gold tooth-pick, and a silver match-box.

He put these things in the chest for the present, as his clothes were little more than rags, which hung upon him like wet weed on a rock, and his pockets broken and useless, and then removed the coat, waistcoat, and trousers. This done, with trembling hands and a sobbing heart he gently and reverentially dragged the body down the slope to the grave he had dug, and after lining the trench with grass, with most pious hands he contrived to let the corpse slide into the grave, where it rested on its back, looking with sweet expression in death up to that God whom in life he had adored. With him was buried his wife's wedding-ring and the ring he wore on his forefinger. Reynolds next covered the body with grass and leaves, and when this was done he knelt and pronounced aloud these simple words: "Father, receive him, and do not forsake me."

He arose and began to shovel in the earth, haunted by this reflection, "If I die here, who will bury me?" And he shuddered again and again to the loathsome image that held aghast the vision of his mind.

The hours passed in this melancholy work, and in the afternoon he had heaped up a sight-catching grave, which he resolved to memorialize. So next day, with the axe, he had hewed down a stout bough and made a cross out of it, and in the next two or three days, during the intervals of providing for his own necessities, he cut these words—

> "JOHN GOODHART, died May 20, 1892.
> Buried by his loving friend and mourner,
> Francis Reynolds.
> Lord have mercy upon us."

The letters were small, for the split surface on which they were traced was narrow. But they were cut deep and well. He was something of an artist with a knife, and in Goodhart's he had a good tool. He could carve model sailing-ships, make toy chests of drawers, and dolls' houses, and had been chased and caned more than once in his youth for cutting his name in church sittings, school-desks, park-seats, and the like.

He was once again alone—lonelier than when he was formerly alone, lonelier by virtue of the knowledge he had gained that ships might pass and he would not see them unless they came close in.

CHAPTER XI

THE "CHANTICLEER"

CAPTAIN FRANCIS REYNOLDS, bankrupt by shipwreck, was now a rich man ; that is to say, he was rich beyond any dreams of avarice which had ever entered his head. For how long does a master in the Merchant Service take as a rule to save out of perhaps the poorest-paid calling in the world the handsome sum of eleven thousand pounds, with a few hundred pounds on top in notes and gold ; just enough to open a pretty little banking account with ?

But Reynolds did not happen to take an inspiriting view of the noble turn which fortune had done him. He was never once visited by a single heart-beat of exultation. The solemn and sturdy sense of satisfaction and repose of spirit which attend competence did not come to swell his heart. On the contrary, he regarded himself as a miserable hopeless castaway, as a wretch whose hideous doom prayer was not likely to avert ; and the bonds in the cave, and the notes and property in the chest, were as worthless in his sight as the leaf on the tree, or the empty sea-shell on the sand.

At the same time, he was sensible that he had most honourably come by this little estate, and he would sit and lament that he could make no use of it. The desire of his soul was that Lucretia should get it, and learn from whom it came, and in what state the husband she had forsaken had been when he contrived that she should receive it. Mrs. Lane was by no means well off. Dr. Lane in his day had been tempted to gamble on the Stock Exchange. "The old fool went into mines," his friends said. He could not ask for a simpler and surer grave for the everlasting entombment of his capital, which he had gotten by painful toil, by tedious, anxious vigils in sick-rooms, by exposure to weather, and to the many morbific diseases to which flesh is heir. Panic seized him. To rescue himself, his wife, and daughter from the workhouse he purchased an annuity on his own and Mrs. Lane's life, on which, and about one hundred a year, which Lucretia would come into on her mother's death, and which represented money that had not gone to the jobbers, Mrs. Lane and Lucretia lived.

All this was known to Reynolds, and whenever he thought of the bonds in the cave, he longed to give them to his wife, though convinced he would never meet her again. But how was this to be done? He pondered in vain. It was an end impossible to arrive at. Ideas occurred to him which he considered absurd. He had Goodhart's gold pencil, and there was a flat pencil in the chest; a roll of paper was there, and in that chest were blank leaves of letters—Mrs. Goodhart's, and a few of Lucretia's to him; his wife's letters had been in his pocket when he was washed ashore. The ink had run, the writing was indecipherable; but he had kept the letters, nevertheless, and they had dried long ago, and were fit where they were blank to receive pen or pencil.

He said to himself: "If I write my wishes, how am I to despatch them? I have not even an empty bottle to cork the missive up in, and send it afloat. But suppose this could be managed; the man who picked up the bottle (if it did not go washing about till the crack of doom) might value the secret too highly to betray it, come to the island, and carry off the bonds."

It will be seen that in these speculations he conceived himself dead. But one day, being vastly exercised by thoughts of his wife and the bonds, he formed a resolution. He said to himself: " I will write a sort of will, and take my chance of its being found by one who will prove honest enough to carry out the instructions it contains."

For he clearly understood that if he was to die on the island, the buried bonds must remain a secret for ever ; and eleven thousand pounds would be left to rot in a cave, of no good to mortal man, when, by leaving a declaration of the existence of the treasure—which it truly was—it might, peradventure, come safely into his wife's hands, and benefit the honest fellow who delivered it to her.

He took the roll of old paper from the shelf in the chest, and using Goodhart's pencil-case, he sat down on the grass, employing the back of the shovel as a table. A useful shovel! It had served as a frying-pan, as a mattock for the burial of a man's bonds, and then the man himself, and now it was to supply the place of a desk. He wrote thus :—

" June 15, 1892. I who write this am Captain Francis Reynolds. I commanded the ship *Flying Spur*, which sailed from Falmouth, October 13, 1890, and was lost off this island through fire, and in half a gale of wind, February 2, 1891. I am the sole survivor of the whole ship's company. This, at least, is my conviction. I remained alone till September 14, seven months of solitude, when a boat arrived with six seamen of the crew of the *Esmond*, that had gone down through a collision, and Mr. John Goodhart, of Sydney, New South Wales. The sailors stayed on the island until October 2, on which day they chased a ship, but the boat was without mast or sail, and I am certain that she never came up with that ship, and I am also persuaded that she will not again be heard of. Had her people been rescued, they would have reported Mr. Goodhart and me as being left, and we would have been fetched, not necessarily by the ship that received the men, but through the report of her master; plenty of time having elapsed to allow for that report to reach the ears of a British Consul, who would consider it his duty to communicate with the commander-in-chief on the Pacific station.

"When the boat had left the island, Mr. Goodhart showed me, in a couple of waterproof sacks, eleven Victoria 4 per cent. bonds, each of the value of one thousand pounds. He informed me that his wife had died in childbed at Sydney, and that he was absolutely without kith or kin. We conceived a great liking for each other. We were one in sympathy and tastes. But his was a very great and noble mind. Our comradeship in privation, and the sufferings which attend shipwreck, heightened our affection, and endeared us to each other. He told me that if he died on the island I was to consider myself as his heir, and take possession, not only of his bonds, but also of all the property which was upon his person. As I shall continue to carry that property about with me in his clothes, which I am wearing, it will be found upon my remains, which cannot lie far away from this spot, if, indeed, I do not die in the cave; and the discoverer of this letter must seek my body, and take what is on it; and I implore him, in God's name, to bury me.

"To provide against the risk of a landing being effected unseen by us, in which case the cave might be entered, the chest explored, and the bonds removed, I buried them with the approval of Mr. Goodhart, and the place where they lie will be found marked by a short spade-shaped stake, which I drove into the ground, to help me should my memory come to be weakened. My wife, Lucretia, when I left England, was living with her mother, Mrs. Lane, in Chepstow Place, Bayswater, London, W., and it is my earnest wish that she should be the recipient of these bonds and the property that may be found upon me. To which end I, a broken-hearted, desolate, dying man, humbly and affectionately greet the reader of this letter, and do entreat him, as he loves God and the truth and honour, to convey these words and the property to my wife, Lucretia Reynolds, who, for the trouble he is at in finding her, if she has removed, and in acting as my emissary, will receive fifteen hundred pounds, which he will more greatly enjoy, as money honourably and virtuously gained, than if he kept the whole sum, thereby robbing the widow, and blasting the only hope which keeps warm and alive the heart that dictates these words. Again I greet and bless you, and thank you for the noble service you will be doing me.

"FRANCIS REYNOLDS."

The mere writing this letter was almost as good as a talk, almost as comforting to the poor fellow as the sound of a voice. He was even warmed, when he ended it and had read it over, by a little glow of hope. It was a something done, an act with a possibility attached to it. He went into the cave, and, opening the chest, took out an envelope that had been addressed to him by Lucretia ; but the ink had been dissolved by immersion into mere stains. The envelope was dry, and he wrote upon it—

"TO THE HONOURABLE STRANGER."

He put his letter into the envelope, and, by working it with his knife, drew a nail out of the ruptured lock, and nailed the missive to the lid of the chest.

This was a great day's work, and he had not felt easier in spirits for many a long hour. He diverted, or rather distracted his mind by conceiving the sort of person who would find the letter. But his face lengthened, the faint tinge of colour deserted his hollow cheek, when Fancy, exerting her brush, painted the image of a man cautiously entering the cave, then staring at the old sea-chest, then bringing the letter away from the nail to the mouth of the cave to read it, then picking up the shovel and digging out the bonds, then proceeding to search for—Reynolds' dead body! He did not fear the passage from life into negation. He could not suppose it difficult to die. He was certain that in nearly all cases Nature gently slopes the way, and puts her child to rest as a mother her baby. And he was fond of these lines—

> " To die is landing on some silent shore
> Where billows never beat nor tempests roar ;
> Ere well we feel the friendly stroke, 'tis o'er."

Doubtless it was the human instinct of decency, or

o

maybe it was the secret passion in most of us that our ashes shall be honourably used, that stirred in him. Somehow his very soul recoiled from the idea of his body lying unburied, submitting a pitiful shocking spectacle to him who met with it. It is the pride of the spirit which demands that its earthly tabernacle shall not be dishonoured when life is fled. There is nothing of human weakness in this quality. It is in true keeping with our most exalted thoughts that the spirit of man should desire that the shape of flesh which it warmed, which it informed, which expressed in brilliance of eye, in colouration of cheek, in play of mouth, in motion of limbs, the animation of its soul, should, when that soul has departed, be reverently composed and decently draped for death, and piously memorialized.

This same day, being full of his will, as he chose to think of his letter, he took the guineas and silver out of the shelf in the chest, and dropped them into Goodhart's purse, which he returned to his pocket. Goodhart's clothes had been fairly new and of excellent quality, and they fitted Reynolds. But who would have recognized in that pale, hollow, bearded, scarred face, the lustreless left eye, the ruined cheek at the corner of the mouth, in the long hair streaked with grey, in that sad, wistful, hearkening expression which attends long watching and hope deferred, the good-looking, erect, close-shaven man, who had stood before the altar in St. Stephen's Church with Lucretia Lane on Wednesday afternoon, September 16, 1890?

But not yet was Goodhart's prediction to be verified, and Reynolds released from his long captivity and bitter solitude ; from his sad and solemn contemplations

of the awful and stupendous chasms of silence in inter-
stellar space; from the voice of the sea sobbing in the
calm or bellowing in the gale ; from the whispers as of
spirit-tongues in the trees, often to his visionary ear
syllabling his name as though he were summoned ; from
the weariness of his lonely strolls, his solitary labour in
the creek and over the fire-pit, the waking to the cold
and desolate grey of the dawn, the going to rest with
the sea-bird at the mandate of the dusk and the first
of the stars.

Came September 4, 1892. A cool fair morning,
light clouds moving lazily, a note of languor in the blow
of the surge. Reynolds went for his bath and a drink
of cold water. In returning he stepped from the shorter
way to the cave to ascend an elevation. The first thing
he saw, on looking at the sea, was a small brig heading
in. She bore about north-north-west. The wind was
about west, and she flapped and curtseyed as she floated
softly onwards.

At sight of her Reynolds was transfixed for the
space of a minute, then the powerful instinct of self-
preservation broke the hysteric spell ; with the speed
of a madman he rushed to the cave, picking up the
shovel near the cook-pit as he went, drove with weight
of foot and rage of muscle into the earth, exposed the
bonds, tore off his coat and waistcoat, slung the sacks
upon his chest and back, and, struggling into his waistcoat, ran headlong to the beach, wrestling into his coat,
as he dashed down the slope. On the brilliant whiteness
of that foreshore of coral nothing could have been more
visible—not even the hill behind of three hundred feet
—than Reynolds' figure, motioning like a firework in
frenzied dumb-show. Had his sight been good he
would have known he was seen. Invisible to him, but

easily within reach of a good eye, a man stood near
the wheel of the brig, waving a white grass hat above
the bulwark-rail.   She was a little vessel of about two
hundred and fifty tons: her white breasts panted, as
she sank and rose upon the tireless swell of the sea;
a band of white ran round her, broken by painted ports;
the sun flashed a lightning glance from the metal dog-
vane at the royal masthead.

In about half an hour she shifted her helm and came
slowly round into the wind, bracing her fore yards
forward and her after yards aback: and there she lay,
swaying her toy-like milky softness of cloths against
the morning sky with the firm sea-line ruling in indigo
from either hand, whilst a boat sank from her port
davits, and two men and a man steering with an oar
came along.

"Head for the creek!" shouted Reynolds, when they
were within earshot, and he motioned in the direction
of that familiar spot, walking rapidly towards it whilst
the boat swerved and went that way in obedience to his
diverting gestures.

She entered the creek and Reynolds stood waiting
for her, ready to jump in from the low shore, and even
before she had lost way, when three or four feet
separated her from the bank side, even before the two
men had thrown in their oars, Reynolds with a wild
convulsive shout of joy sprang and was in the boat
with arms out to shake hands with them all.

The fellow who had steered with an oar, had a cast
in his eye, and the red beard on his chin was stiff as
a tooth-brush.

"You don't mean to lose no time," said he, gazing
with the others with great curiosity at the figure of the
man.   "Who might you be?"

"A shipwrecked sailor," answered Reynolds. "A man who was in command of a ship that foundered off here twenty months ago. Thank God, you are Englishmen. I can talk to you."

One of them who was a Swede grinned, but his face sank instantly into its former stare of astonishment at the long hair and wild and rugged appearance of this newcomer.

"Twenty months?" said the man of the tooth-brush beard. "Are you alone, sir?"

"All alone."

"This is a non-inhabited island, then?"

"Oh my God, yes."

"Is there any fruit or vegetables to be got? That's what we've been sent ashore to find out, and to bring off."

"You'll find nothing to eat ashore," said Reynolds.

"What have you kept yourself alive on, then, sir?"

"Fish. Look over the side! That's how I have fared."

"Any fresh water?"

"Abundance. Two cataracts of delicious cold-bright water."

"Johnny," said the man, addressing one of his companions, "I'll just step ashore and have a look round, and then we'll put you aboard, sir. Gord bless me, twenty months!"

His face, hard as leather with weather and seafaring, softened its expression as he looked at Reynolds and he said—

"What might have been the name of your ship, sir?"

"*The Flying Spur.*"

"'Ailing from where?"

"From London."

"We are the brig *Chanticleer* from Hobart to Santiago, Muddell, master, and I'm her mate, and my name's Frost. You keep all on down 'ere, sir, whilst I takes a look round. Th' old man will expect a report."

He got upon the shore and walked up the slope. Reynolds sank into the stern sheets. He was trembling now as he had trembled when he first beheld the apparition of the boatswain of the *Esmond* looking down upon him as he sat with a slice of fish breaking his fast in the dell. His eyes were moist, his respiration short and distressing. The two men who remained observed his state, and humanely let him be for a little, with the taste which would have done honour to well-bred gentlemen, directing their gaze at the island, or at the water over the side, in whose glass-clear depths shapes of fish could be seen moving slowly. The sailors viewed anything rather than this rescued man, who was broken down with the joy of release, the transports of deliverance; for extremes of human passions are in close touch, and great griefs and great delights often affect us in the same way.

"I hope," exclaimed Reynolds, "that Mr. Frost won't be long. You can't guess how mad I am to feel your brig's decks under my feet."

"He'll not be long," said the Swede, soothingly. "He vhas bount to gif a look rount, or der ole man vould haze him. He can haze, can dot ole man. Hey, Shonnie?" His shipmate grinned. "I tink," continued the Swede, "I dit know der *Flying Spur*. She vhas a barque?"

"No, she was a ship."

"Den she vhas annudder."

"I don't reckon you've done much smoking 'ere, sir," said Johnnie. "It's always baccy that men miss most when they're locked up. I've got a pipe and baccy on me 'ere. Would you like a draw?" he added with a sailor's politeness.

"I have not smoked for many months," answered Reynolds, "and, thanking you much, will not start just now." He sent an impatient look at the island for Frost. "I have had no news for nearly two years," said he, after a pause. "Have you any to give me? What's happened in all these months?"

"There was a strike on amongst the sailors at Hobart, when we sailed," said Johnnie. "I don't believe in Unions myself."

"It vhas der same 'ere," said the Swede.

"They make you pay to become members," said Johnnie, "and then keeps you out of work."

"No European, no English news?" asked Reynolds.

"I reads a piece in a paper before I leaf, how dot they hov open a new dock at Cartiff, und dot a French tramp roons into der Goodwin lightship und sink her."

Reynolds could not forbear a smile. After twenty months of ocean solitude, this was to be his news of the world!

"One thing you'll find ain't much changed since you was wrecked," said Johnnie, "and that's sailors' wages."

"Und sailors' groob," said the Swede.

"Them's a nice show of oysters," exclaimed Johnnie, looking at a richly dyed cluster on some rocks projecting from the shore of the creek.

"Jump on that rock," said Reynolds, "and you'll

find a stone shaped like a cucumber. Knock them off with it. They are good eating."

He did not need to ask if they had knives; each man carried a blade in a sheath, belted to his hip. They sprang ashore, and were soon busy in hammering oysters and swallowing morsels truly delicious after pease-soup and salt pork.

It would be impossible to describe, though not hard to imagine, the dance of sensations, passions, and emotions in the mind of Reynolds whilst he sat waiting for the others in that boat. The island uprose before him, Goodhart was there in memory, and himself in his solitude; and again he beheld, with the vision of the spirit, the shadowless form that had walked bareheaded in the dell. How often had he watched those cascades, those birds out yonder, the ponderous coil of the surf rushing its load of splendour up the beach? He thought of the gloomy cave, his bed in the fissure, the stars beyond which his thoughts had winged to God, the grave he had dug, the cross he had made, the words he had cut upon it. And now he was to be rescued! He was seated in the boat. Men were hammering and swallowing and talking hard by. Yonder was a brig to bear him back to civilization and liberty, and the life of man in town or country. It was so much like a dream that he sweated with fear that it was, and got up and stepped into the bows of the boat, returned, picked up an oar, opened a little locker under the stern sheets, all to make sure that he was awake.

Mr. Frost came leisurely along to the creek with a deep sea-roll, and his arms curved like spouting water, and, seeing that his men were eating oysters, joined them, calling to Reynolds, "Won't you partake of some before we go on board?"

Reynolds called back, " I've eaten enough, and want no more."

Indeed, he stuck to that boat as a barnacle to a ship. And, grappling the thwarts, he might have defied the united efforts of the three men to heave him out. For this man had been shipwrecked, and the *Chanticleer* was the first vessel that had come to look at the island in twenty months, and God knows how much longer, and he sat in that boat with the intention to stop. Impatience was worked up into agony in him whilst the three feasted. The *Chanticleer* was a little brig ; the discipline was not severe. If Mr. Frost was mate, he was man too, and was Jimmy ashore, though Mister on board. When this mate and his men had banqueted, they must needs linger to knock off a little freight of oysters for the old man ; but whilst they were thus employed the old man appeared to be visited by some of Reynolds' impatience, for, sending for his gun, he loaded and discharged it at the island over the lifting and sinking rail.

"All right," said Mr. Frost, "we're a-coming."

They entered the boat, and shoved out of the creek with about four dozen oysters at Reynolds' feet.

"You must have found it pretty dull," said Mr. Frost.

" Deadly dull."

"Worese'n a lighthouse, I guess. I came across a grave ; was that of your h'erecting ? "

" Yes."

" Ain't bin alone all along, then ? "

"No."

" I likewise looked into a cave ; it 'ad a broken chest in it with a few old pipes in the shelf, and there was a hole in the corner of the ground as if something had been buried and then dug up. Did you sleep in that there cave?"

"Sometimes. Did you observe a letter nailed to the lid of the box?"

"I can't say that I did. Oh, why, yes, now that I come to think of it, I did take notice of what I thought was a label—sort of address card."

"You left it there?"

"Why, certainly."

"Thanks."

His answers were short. He scarcely listened. The man's heart was burning for the brig, to get aboard her, to sit safe and deep in her bound for a port and human life.

"Six months," said the mate, gazing grimly behind him at the receding island. "If I was cast away alone upon a bit of a water-tight backyard like that, blowed if I know how I should be able to pass the time. Nobody to play cards with, even if a pack was to be 'ad or invented, n'er a parrot in sight to tame and larn to talk. There's no signs of life anywhere, not even that durned old goat which every man expects to fall in with when he's cast away."

"If a man vhas cast away mit a fine young female, I doan know but dot shipwreck vhas goodt," said the Swede.

"You might stow that swash," said the mate, with a very bristling, rugged nod.

Several figures leaned over the side of the brig watching the approaching boat. What product of the island, dressed as a man, was Jimmy Frost bringing aboard? The boat's bows struck the vessel, and in a breath or two Reynolds had leapt the rail and was standing on the deck. Captain Muddell was a very short man, clad in a long coat, whose swelling skirts descended to midway the calves of his legs. When you took a back view of him and did not observe the projection of his long feet, whose toes curved upwards, you beheld the travesty of some provincial academic figure, say a village schoolmaster; it was a coat, a head, and a wide straw hat fixed securely on two stout wooden pegs. Nothing more at variance with the traditions of the beef-face of the sea could be imagined than this singular little creature, who wore a beard, who curled into a coil with soap the extremities of his moustachios, and who gazed at you through a pair of heavily rimmed spectacles. He was stepping his piece of quarter-deck with a sort of skating or sliding motion with the dignity of an admiral taking the air in his stern-walk, but stopped when Reynolds, jumping from the rail, sprang almost on top of him. The recoil of the short left leg in its trouser was an involuntary melodramatic stroke, an example to the tragedian who starts at a ghost, and the little man's magnified eyes glared at the wild and hairy figure that confronted him.

"Are you Captain Muddell?" exclaimed Reynolds, who was so profoundly affected by the sense of salvation and the knowledge of absolute safety, that he was without control of his voice; he spoke in gasps; the whole fabric of his nerves appeared to have fallen to pieces.

"Yes, sir; my name *is* Muddell," answered the little skipper, viewing the nearly two years' growth of hair, the long beard, the bloodless, haggard, injured face, the worn-out raiment of his visitor with a most risible expression of astonishment, not wholly uncoloured by awe.

Reynolds grasped his hand.

"May the merciful God bless you," he said, "as the only man whose ship has touched at this island in twenty long months, during most of which time I have been alone. Here—about here—twenty months ago my ship, in flames, the *Flying Spur*, foundered. I commanded her. Where are you bound to? Oh yes, I remember—Santiago. Am I awake? My God, am I awake?"

He looked around him, and up at the brig's canvas.

The sailors forward who were viewing him spoke not, did not smile, nor nudge, nor give expression to any other emotion than that of the sensations with which their little skipper was filled, by the pathetic pallor and worn and sorrowful countenance of this long-bearded man who pleaded as a castaway, who was imperiously significant, even to the most ignoble instinct by the magnitude of his twenty months of almost lonely confinement to yonder little island, with its silver threads of cascades, its lifeless slopes, its dazzle of foreshore.

"I am very glad to receive you," said Captain Muddell. "I was a bit out of my reckoning, and seeing this island close aboard at daylight, I thought I'd look in to find something that would give us a fresh mess. What's to be had?" he asked, addressing the mate.

"I've brought off a few oysters," answered Mr. Frost. "There's nothing else worth mentioning. There's fish, but fishes want catching, and catching means waiting."

"Is that water good that's spouting down that hill?" said Captain Muddell.

"Deliciously pure and cold and bright," answered Reynolds.

Muddell sent a look at the oysters which the men had handed up.

"We might do with some more of them," said he; "and suppose you turn to, James, and lower a couple of casks into the boat. We can do with a little pure, cold bright fresh water. It may be all a week's sail yet, and fresh water at sea is fresh water if its fresh water anywhere, bar no place in this globe, though you shall call it Sahara. Have you eaten any breakfast, captain?" he continued, expressing much kindness in tone and manner, and some culture in enunciation.

"No, I've eaten nothing since yesterday," answered Reynolds.

"Then step below, sir. Joe!" he shouted.

A young sailor started from the rail over which he had been hanging in the lazy lounging posture of the merchant seaman when he is idle on board ship.

"Bring some hot tea aft to the cabin. Get some coffee made. Tell the cook to fry some bacon, and put some salt beef and marmalade and ship's bread on the table."

And he led the way down into the cabin through the little companion-hatch, a brown, dusky interior with lockers for seats and a chair for the skipper at the head of the table; a dingy skylight, a stove, and two little cabins aft, and two little holes of berths in the fore part.

Reynolds, cap in hand, stood gazing around him dumb with the transport with which the sight of the cabin fired him. This interior, gloomy as it was, was raised to the spirit of this rescued man to the magnificence of a palace by the royal quality of liberty with which its darkling atmosphere was instinct.

"I thank Thee, O God!" his heart said mutely, and he turned up his eyes with a beautiful and touching look of adoration and gratitude.

CHAPTER XII

AFTER EIGHT YEARS

ONE morning in May, 1898, a gentleman was driven to the Tavistock Hotel, Covent Garden. He alighted, and entered the house, and having viewed his bedroom, proceeded to the coffee-room and opened the London Directory. His beard and mustache were scissors-trimmed; he wore his hair short, but this was white, whilst his beard was iron grey, dappled with white. The change which the hurl of the breaker had wrought in his face had been confirmed by time, and no two men could have been more dissimilar than the Frank Reynolds who had married Lucretia Lane in 1890 and the Francis Reynolds who had driven to the Tavistock Hotel on the morning of May 14, 1898.

He turned to the addresses under the heading "Chepstow Place." The house in which Mrs. Lane had lived was now occupied by one William Johnson. He looked down the list of court addresses, and found so many Mrs. Lanes that he easily saw he might spend a fortnight in driving about all over London, only to fail to verify the individual he had in his mind. He shut the immense volume, and went to eat the breakfast he had ordered.

There was no need for him to report his safe arrival to the owner of the *Flying Spur*, Mr. George Blaney. Long before, whilst in Australia, he had learnt that this

gentleman, like his ship, had gone under, and that Mr.
Blaney, as man and owner, was as extinct as the crew
who had never returned to take up their wages.

Whilst he breakfasted his thoughts were with his
wife. He did not intend to justify Goodhart's prophecy
that he would seek her out if living, and endeavour to
woo her back to him, but he most passionately desired
to know if she was alive, where she was, if she was
married, if she was well or badly off. The mould of his
character was very visible in his face. You witnessed
habitual melancholy, a habit of thought that was often
carried into the recondite, deep sensibility, the look that
the practice of patience paints upon the human countenance, with a firm cohesion of the whole in a spiritual
tissue of resolution. This, in a brief survey, the gifted
eye could easily construe.

No, it was not his intention to woo his wife afresh,
if she was still in a state of life to be won. But he
could not be in London, he could not see, and hear, and
smell, and taste London without the sensations thus
excited attacking memory and troubling it into the
presentment of hot and oppressive images : the marriage,
the delirious refusal to see or have anything to do with
him, his visit to a solicitor, the stratagem that had
decoyed her to the ship, her insensate, unwomanly,
unwifely aversion whilst on board, and the inglorious
victory of her departure at Falmouth.

After breakfast he called a cab and drove to the
office of a shipping paper off Gracechurch Street. He
said to a clerk—

"Do you know if there is any reference to the loss
of a full-rigged ship called the *Flying Spur* in one of
your back numbers ? "

"What date, sir ? "

" She was lost February 2nd, 1891. But I could not
tell you the date when the news was published." .

"They'll know all about it at Lloyd's," said the
clerk.

" I want to know if the news was published in the
papers."

"You're welcome to turn over those back numbers,
sir," said the clerk, eyeing him with some curiosity, and
indicating a table on which reposed a number of bound
copies of the journal, going back some years.

Now, Reynolds never had a doubt in his mind that
all hands of the ship's company, saving himself, had
perished; in which case, having regard to his own
situation on the island, the ship's loss could only have
been assumed: she would have been posted at Lloyd's,
ranked amongst the missing, and then dismissed from
commercial memory as something extinct. But the
boat of the *Esmond*, it will be remembered, had gone
away to intercept a distant ship on October 2nd, 1891,
and it was possible that her people had been taken out of
her, in which case they would report that the *Flying Spur*
had been lost off the island of Santo Cristo, and that
out of her whole crew the captain alone had survived
by being cast in a life-belt upon the island.

So Reynolds turned to the volumes containing the
issues of November and December, 1891, and to the
succeeding volumes of 1892 and 1893. These he painfully and laboriously examined through a pair of spectacles, and spent nearly two hours in this study, but
found not the smallest reference to his ship or her loss,
nor to the escape of the *Esmond's* crew that had left the
island. It was clear from this that Captain Muddell
had omitted to report the circumstance of Reynolds'
escape, and Reynolds himself had been silent. The

P

clerk said there was no fee. The volumes were for the
convenience of the public, particularly subscribers, and
Reynolds departed.

It was quite certain that if the *Shipping Gazette*,
which records everything about the merchant service,
had made no reference to the loss of the *Flying Spur*,
all papers in any way likely to meet the eye of Lucretia
would be, and had been, silent also.

Next morning Reynolds travelled by railway to
Bayswater, and walked from the station to Chepstow
Place. His breath grew somewhat difficult as he approached the house. All that had happened between
pressed heavily about his heart in a sensible weight of
intellectual atmosphere. This was the pavement they
had walked on when they returned from church, she
with arms hanging by her side, as inflexibly mute as
the corpse in its grave. What had provoked this cruelty
in her? Why had she married him? Everything was
present as though all were of to-day. But the chasm
demanded for its passage a bridge of sighs that had
taken eight years to make; and was it for him, a husband
scorned, humiliated, forsaken, on one side, to measure
that length, or for her, on the other side, to cross, if
alive?

He summoned the servant, and was admitted. The
card he gave her was plain, and on it he had written,
"Mr. John Goodhart, Tavistock Hotel, Covent Garden."
He was shown into the parlour. This was the little room
in which Mrs. Lane had displayed those refreshments
of which the wedding guests had not partaken. The
image of Lucretia shaped itself with the velocity of
memory upon the eyes of his spirit. He was alone, and
there she stood—in the doorway, at the window, at the
table—as she had again and again stood, tall, nobly

moulded, with a light that should have been love in the luminous gloom of her eyes, with glowing hair and firm lips, and a demeanour of tranquillity which he had long ago translated into a passionless nature, ice-cold in chastity, bleak and sterile by refrigeration of virginal impulse ; a beautiful flower without odour, a lovely star without heat, a woman into whose creation entered many of the perfections of her sex, but from whom had been withheld the sanctifying touch that creates womanliness.

Mr. William Johnson walked in, a white-whiskered man and bald, who apologized for presenting himself in a dressing-gown.

"This house," said Reynolds, after a few sentences had been exchanged, "was occupied a few years ago by a widow named Lane—Mrs. Lane."

"Yes ; I took it after her death."

"Oh, she is dead, then ? " exclaimed Reynolds, with the calmness that betrayed the preconcerted arrangement between the nerves and the understanding.

"Yes ; I happen to know something about her. As a matter of fact, I am the late manager of the insurance office in which Dr. Lane purchased an annuity on the joint lives of self and wife."

"There was a Miss Lane."

" I believe there was."

"Do you know if she's alive ? "

" I am afraid I can tell you nothing. I merely happen to remember the name of Lane as a client of the office."

" I know a friend of hers," said Reynolds, "who wants to hear about her. How shall I go to work to obtain information ? "

Mr. Johnson studied Reynolds' face with some

attention, with the attention of a man who has passed his life in "taking lives;" it was an interesting, a striking, in all respects a very remarkable face.

"I rather fancy," said he, after a little reflection, "that if you were to call at my old office they will be able to give you the name of Mrs. Lane's solicitor, who had something to do with her will, for I remember that he wrote to us about the annuity."

"I am greatly obliged. How long has Mrs. Lane been dead do you suppose?"

"I took possession here in February, 1895. I was her immediate successor, and as these houses do not long remain empty, we may assume that her death was then comparatively recent."

Reynolds bowed and left the house. After transacting certain business at the London and Westminster Bank, he walked to the insurance office, which was within a couple of streets. The letter-book was examined, and the address of the late Mrs. Lane's solicitor found. He was Mr. J. Wembly-Jones, Lincoln's Inn Fields. It was too late to call that day. Reynolds returned to the hotel.

A man alone in London, without friends or acquaintances, seldom feels lonelier than when in a London hotel. The bigger the hotel, the vaster the desert, the wider the amplitude of the swing of the pendulum of dulness. And perhaps what is least agreeable of London in flavour, sound, and sight you will discover by putting up at a hotel in Covent Garden. The prevalent property of the district is cabbage. The residual music is the 'Ebrew throat of the salesman and the bray of the coster's donkey. The climate is fog, and the prospect strictly limited. Reynolds had felt with crushing severity the burden of solitude imposed by his island;

but the feeling of loneliness which depressed him that evening as he sat, now in the coffee-room, now in the smoking-room of the hotel, though differing in kind, was not in degree very remote from the feeling that had weighed him down in Santo Cristo.

Was his wife alive ?   He could form no reasons to suppose her dead.   He assumed her living, and logically thought, therefore, of her as alive, and, it must be added, alone.   For to presume her married, in the belief that he was dead, was to mangle and ruin his theory of her. That bayonet-keen principle of chastity that had kept him at bay, that had despatched him to a remote part of the globe as much a bachelor as if there was not a woman in the world, must surely have kept another off —all others off—unless, indeed, the cold and pitiless weapon had sunk at the cat-call of poverty, or to the rainbow eloquence of title and estate.   But it was his habit to think of Lucretia as alive and alone, and this conception, working in him as a truth, troubled him by the creation of a subtle yearning, a straining of mind which his consciousness refused to heed, because he had resolved not to seek nor to have relations with her ; but desire was in him, nevertheless, as pain is in sleep, causing the sufferer to moan and toss.

He sent in the same sort of card he had delivered at Chepstow Place next day to Mr. Wembly-Jones in Lincoln's Inn Fields, and entered an office, where he was received by a tall, thin, whiskered man, with a big hooked nose and a Caspian Sea of shirt-front, on the top of which, under stiff stand-up collars, sat a black bow.   He took a chair, and Mr. Wembly-Jones examined him with keen attention.

"I have ascertained," said Reynolds, "that you were the late Dr. Lane's solicitor."

"That is so."

"Dr. Lane apparently had a daughter," continued Reynolds, "who became Mrs. Reynolds, and as I have a communication to make to her, I should feel obliged if you would give me her address."

Mr. Wembly-Jones summoned a clerk from the adjacent office.

"Find out, if you can, in the letter-book Mrs. Reynolds' last address—the Mrs. Reynolds who is daughter of Dr. Lane."

"I will explain to you as briefly as I can the object of this visit," said Reynolds. "I happened to be off the island of Santo Cristo becalmed and sent the mate ashore to examine and report with respect to fresh water and provisions."

"When was that, sir?"

"Last year."

Mr. Wembly-Jones bowed.

"The mate returned and brought a letter which he said he had found nailed to the lid of a chest in a cave. It was addressed to *The Honourable Stranger*. It contained one hundred and fifty pounds in bank-notes and a letter signed by one Francis Reynolds, begging the finder to send the money to his wife, Mrs. Reynolds." Here Reynolds pulled out a pocket-book and seemed to refer—"Care of Mrs. Lane, Chepstow Place, Bayswater. These are the notes," said he, taking them from the pocket-book.

"Have you the letter?"

"I put it into a locker for safe keeping, and when I wanted it I could not find it."

"These notes were nailed to the lid of the chest, but you'll observe that they are not perforated," said

Mr. Wembly-Jones, blandly, but with professional suspicion colouring his smile.

"The notes were folded thus," said Reynolds, with
dramatic emphasis and a warm cheek. "The envelope
was large; the nail obviously missed the notes. How
else should it have been, pray?"

"Do you know what has become of Francis Reynolds?" inquired the solicitor.

Reynolds shrugged his shoulders.

"Do you think that he died on the island?"

"A man who writes such a letter as I read is not
far from his end," was the answer.

"But, all the same, he might have been rescued.
Certainly, in the face of this evidence, he would not, in
the eyes of the law, be considered as dead."

"How about the disposal of the money, sir?" said
Reynolds, with an air of carelessness, as though he
wished to complete his mission without further trouble.

At that moment the clerk entered with the letter-
book.

"Yes," said Mr. Wembly-Jones, after humming
through the impression of a letter which the clerk had
placed before him. "Mrs. Reynolds had occasion to
write to me about an investment under her father's
will. The date, I see, is June, 1896. Her address then
was—Mrs. Reynolds, Ladies' School, Cathedral Place,
Canterbury. I have not heard of or from her since."

"Will you take charge of this money on her
account?" said Reynolds, with the tranquillity of a man
whom many months of ocean solitude had converted
into an admirable artist in self-control and facial tokens.

"I'll first ascertain if she's in Canterbury," answered
the solicitor, "and then communicate with you," he
added, picking up the card; "you will then instruct me

or act for yourself as you think proper. Did the officer you sent on shore observe no signs whatever of human life upon the island?"

"The place was as empty of life as that hat," said Reynolds.

"It is important that Mrs. Reynolds should be made acquainted with what you have told me. It might rescue her from a very disagreeable position. We cannot be convinced by your statement that Francis Reynolds is dead, and his wife should be advised not to entertain the idea of a second marriage for some time to come."

Reynolds inclined his head as though he should say, "This is no business of mine."

"Are you making any stay in town?" inquired the solicitor.

"I shall stop at the hotel for a few days."

"Then, Mr. Goodhart, you shall hear from me when I have news to send you about Mrs. Reynolds."

Reynolds rose, bowed, and walked out.

"Mr. Simpson," said Mr. Wembly-Jones to the clerk, who had been a silent auditor since his arrival with the letter-book. "Did you ever see a more remarkable-looking man?"

"Never, sir. I was thinking so."

"That man," said the solicitor, "has known trouble; he has suffered hardships."

"What's his calling, sir?"

"Why, the sea, I suppose. He talked of being off an island and sending his mate on shore. An interesting face—almost fascinating. A very honourable man, too, to bring the handsome sum of a hundred and fifty pounds in notes for remittance to a stranger."

He drummed on the table for a minute, lost in

thought, with his eyes planted on the window like a doctor thinking of a prescription whilst the patient waits. "Send Mr. Wilkins here, please."

Five days after his visit to Mr. Wembly-Jones, Reynolds received a letter from that gentleman, informing him that Mrs. Reynolds had left Canterbury in October, 1896, and taken a situation as governess at Margate. She was there in August, 1897. He had written to her at Margate, but down to the present had received no reply. Reynolds in answer said he would place the amount in his bank, that letters addressed to him at the hotel in Covent Garden would be forwarded, and that on his hearing that Mrs. Reynolds' address was known he would send Mr. Wembly-Jones a cheque.

All this seems little better than beadle's talk ; but it is necessary as containing particulars which are links that must be made visible in this chain of sequences.

Two facts Reynolds had come to discover : first that his wife was alive, next that she was poor. Poor she certainly must be, because had her income been sufficient to enable her to live without work, she, though a clever, well-read, even an accomplished woman, by which is meant that she sang well, played the piano well, danced with splendid grace, could speak French and read in German, a language she had taught herself, and had covered a range of English literature which very few young ladies have ever heard about,—was one of the last of her sex to have dreamt of offering her services in a walk of life whose thankless and underpaid toil she would speak of with pity and aversion. Evidently she had started a school and failed. He was moved to think of her as alone and struggling, as alone and poor in a world where to be poor is to entitle man or woman to the sympathy of the mongrel dog, that despite fleas and the mange is taught by Nature how to earn a living, to rejoice in the sunshine and exalt with complacency its stumpy vibrio of tail. And the emotion thus induced quickened yet that subtle and finely burning desire which his reason declined to recognize. But then he would argue in varying terms over and over again, " If suddenly she found me loathsome enough to abandon eight years ago, when I was comely and younger, how shall it be now, if she meets me and sees me with this broken face, this changed and charged expression ? if she should see the man she had shrunk from and hissed at and forsaken, clothed in a trunk of flesh moulded by the fingers of the breaker and painted by the viewless brush of the island's spirit of solitude !" In short, he feared to meet her, dreading the horror and wrath which would flame in him and consume him and make a pitiful wretch of him, if, forgiving the past, he opened his arms to her, and if, neglectful of that past, she spurned him and turned from him as at Chepstow Place, as on board the *Flying Spur*, as at Falmouth, when she departed without giving him a single look.

When he was on the island his heart clamoured for the civilization of great cities. His dreams were of crowded streets and bustling shops. Now that he was in the middle of the greatest city the world has ever probably known, he began to pine for the repose of the country, or the hundred pictures of the coast. He was consistent, however, in his dislike of London. His might have been likened to the case of a man who, having received a blow on the head, loses a sense, it may be taste or smell, or both. Reynolds associated London with his marriage. His marriage was intellectually a knock on the head, and it extinguished all capacity of relishing London. It was not because he believed his wife to be in Margate that he resolved to spend a month or two in Ramsgate. As you have just heard, he trembled at the idea of meeting her, not because he did not most passionately desire to behold her, but because he feared the moral, the ruining consequences to himself of an encounter. But even supposing Lucretia to be in Margate, that town was as far from Ramsgate as Ramsgate from Deal, or Deal from Dover, and there was no more reason why he should come across her in Ramsgate than if he remained in London or vindicated his pre-nuptial aspirations by making the tour he had planned for his honeymoon.

He liked the old town of Ramsgate; he had spent many a holiday there in his boyhood. His recollection of its embracing piers, the bright enfolded water of the harbour reflecting the red or brown of the drooping sail of the smack or collier, the sparkle of windows looking eastwards over the edge of the low white ramparts, the placid hours he had passed in fishing over the side of a boat when to the thrilling tug at the baited hook he would strike and haul up hand over hand a plaice as big as a turbot who made sport choice and delicious by the resistance of its heavy curved shape in the water; his recollection of these and more, when life was young and the blood romped through his heart, and the horizon of the passing year was gay with the pennons hoisted by hope, or remembered as pleasures, freshened him to the very spirit, as the salt sweet breath of the sea vivifies and enriches to the inmost depths of existence; and one morning about three weeks after his arrival in London he packed his portmanteau and drove to Charing Cross Station.

It was the month of June, a pleasant month in Old England, nowhere pleasanter than by the sea when the

ocean blends her gifts of weed and shell and sand with
the coloured and odorous produce of the land. In
Australia he had added four thousand pounds to the
value of Goodhart's bonds by prudent speculation or
wise investment, and his income was about six hundred
a year.   On this amount a single man may, if he is dis-
creet, make a figure.   He cannot, indeed, run a theatre,
or start a London daily paper, or race, or keep a yacht,
but he can, for instance, when he arrives at such a place
as Ramsgate, treat himself to the best hotel, and this
Reynolds did, putting his name down as John Goodhart.
This hotel is situated on the East Cliff, and bears the
name of a bland old politician who was long a Lord
Warden and rememberable for his affirmation : "That
on the advice of his doctors he dropped port for a
year, at the end of which the gout had not only returned
in full force, but had made room for seven even worse
fiends, so that he not only had to writhe under his
disease but also under the memory of having lost twelve
months of port wine to no purpose."

Reynolds arrived in time for the *table d'hôte*, and
then strolled out to view the place.   Ramsgate, it is
said, has been greatly improved by its new road and
the disappearance of parts of the old town.   The im-
provement is much the same as that made by the
erection of a red-brick jerry-built villa in the midst of
houses whose architecture is Tudor or older yet, where
everything but this flaunting piece of worse than cockney
impertinence, with its farthing affectations of porch and
pillar, its carrot-haired roof and impudent assertion of
bay window, where everything else breathes in a poetry
of soft and happy keeping, style blending with style,
shadow with shadow, decay with decay, until the soft
and pure rhythm, the adjustment of harmonies, the

gradual but beautiful revelation of meaning both in man's work and time's relation with his work, make an idyl or sonnet of the spot.

This was much about Reynolds' judgment of the improved Ramsgate he viewed as he strolled, with memory eagerly and fondly painting the old sea town, with its gap of harbour street betwixt two cliffs, like Dumpton Gap a little way beyond, its terraces of chalk, in those days undisfigured by the railway station and the black hole of tunnel that belches sulphurous vapour at the glaring advertisements hung up just outside, its spacious stage of sands on which were enacted a hundred agreeable buffooneries—the fat women screaming with laughter on the galloping donkey; the milkman limping under cans and yelping "Goat's milk fresh from the cow;" the sweet song of the brandy-ball man; the orgies in the surf "where shrieked the timid and stood still the brave;" where elderly men fell out of machines like little cottages, and disappeared in foam; where figures of blubber bobbed and vanished; where girls who, when apparelled for the esplanade looked a dream of fair women, emerged in shrunk and clinging shapes, pallid, hair-wrenched, and sexless to the male eye.

It was the hour of sunset. Over the levels between Minster and Sandwich the red light was streaming in pennons of glory which certain large clouds over the town reverberated and despatched in a delicate orange into the liquid velvet softness over France. Yonder, opposite Deal and Walmer, were the Downs with a sea-line covered with small dim sketches of ships motionless in the distance. Reynolds leaned upon the rail that stops people from falling over the cliff, and gazed at that remote prospect of water. A head wind had forced him to bring up there eight years ago in the *Flying Spur*, with Lucretia on board disdaining him, acting indeed as though she loathed him. Eight years ago! Right opposite, a collier was slowly flapping along for Ramsgate harbour; her sails were coloured by the sun-glow, and they panted like the human breast as she strove with the stream of tide. Eight years ago! Where was Lucretia now? To-morrow he would go to work to find out if she was at Margate, and if she was in that town he would instruct Mr. Wembly-Jones to send her the money, for which he would remit his cheque. He could not endure to think of her as alone and poor and struggling. How could he tell but that she might be in actual want?

The dusk drew down and found him watching the sea. A few people paced the esplanade to and fro. The lights of the Goodwins sparkled, and the Calais lantern glanced its lightning into the distant gloom. Yonder lurid spark is the brilliant star which the Frenchman's kindly hand has set upon the forehead of his rock of Gris Nez. A band was playing somewhere, but not too near to trouble the weaving mind. Lights, like the glowing tips of cigars, burnt at the ends of the piers, whose dark curves framed a gleaming shadow, restful with slumbering shapes of moored craft, a rest not broken by a vision of white wing creeping from seawards betwixt the pier-heads like a wreath of mist in the sad colour of the dawn.

What was that light making the dark atmosphere look sultry with its tincture as of volcanic vomit beyond the Goodwins? It was the rising moon. She lifted a swollen, distorted bulk, freed herself from the clinging draperies of the atmosphere and soared into an orb of brilliance, rolling down the water under her a fan-shaped river of brightness.

Some one stopped just behind Reynolds. He turned to see who it was who stood so close, and beheld his wife, in the cold clear glow, watching the moon.

CHAPTER XIII

AT RAMSGATE

SHE stood so close that he could see the stars of
the moonlight in her eyes. Her face was pale
as marble in that sheen. She was dressed in dark
clothes that expressed her figure, and her sailor hat
was of coloured straw. She gave him no more heed
than she bestowed on the people who passed. The
lovely picture of the rising moon and its rippling
reflection, and the black brig sulkily stemming and
panting to the right of the flowing radiance in the sea,
appeared to have fascinated her.

A sensation of tightness was about his heart, and
its pulse throbbed half strangled. His throat grew dry
as in fever, and the sudden passion of his spirit ran a
momentary paralysis through him, and he stood as one
seized with tetanus after taking poison. She was before
him even as he had viewed her spiritually from his
fissure in the dell, pallid in the star-white light that
clothed her.

Who is the artist that can throw such a passage
of life upon the mental gaze of his reader without
shrinking from the dread of the derision that attends
exaggeration?

She passed on without noticing him, for this was
a figure to court the male eye, and she was used to
being stared at. He watched, and then followed her.

That "old mole i' th' earth," Goodhart! Was his prophecy to be fulfilled? Was the old magic to exert the old spell now that she was there, stately in form, unchanged—unless the moon lied—by so much as a single stroke of the pencil of time?

She stopped again to look at the sea, and he halted and turned his back, again followed when she moved, and so kept her in sight down Augusta Road into the Bellevue Road, where she vanished. But he had marked the house she entered, and presently passed it and read the number. It was a road mainly of poor lodging-houses.

He returned to the esplanade and sat down to think. His heart had cooled; memory had flooded and chilled him as the night with its cold moisture descends upon the sea.

Moonlight makes all things beautiful. Says Wordsworth—

> " The moon doth with delight
> Look round her when the heavens are bare."

But it had not adorned the beauty of Lucretia by throwing over her its concealing ethereal veil of silver. In eight years she had not physically changed; he was sure of that. If materially she had not altered, why should he expect or hope that she had morally altered? What right had he to believe that her passionless nature was not still as frosty as it was eight years ago, with its ice-bleak presence of a form of chastity that was a distemper of mind? And if this was true, would it not be equally true to predict that the revelation of his identity, the confession of his individuality as Francis Reynolds would provoke precisely the same disgust, induce exactly the same horror

Q

and revulsion which had attended her marriage and
made of her a moral phenomenon?

This was a consideration that brought his brows
together, and his hand tightened upon his stick. For
he knew himself well enough to understand that his
self-respect as a man, that the honour in which it is the
duty of every man to hold his own character, seeing that
to the degree of honour a man does himself is the
dignity of his manhood lifted, must fall irretrievably
into ruin if he again courted and gained the aversion
which had despatched her to her bedroom from the
church, and filled his arms with the killing mockery of a
phantom.

He resolved to pursue a course, and walked to the
hotel. He entered the reading-room, and seated himself
at a desk at a table and wrote to Mr. Wembly-Jones:
" I am here, and by accident have discovered that the
Mrs. Reynolds whom you were good enough to inquire
about is lodging at 28, Belle Vue Road, in this town.
Will you kindly send her the enclosed draft for £150,
stating the facts as I related them to you, and oblige,
etc.?" He signed the name of John Goodhart.

He mused a bit after writing and stamping his letter.
Suppose, he thought, on receipt of this money Lucretia
leaves Ramsgate? I may be unable to trace her again.
And he plausibly represented to himself that his desire
to hold her in view was because she was obviously poor
and apparently alone and might want a friend. The
judgment is always willing to be betrayed by one's tastes
rather than be controlled by one's interests. He entered
the hall and posted the letter.

" The morning," said a gentleman who next day was
seated at breakfast at the same table with Reynolds,
" is always the pleasantest part of the seaside in June,

when fine. The dip, then the breakfast, then the pipe.
Where does tobacco discharge so delicate a richness,
so nutty an aroma, as by the sea? The fresh fried
sole for breakfast yields a sweetness and flavour it
never delivers inland. There is a savouriness, by the
sea, in the incense sent up by the dish of eggs and
bacon which must often make the gods lament their
divinity as a form of being which requires neither palate
nor stomach."

This rhapsodist, who was rather deaf, and who had
told Reynolds that he was a stockbroker with a great
taste for literature, in which he had sought eminence
without achieving it; this man who had informed
Reynolds in the smoking-room that he had read
Burton's "Anatomy" fourteen times, that he possessed
the first folio edition of Beaumont and Fletcher, and that
he had refused six hundred pounds for a collection of
autographs from Wycliff to the Prince Consort, might have
added to his list of the engaging pleasures of the seaside on a fine June morning, the breakfasting at an open
window which frames a broad plain of water sparkling
with sun-stars, over whose surface, firm ruled against the
sky, glide shapes of steamer and sailing-ships—the
solemn mail-boat, stately in sentiency of human life, of
precious freight, of beautiful enginery, of elegance in
mould of hull; the cargo tramp that, perceptive of the
under-manned look-out aboard her, strains the eyes of
her hawse-pipes at the sea from her rearing bows; that
coster of the coast, the barge, discolouring the water
under her with dyes of red mainsail and white topsail.
Pleasant, also, is it to breakfast in the fanning of the
fresh salt air, to the stealthy seething of waters upon
the sands and rocks, to the thin undistracting orchestra
composed of the town band afar, piano organs muffled

round the corner, blackened minstrels upon the beach, human voices calling or singing, the vibration of bells, the cries of the hawker, faint as though in partial vacuo, blending and contained within that frame of open window, with the hollow dome on high full of blue air and moving clouds.

Before and during breakfast Reynolds had kept a look-out for his wife. He was consumed with the desire to behold her by daylight. One road to the town, from the place where she lived, would carry her past the north and east windows of the hotel. How did she occupy the day? Did she teach, and if so, at a school, or did she receive pupils? After breakfast he went for a walk. His heart prompted his legs, and he made for the harbour by way of Augusta Road and the road in which Lucretia lodged. He looked at the house as he slowly passed—a somewhat dingy, poorly draped, fifth-rate lodging-house, whose character was not improved by the yells of a man gutting fish at a barrow opposite the door, with a couple of cats rubbing themselves against his fearnaught trousers, and by another fellow with a basket on his arm, trying to burst through the first man's shouts of "Beautiful fresh soles" by bawling, in ear-splitting notes, "Ho, the beautiful fresh Pegwell Bay shrimps." Lucretia was not to be seen.

He walked on, lost in thought about her, and passed through the pier gates into a scene that was as familiar to him then as it had been a quarter of a century before. It was a richly coloured picture of English longshore life. The breeze filled it with motion. In places it was a dance of prisms. Every flag rippled and waved sea-wards ; the wherries swayed upon the pulsation of the waters ; shadows like that of gigantic fingers ran through the white heights of hoisted canvas ; marble-like forms of sea-gulls hovered on tremorless wings between the pier-heads, where the surface of the brine glanced and frolicked with the splendour of a herring shoal. Reynolds, pensive with memories of boyhood, watched a tug head slowly out, slapping her wake of foam at the mud-barge she towed. A cluster of large pleasure-boats called yachts lay at the pier steps, and their captains were competing for fares in voices which could be heard half a mile off. Some way this side lay the lifeboat reposing peacefully at her buoy, a noble, a significant symbol of the life of the sea to the sailor. One of those yacht-masters on the pier was exhorting the public to step on board his swift and lovely ship and sail to the Goodwin Sands, where they would land to play at cricket—an incident of travel to boast of on their return home; and hard by was the lifeboat, so fraught with memories of those same deadly Goodwins that you might almost fancy, if you pressed your ear against one of her thwarts, whispers of tragedies, breathings such as fabrics made sentient by their burden and business of humanity converse with would penetrate to your consciousness and group upon your spiritual retina many shocking, many wild, many ghastly visions. What sailor but knows them? The dead bodies lashed in the lee mizzen-rigging, men who had drowned in the freezing foam when the mast went, watched by a shivering crowd of wretches in the fore-top; the saloon of the stranded liner with the dead bodies of nuns and others floating about; the streaming, reddening flare that lights up the sea for miles, and flings upon the flying raven wings of the storm a low sullen radiance, in which the rocket of the lightship flashes and fades.

"Would you like to go for an hour's row, sir? Beautiful day for a sail. Some nice fishin' ter be 'ad—

very fine poutin', codlin's long as my arm," said an
elderly man, coming up to Reynolds.

His face was like the inside of a crumpet with its
recollections of small-pox, and, though the dog days
were not far off, he wore a yellow sou'wester, and
lounged in breeches as heavy as winter blankets.

"Aren't you Joe Cooper?" said Reynolds.

"Yes."

"I remember you twenty-five years ago. Have you
been here ever since?"

"Ay, ever since I was born. So'd father. So'd his
father. Shall I get the bort ready, sir?"

"How's old John Goldsmith?"

"Old John! him as 'ad the *Pilot!* Why, e' comes
down 'ere three years ago, just where we're a-standin',
and, arter lookin' at 'is *Pilot*, 'e says, 'Joe,' he says says
he, 'the ole bort lies safe.' 'Ay, safe enough,' says I.
'I feels a bit tired,' says he, in a soft way. 'I think I'll
go and loy down.' Loy down he did, and he's still
aloyin'. William," he bawled, "got any bait in that
there can?"

Reynolds gave him two shillings, and walked away.
He had fished so much in his day that he wanted no
more of that sport. He went on the pier, but all the
time that he walked his eyes hunted for a sight of
Lucretia. But throughout that day he saw nothing of
her, though he was studiously much about, on the
sands, on the west pier and west cliff, and at ten o'clock
that night, when he sat in the smoking-room conversing
with the stockbroker and one or two others, he had not
seen her.

Next morning he received a letter from Mr. Wembly-
Jones, acknowledging the receipt of his cheque for one
hundred and fifty pounds, and informing him that he

had sent the money to Mrs. Reynolds at the address given by Mr. Goodhart, together with the particulars which he had been asked to communicate. He added that he did not doubt that Mrs. Reynolds would do herself the pleasure to call upon Mr. Goodhart to personally thank him for his kindness. This was naturally Reynolds' expectation, but he did not suppose that she would call in the morning.

On his return, however, to the hotel to lunch, a card was given to him, and the porter said that a lady had called to see him, and that she would come again at half-past four. The card bore the engraved name of Mrs. Reynolds, and she had written her address in the corner. He had flattered himself that he had schooled his face and drilled his spirit into qualifying him for such a meeting as to betray on his side no more than if indeed he was veritably the man he personated, but as he walked to the luncheon-table with his wife's card in his hand he was conscious of a perturbation, a hurry and tumult of mind, a collision and recoil of sensations which assured him it was vastly well, truly, that he had not met his wife without this advice of her coming. Indeed, he could scarcely swallow the meal he ordered, and when his acquaintance, the literary stockbroker, asked from an adjacent table if he would join him in a shilling trip in one of the pleasure-boats that afternoon, the answer he received was so abrupt in a person whose demeanour was uniformly mild, somewhat melancholy, but pleasantly flavoured with geniality, that the stockbroker thought that Mr. Goodhart must be feeling ill, and looked at him for a little while in friendly inquiry.

Reynolds, conceiving that the ordeal of the first meeting with his wife would lose in tension if it were

unwitnessed, asked for a private room in which to
receive his visitor, and at half-past four he was pacing
its carpet. Precisely at the time named in the message
the knuckles of a waiter drummed on the door, which
was flung wide open and "Mrs. Reynolds, sir," was
announced in a strong German accent.

Reynolds stood with his back to the light, and bowed
low with a tranquillity that would have reassured any
secret spectator who had been his well-wisher. Had
the moon the night before last told a flattering tale?
Had she deceived him with her cold pencils of white
brightness? It is a fact that eight years had robbed
Lucretia of nothing and had added something; as the
red rose of June is to the same red rose of July, was
Lucretia of the altar in St. Stephen's Church to the Mrs.
Reynolds who sank her head in a queenly movement to
Mr. Goodhart. Hers indeed had been some trial of
poverty, not severe; but no discipline of maternity, no
death of babe nor anxiety of always ailing child, no
kitchen murmurous with grievances and the poor pay
of a shipmaster as a thread for the pearls of the faith of
Hymen. She was richer in colour, fuller and rounder
in figure than when they had parted; but one characteristic time had wrought no change in, and this was
the inherent quality of coldness in the residual expression of her face, which, had she been ugly, would have
ascended to the degree of a virile austerity. But though
her beauty held this element in solution, it was present
and visible as the label of her nature, and Reynolds at
a glance saw that if Lucretia had not lost in external
charm as a woman, neither had anything come on the
spiritual side to help her as a woman.

Her sailor's hat suited her, and her dress fitted her.
Her left hand was gloved. He could not know at once

if she wore his ring. She put her right hand behind her in search of her pocket, and said, with calmness a little coloured with the glow of gratitude, " I have the pleasure of addressing Mr. Goodhart ? "

Again he bowed, and begged her to sit. There was clearly nothing in the sound of his voice that struck her. Her demeanour proved this; it was the self-possession of a lady in the presence of a stranger.

" I received this morning this letter," she said, producing it, " from my father's solicitor, Mr. Wembly-Jones. He enclosed your cheque for one hundred and fifty pounds, for which I do not know how to express my gratitude to you. The story you told him is naturally of the deepest interest to me, and I shall feel greatly obliged if you can add anything to what Mr. Wembly-Jones writes."

" I fear I can add nothing," said Reynolds, in a low but steady voice. " It was my duty as a man and a sailor to carry out this poor shipwrecked fellow's wishes. It has given me no trouble; it has been a pleasure. I could enter into the feelings that governed him as he wrote. I wish I had preserved his letter."

So far absolutely nothing in his voice nor in his aspect to invite her regard outside the interest of the subject she had called about.

" You may have been told," she said, " that Captain Reynolds was my husband."

" Oh yes."

" Do you believe he is dead ? Mr. Wembly-Jones does not seem to consider your discovery of his letter a proof of his death."

" He wrote in words such as only a man who is convinced that his death is at hand would use."

"And yet that is no proof. He might have been taken off the island."

"Would not you have heard from him?"

She was silent whilst she looked at the letter she held, and he watched her.

"Can you tell me when his letter was dated?" she asked.

"To the best of my recollection," he answered, "it was dated January, 1892."

"Six years ago!" she exclaimed, and the shadow of thought was on her face as her large dark eyes fastened themselves on the carpet. She looked up and exclaimed, "There has not been a line of reference to the loss of his ship in the papers! The uncertainty has been very hard to bear. But time reconciles us to much."

The waiter entered with a tea-tray. Lucretia took off her gloves, and Reynolds saw his wedding-ring.

"May I give you a cup, Mr. Goodhart?" said she.

The same graceful posture at table; the same fine motions of arm, like the swaying of stately branches in summer winds; the same flower-like curve of neck; the same glow of hair and brilliancy of teeth! The magic was there, and the spell was working—but in a way.

"Shall I call you Captain Goodhart?"

"No, madam; I have given up the sea."

"You retired as captain?"

"I am Mr. John Goodhart. In the Merchant Service we are not entitled to be called captains; we are master mariners."

"Will you tell me about that island?"

"I will tell you what I saw, and what my chief officer reported."

When he used the words " chief officer," she looked at him intently, under slightly knitted brows, as though something in the tone in which he pronounced the words affected her; but the expression vanished like the shadow of a cloud crossing a brook, and she listened with single-hearted attention.

" The island is called Santo Cristo. It is about a mile long, and not a mile broad. It rears a green hill in the middle, out of which, halfway down, spout two cascades. Its foreshore is of white coral sand. It's an island of which something could be made were it situated in a lake on an estate."

" Did the officer see no signs of Captain Reynolds?"

" None."

" If he died on the island——" She did not like to continue.

" Nature is kind," said Reynolds, calmly and gravely, "and in six years she would not only have found him a tomb, but ornamented his resting-place with a memorial —a bush, a little growth of flowers."

" It is shocking to me to think of his dying on that island. Was he alone, do you think?"

" I should say so. Few ships sight that bit of land. Had we not been blown out of our course, we should not have come within fifty miles of it. Then, again, the mere circumstance of his letter about you lying nailed on top of a chest in a cave for nearly six years proves that the island was unvisited. Anybody who landed and explored the island would find the cave and take the letter." He paused and added, " Have you any children?"

" No," she answered, with an expression of face which he readily translated into an emotion of tingling self-consciousness, but it never could have been so construed by a stranger. " How did you find out where I lived, Mr. Goodhart ? "

It was necessary to fib. He was acting a part ; the actor must tell lies off the stage as well as on. He was Goodhart to this spectator, and he must play up to the part, just as though he was King Lear or Joseph Surface, watched by rows and tiers.

" I saw you on the esplanade the other evening, and ascertained your name, which induced me to inquire after your address, in the conviction that, if I was mistaken, a plain explanation of the facts would be accepted by you as my apology."

Never was falsehood nearer the truth nor more satisfying. He saw that she was not displeased by the initial curiosity the incident implied. He had manifestly been attracted by her appearance, had asked who she was, had been surprised on hearing her name, sought her address, and taken his chance of her proving the woman he wanted. She began to put on her gloves.

" How do you think," she asked, " did my poor unfortunate husband contrive to clothe and feed himself on that wretched lonely island ? "

Reynolds gravely shook his head, and slightly shrugged his shoulders, as though he should say, " How can I tell ? "

She rose. " Is Mrs. Goodhart with you ? " she asked, with a smile that was easily interpreted into meaning that " if Mrs. Goodhart is here, I will formally call upon her."

" Mrs. Goodhart has been lying in her grave in Sydney since 1878," answered Reynolds.

She bowed her head in apology for asking the question.

"I wish you to believe, Mr. Goodhart, that I am deeply obliged to you for your kindness."

"Nothing could have given me more pleasure. I trust this may not be our only meeting."

"Are you making any stay here?"

"I like the place, and shall linger until I weary of it. And you, Mrs. Reynolds?"

"Oh, I'm a fixture, I'm afraid. My mornings and afternoons are occupied. One must live, Mr. Goodhart. Women's opportunities are fearfully limited. If I had been born a man, I should not teach for a living. This money is a great godsend." She looked away to the window, and her fine eyes wore the softened glow which tells of abstraction, but she was back again in a second. "So many, many thanks for your kindness."

She extended her hand. He clasped but released it swiftly; then opened the door and attended her as far as a corridor that led to the hall, bowed, and returned to sit down and think.

It will seem incredible that Lucretia should not have recognized her husband. Put it thus: for six or seven years you have thought of a man as dead. The conviction of his death is a custom, and custom lies upon us "like a weight, heavy as frost and deep almost as life." Suppose this man to reappear, absolutely transformed in aspect, would you, without information, accept him as the person you know is dead? You might witness features physiological and moral to suggest resemblance, but this resemblance would be accident, and not revelation; and, short of revelation, you are bound by the custom of your thought to believe the person you knew dead, and the same man, when he presents himself, another. How stood the thing

with this couple? In the first place, it had been a
sailor's courtship. She had not seen half as much of
him in the wooing-time as she would have seen had he
filled a shore appointment. Next, she had not been a
wife to him. She could not found herself on such
knowledge as would have been hers had they lived
together. She had abandoned him on her wedding-
day, and believed him dead after eight years, during
which time she had not heard of him or set eyes on
him, and memory now was holding only the image of
him as he figured whilst he courted her—a fugitive
figure, thanks to his calling. Here he was now as
Goodhart, not as Reynolds ; so changed in face, he had
started and not known himself when, for the first time
after twenty months, he had looked at himself in a
looking-glass in a cabin in the *Chanticleer*. The sight
of his left eye was so impaired that he could barely see
with it. The orb was lustreless and charged the face
with a new expression. He used spectacles for reading,
and pince-nez for surveying distant objects. His left
eyebrow and side of the head were warped by the
healing of the wound, and this, combined with the
blow which had wrecked one side of the mouth, completed a metamorphosis, of which other features were
the white hair and grey beard and mustache, a singular
modification in his normal enunciation owing to the
damage done to the mouth, a shadow of melancholy
that had never before been visible—that is, in Lucretia's
time. It was inconceivable that the wife, believing the
man dead, should translate this unfamiliar figure of
Mr. John Goodhart into her husband, Frank Reynolds.
She had not done so, and when Reynolds returned to
the private sitting-room, whose atmosphere still cherished
the memory in fragrance of her presence, he felt that

he was as dead to her as though he occupied the grave he had dug for his friend.

This had been a meeting that had imposed a desperate restraint on him, and now that the pressure was removed, his spirits and feelings swelled into turbulency, and he paced the room deeply agitated. As his passions cooled, he asked himself, What should he do? Nothing was more certain than that his wife, unchanged by time, unsoftened by experiences, was still that same Lucretia of the altar, who had repulsed him after she had vowed before God to love, honour, and obey him. But he loved her; he desired her. The secret of his heart was not to be concealed from his understanding. He thought her a nobler-looking, a more beautiful woman now than when he had first met and fallen in love with her. What depth of spirituality in those dark eyes! How sudden, like the play of light, was the sweetness of her smile! How tranquil her brow, as virginal to his, her husband's eyes, as an angel's who in this world was a little child! How resolved the expression of her bright lips! How excellent, in this ignoble world of carnal sensation, whether of finger, or nose, or eye, that spirit of chastity which had held her from him! He must woo and try to win her as Goodhart.

But though in his wife's unchanged nature he thought he saw the necessity for this, it was a prospect his vanity by no means relished. Good God! what would be his feelings to find himself accepted as Goodhart, when he had been spurned as Reynolds? to find himself accepted as another man by the wife who would have none of the real man? It was enough to make him feel jealous of himself as Goodhart!

Next afternoon, at about five o'clock, Reynolds was seated with his acquaintance the stockbroker on a

bench on the East Cliff. A very flowery young lady
of about thirty-eight passed. She was powdered and
vermillioned under a white veil to the aspect of about
twenty; eyes doctored by pigments into an expression
of lickerish langour, dangerous to old and middle-aged
men; round in hip, plump and clean in waist, ripe in
bust.

"Ha!" exclaimed the stockbroker, fetching a sigh,
and following the gaudy nymph with his eyes; and the
rhapsodist burst out, "How beautiful and mysterious
is that creature—Woman! Think of the loveliness of
her shape, its marvellous adaptability to the purposes
for which it is intended, her power of germinating, the
rapture she can excite, the inspiration she can fire the
imagination with, the mighty or the mean actions she
can induce the performance of; think of her, too, as
incarnating that holy mundane trinity—wife, mother,
sister! Mr. Goodhart, of all God's miracles, woman is
the greatest."

"And what is your opinion of man?" asked
Reynolds, a little drily.

"I have the highest opinion of man in the aggregate;
but the individual man does not always recommend
himself to me. He does not always pay his bills; he
tells lies; he runs away with your wife."

"With the greatest of all miracles?"

"Yes, he'll even go so far as that. But the aggregate
man! Look at that noble steamer yonder. Look at
that pier down there. Feel the rumble of the train
passing through the tunnel cut in the solid chalk on
which we are seated. It's not man's failures that should
dismay us; it is his achievements that should astonish
and stimulate us. He comes into the world with five
senses only; in most cases these senses are defective.

His knowledge is limited to his capacity of perceiving
by these senses. And their doubtful reports are to be
construed by that fallible organ the brain. Thus
slenderly and, indeed, almost impotently equipped, the
man you ask me my opinion of points to the noble
bridge that spans the river, to the locomotive shrieking
into the tunnel, to the steamship tearing with iron tooth
through the mad heart of the living gale, to the message
that passes to the Antipodes in the twinkling of a star.
Think of these products of five senses only, two or three
of them abortive, depending in their poor efforts to
report aright on the interpretation of that misleading
condition of life, the human reason. I say that, on the
terms of his existence, man's achievements are god-like."

"Not bad for a stockbroker," thought Reynolds, who
sincerely agreed with the rhapsodist.

Just then Lucretia turned the corner of the esplanade.
As she approached, Reynolds stood up, and raised his
cap. The stockbroker, after a glance at this further
illustration of the greatest miracle, walked off. They
saluted each other. They agreed that it was a fine
evening.

"I should like to hear more of—— What's the
name of the island?" said she.

"Santo Cristo. Won't you sit?"

She took the place vacated by the rhapsodist. She
was slightly flushed; it was not the heat. She was fresh
from teaching, and all the while she had walked from
the house, she was secretly resenting the manner in
which her two pupils' mamma had expressed her regret
that Lilian's handwriting should show no signs of im-
provement, and that Violet's spelling should continue
wretched.

"As if *I* had had any share in giving those creatures

R

their brains!" thought the proud and passionless Lucretia as she left the house, which was in Wellington Crescent.

"I don't think that I could add a sentence to the description I gave you yesterday," said Reynolds. "It's just a poor little uninhabited island. Nothing, I should suppose, could live upon it but a man or a sea-bird."

"If my husband had been taken off by a ship, should not I have heard?"

"Undoubtedly, either through the owners of his ship or from himself."

"What do you really think?" she asked, fastening her full dark eyes upon him.

"You are reconciled to the idea of his death?"

"His ship was never accounted for after she sailed, and I am forced to believe that he is dead."

"Since you are reconciled, I should hold to that view if I were you. Had you been married long before he sailed?"

"No," she answered, slightly contracting her brow as she looked at the French coast, which was lifted in a delicate orange mirage, and hovered like a cloud over the sea-line.

"Do you like Ramsgate?" he asked.

"Yes, but not the reason that keeps me in it. There is nothing that worries the nerves so much as teaching stupid children, whose mothers think them clever and capable of rapid progress."

He looked at her with a quiet face, when again she gave him a steady view of her profile, which was the aspect of her beauty he most admired, whilst she gazed at the French coast.

"You have friends here, of course?"

"None; I have not been here long enough to form acquaintances. Besides, teaching makes one unsociable.

I used to think schoolmasters disagreeable company, because they bring with them the peremptory, domineering, correcting ways they employ in the schoolroom. I am afraid, if I went into society, people would find me objectionable for the same reason—which, indeed, I can't help, for one contracts bad habits insensibly in this world of all sorts of misdemeanours." She rose. "Good afternoon, Mr. Goodhart."

"I am sorry you should be in a hurry."

"I am not in a hurry. I am going to my lodgings to drink a cup of tea," said she, with a smile.

"Will you do me the pleasure to drink tea with me at the hotel? I am a stranger here, and I assure you your society is a singular privilege which you will not allow me to lose for a cup of tea?"

"I shall be very pleased," she answered, without hesitation. "I'm sure your thoughtful kindness, the trouble you have taken in carrying out my husband's wishes, make me very glad, indeed, to meet you."

Naturally, as a lady whose income was very limited indeed, and who was obliged to teach in order to live she was greatly touched by the kindness of the man who had taken the trouble to find her out that he might hand her the handsome and welcome sum of one hundred and fifty pounds, her husband's farewell gift.

They walked slowly to the hotel.

CHAPTER XIV

A RESCUE

A S they walked, Reynolds said to Lucretia, "It is sad that you should be obliged to follow an uncongenial calling for a living. Mr. Wembly-Jones told me that your income was small—I think he said seventy pounds a year."

Mr. Wembly-Jones had said nothing of the sort; but then, Reynolds thought that he knew what he was talking about.

"It is less than that," answered Lucretia, with her cheek warmed by a little colour discharged into it by half a dozen different feelings. "Indeed, it is barely sixty."

Their eyes met as she spoke, and she witnessed a sympathy that was deeper than any that could give life to pity in a stranger in his look. He saw a sudden trouble of mind as of perplexity in the shadow her brow took, and in the compression of her lips.

"Had I thought of it," said he, "I might, on learning the name of your father, have found out where you lived by looking at his will. Your trustee would have given me your address."

"There were two, and both are dead."

"Who sends you your money?"

"It is received by the bank and forwarded to me. Mr. Wembly-Jones told me that you were an Australian."

Reynolds did not speak.

"The income I receive," she said, "is derived from Australian bonds. I should know what they are called if I heard the name."

"New South Wales?"

"No."

"Victoria?"

"Yes."

"I also hold in Victoria. They are very safe."

She asked him some questions about Australia, and this brought them to the hotel.

As they entered, one of two men who were conversing in the hall shrieked like a locomotive whistle and fell in a fit. From all parts, from offices and rooms, people rushed. Who was it? Only his grace the Duke of ——. When a duke has a fit the flap is usually great in the barnyard that is the theatre of his exploit. A duke's a duke. Reynolds and Lucretia blended their gaze in an expression of awe at the noble figure (five feet eight) as it was lifted and carried away.

"Who is it?" asked Reynolds of a waiter.

The fellow told him.

"What was the matter?"

"A fit, sir. But it's well known his viscera's wore out."

After an uncontrollable fit of laughter, Reynolds ordered tea for two and passed with Lucretia into a great room and sat down with her at a table at an open window which framed the sea. When events come to pass, they lose the weight of meaning they held whilst in contemplation. Had Reynolds been told, whilst on the island of Santo Cristo, that a day might come when he would be sitting at tea opposite his wife in a hotel at Ramsgate, he personating the part of Goodhart, and she accepting it to the very root of the credulity in her, he might, with a shrug and a smile, have held such a circumstance faintly possible, but in the uttermost degree improbable. Now that they were together he found the situation reasonable, logical, easy, though, to be sure, curious. Very soon after they had seated themselves, she said to him—

"Do you know, Mr. Goodhart, that in some way I'm not able to explain you recall my husband."

"And do you know, Mrs. Reynolds," he replied, "that in some way I can explain you recall my wife."

"Not that you are a bit like Captain Reynolds," she went on. "And yet you have that sort of resemblance which, if you were his brother, would be called a family likeness."

"You are like my wife in eyes, hair, colour, and figure," said he. "But she was slimmer, and had not your voice nor the power of expression I find in your eyes."

Lucretia believed that she concealed her pleasure, the pleasure of tickled vanity: but it is seldom that gratification can be so obscured that its light shall not appear in the face.

Reynolds' instructions for tea had been liberal. Strawberries and cream, prawns, brown and white bread, butter, cakes, and such things. He easily guessed that Lucretia dined in the middle of the day, and that her lonely repast would be very homely indeed—a mutton-chop say, cooked in a frying-pan, ill-dressed and ill-served, a lone lorn Mrs. Gummidge of a potato, and perhaps a sponge-cake for pudding. He had fed for twenty months upon fish fried in a shovel, and he was naturally in sympathy with Lucretia, who lived in a fifth-rate lodging-house.

If he had been pleased with his breakfast at an open window with a London stockbroker, we may conceive him immeasurably happier at tea at an open window with Lucretia. It was the singular case of a man who had resolved to woo and win, in another name, and in an unrecognized aspect, the handsome and indecorously chaste woman who had married him, and then cast him out as though he had been one of those abominable fiends whose misdeeds are recounted in Holy Writ. They had been married eight years. Commonly after eight years the most impassioned couple grow a little used to, if not a little tired of, each other. But here was a man who had got married, and had been immediately prohibited to find out what a wife meant, or what marriage was like. The painted dust still glorified this butterfly. The first love of his life still preserved the freshness and the glory of the dream. The virgin still slept in the shape of the married woman, and the wooing of her was to be made as sweetly and deliciously ardent, as though she had never been won. An odder contradiction in human affairs could not confound the understanding. Nevertheless, there they sat at tea, at an open window in a hotel in Ramsgate.

He opened his purse, and took out two guineas.

"The mate I sent ashore," said he, "found these coins in the old chest to which your husband's letter and enclosures to you had been nailed. As they may have belonged to him, will you allow me to present them to you as mementoes of his shipwreck."

She slightly flushed, bowed with the stateliness her fine figure and shape enabled her to command, and, taking the guineas in her hand and examining them, said—

"I shall value them very much indeed."

"I have no doubt they belonged to him," said Reynolds, "and that he put them into that mysterious old chest in preference to making a hole in the earth as the mariner's custom is when he meets with booty or disburdens himself of treasure. If he was long on the island his clothes would fall into rags, and he would be as badly off for pockets as young Colonel Jack."

She looked pensively out of window, then her eyes came back to the money in her hand ; she examined the coins afresh, and put them in her purse.

"How long were you at sea, Mr. Goodhart?"

"Many years."

"It is a hard calling and badly paid."

"Very—very."

"The only charm of the ocean as a life lies in it making you see the world. How mean I used to feel sometimes when Captain Reynolds was talking about the places he had visited! He'd tell me about Hong Kong, and Calcutta, and Sydney, and Cape Town, and dozens of other places, and all I could answer was, 'Do you know Ramsgate, for I've been there?'"

Reynolds was holding himself under wonderful control; such control as he never could have exercised but for two reasons : First, he was a man of great intelligence, of instant sympathy, and at this particular juncture you will suppose that every instinct bristled in him with the spirit of alertness. Second, he was used, as a sailor, to sudden confusing and amazing confrontments, and had taught himself never to be at a loss, and this professional habit had been matured by his island-isolation, by months of enforced introspection, by frequent contemplation of contingencies, such, for example, as suddenly meeting his wife, and how he should act, and the like. He listened to Lucretia with an unchanged face whilst she talked.

"Though sailors travel far, they see little," said he.

"I want to ask you this question whilst I think of it: do you suppose the sea-chest in the cave belonged to Captain Reynolds?"

"To judge from the chief officer's description of it I should say certainly not. He considered it about a hundred years old."

"I don't think I ever saw his sea-chest," said she, musingly. "And now another question, Mr. Goodhart. What chance do you think would a person, placed as I am, find in Australia?"

"A very poor chance."

"Surely a better chance than England offers?"

"No; you are not a cook or a housemaid. Governesses are not in demand in Australia."

"Where *are* they wanted?" she exclaimed, with a glow of eye, a colour of temper he remembered well, and remembered only to admire as he again admired. "Where is the governess paid as a person who must look like a lady if she is unable to live as one? I started a young ladies' school at Canterbury; two pupils could not maintain me, and I lost money, which reduced my income and drove me to Margate, where I was most unhappy. I cannot see why governesses should not be wanted in Australia."

He laughed softly, and answered that she would be deceiving herself if she acted under that impression.

"Forgive my apparent curiosity," he said, "my desire is to be of use to you. Did not Captain Reynolds leave anything—any property—cash—a house?"

"I believe he had two or three hundred pounds lying in savings at the London and Westminster Bank," she said, viewing him steadfastly as though struck by the idea he had put into her head.

" Have you claimed the money as his widow ? "

" No."

" Why ? "

" Because I never thought of doing so."

" Have you had no adviser in your time ? "

" I have consulted one or two solicitors, but on business that never could have suggested the thought you have given me."

" If you will authorize me to make a claim for this money as Captain Reynolds' widow, I will go to work. How much is it ? "

" Frank told me it was between two and three hundred pounds. But I know that he drew a part of it before he sailed on his last voyage, and perhaps that was the one hundred and fifty pounds he wished me to get, and which, thanks, so many, many thanks to you, I have got."

" Will you address a letter to me here, authorizing me to act for you ? "

" I will most gladly ; indeed, Mr. Goodhart, you are very, very kind," she exclaimed, and her voice trembled, and the extremities of her mouth twitched, and her eyes softened with the shadow of an emotion as the sunbeam on the river gathers tenderness from the shadow of the delicate film of cloud. "But," she continued, after a few moments' consideration, "if my husband is alive, ought I, have I a right to take the money ? "

" My dear madam," he answered, steadily returning her gaze, " I understand that it is eight years since you parted from your husband. His ship has been overdue seven years. In those seven years you have not heard of or from him. If he were alive would not he, on his rescue, have made haste to communicate with you? You must either take it that he is dead or that he has abandoned you. You knew your husband. Was he the man to abandon you?"

Her face expressed the complexity of her mood. She faintly responded—

"I do not know—I should hope not."

"Then, as he was not the man to desert his wife," continued Reynolds, repressing with a violent effort the animation his voice and manner were beginning to betray, "it must be that he is dead. For how is it to stand with you if you are to go on thinking of him as alive, yet never hearing from or knowing where he is? You told me you were newly married when he sailed. You were, so to speak, his bride. Do men desert their brides—and such brides as you? I do not think I could have deserted my wife, whom I loved, and I am sure she would not have thought I deserted her if I had sailed and had not been heard of for eight years."

She listened to him with an attention that made her eauty severe and colourless with the pain of that attention. She sighed suddenly, and gave her body a little shake, as though by the physical effort she could dislodge the gnats of thought which stung her.

"You are extremely kind to take so much interest," she said, feeling in her pocket for her gloves. "I will gladly take your advice."

"You will write authorizing me to apply for the money?"

"Yes—this evening."

"It will save a post if I send for it."

"I will leave it here."

She looked about her for a clock.

Reynolds pulled out Goodhart's splendid gold watch, somewhat ostentatiously surveyed it, and said—

"It is half-past six."

"I will leave the letter at about eight o'clock."

He sprang the lid of the watch as if to inspect the face, so held it that she could not fail to see the monogram, "J.G.," on the back, then closed and pocketed it.

She stood up.

"When shall I have the pleasure of seeing you again?" he said, rising.

"I am engaged morning and afternoon."

"And after?"

"I usually take a walk on the pier after tea."

"Shall we say this hour on the pier to-morrow evening?"

She bowed.

As they walked to the hall of the hotel they met the London stockbroker, who, after staring at Lucretia, thought to himself, "Well, this is coming it a bit thick! A pale, melancholy, white-haired man, well on for sixty, professing to love science and philosophy, and he has not been in Ramsgate a couple of days before he has managed to pick up the handsomest woman in the place!" So accurate are men's judgments one of another!

That evening Reynolds received the following:—

"28, Belle Vue Road, Ramsgate.

"DEAR MR. GOODHART,

"My husband, the late Captain Francis Reynolds, told me before we were married that he had saved up two or three hundred pounds, with which he intended to furnish a little house for me on his return.

This money he said he had placed in the hands of the London and Westminster Bank. I am quite sure this was the name of the bank in London. He sailed in the ship he commanded, the *Flying Spur*, from Falmouth, in October, 1890, and I have never heard of or from him since. As you inform me that I am entitled to this money as his widow, I should feel deeply grateful to you if you would help me to receive it, as I am poor and working as a governess, and this sum, whatever it may be, would be greatly helpful. I believe he drew a portion of it before he sailed. Thanking you again and again,

"Believe me, sincerely and gratefully yours,
"LUCRETIA REYNOLDS."

He slightly smiled, but his face swiftly resumed its habitual grave and melancholy expression, and he put the letter into his pocket with the slow motion of hand which is one of the body's visible tokens that the spirit within it is in labour.

Reynolds was a sailor, but he was also a good man of business. He easily understood that, as a stranger to Lucretia, he could not help her to get the money her husband had left on deposit—the procedure would have involved the starting of the gigantic mill of the law. First, Mrs. Reynolds must apply to the courts for leave to presume her husband's death; and this leave being granted, she must take out letters of administration or obtain probate of her husband's will, and in this case there was no will. The letters of administration, or the probate, would then have to be lodged with the London and Westminster Bank for registration, after which the money standing to the credit of the husband could be withdrawn. Reynolds had no intention to disclose his

identity, and his secret must be imminently jeopardized
if, feigning to be Goodhart, he placed himself within
the radius of the light of that searching bull's-eye, the
law. He quite knew what to do, and how to continue
his appeals to the gratitude and to the deeper emotions
of his wife, by holding her as a lady who would be very
willing to accept Mr. Goodhart's word, providing Mr.
Goodhart's or another's cheque confirmed it.

That was a fine month of June, and the following
day was as brilliant as any of the vanished flock of
sunlit hours. At half-past six Reynolds was on the
East pier. The sun was reddening westwards, and
clouds, as soft and white as foam, came out of the east
from the lips of the wind and floated across the sky to
make more glorious the pavilions and the couch of the
sinking god of day. Many people walked upon the
pier. Here and there, within a mile or two, gambolled
a boat, with men in her, fishing ; and here and there the
canvas of a sailing-boat resembled the breaking head
of a little sea. The Sandwich shore swept along in
purple shadow until it soared in dimming brightness
where the Foreland exalted her star. Whatever took
the eye was rich with the colours of the dying day—the
blue of the sea a deeper blue, the commonplace sail of
the smack a symmetric space of cloth of gold, the
granite of the quay mellow as ancient marble, the staring
chalk of the cliff as bland as the softness of cream, and
every glass-sparkle was a little golden sun, and every
reflection in the water the poetry of what was mirrored.

Reynolds stood at the end of the pier, and looked
down upon the water, which raced with the tide of flood,
and spat and snarled about the solid masonry, leaping
in bayonets of blue brine, foaming in eddies, waltzing
in mimic whirlpools away eastwards with an inward

swirl that made somewhat heavy weather of it close in against the seaward-facing pier-wall; and by looking apace steadfastly down you would have thought that the pier itself was shouldering through it at the rate of knots.

"Good evening, Mr. Goodhart."

Lucretia stood behind him. He could never weary of admiring her. Every time they met she grew in charm; her presence was fairer with beauty. Though English to the root, she had, he always thought, a something French—Parisian—in her several graces of demeanour and attire. Could she, even at this early date, fail to see that Mr. Goodhart was very seriously attracted by her, found her gravely engaging? Though his face was half buried in hair, and one eye lustreless, and the side of his face wrinkled like the shell of a walnut, there was window of countenance enough left for the man inside to peep out of and be detected, and she would not have been Lucretia Reynolds, in short, she would not have been a woman, had she missed the import of Reynolds' spirit that came and went in that facial show-box as an actor struts and withdraws. Was the spirit of chastity, adorable and thrice-blessed in the maid, but bitter and false in its animation of Lucretia as a wife, was the spirit that had expelled her lover and her husband from her life, to influence her afresh with like results on the cognition by her heart of Goodhart's meaning? This was the problem Reynolds intended to solve one way or the other in his own fashion and by the light shed by his past.

"How do you do, Mrs. Reynolds? I received your letter last evening, and the matter is in hand. You shall not be kept waiting, if I can help it."

She thanked him, smiling, and no smile of royalty—

taking its value from homage—could be more gracious than hers.

"Have you been at work?" he asked, whilst they seated themselves on the low coping that protects the extremity of the pier.

"Yes; from half-past two to half-past four. But I have done with that family. Mrs. Kendal is difficult to please. She has thin lips and pale eyes, and is one of those economical women who at table asks you to help the children plentifully to vegetables. She is a second wife, and calls herself number two."

"Who's wife is she?"

"An infatuated old man's, whose only son by his first wife was sent to sea as an apprentice."

"She is naturally proud of her own children, and spends all the money she can afford on them?" said Reynolds.

"Yes; her baby is the most handsomely dressed infant in Ramsgate, and although the old man is always appealing for funds, Mrs. Kendal manages to keep two nurses."

Lucretia spoke with a fine sultry glow of resentment and contempt in voice and eye.

"I'm glad you've done with them. You'll enjoy more liberty," said Reynolds.

"I wish you would encourage me to try my fortune in Australia, Mr. Goodhart. If I come in for any money from my husband—a thing I never should have thought of but for you—that, with the money you kindly sent me, would help me to start a school."

"I cannot encourage you," answered Reynolds.

"This visiting-governess work is a pitiful outlook—

a hand-to-mouth struggle which subjects one to endless mortifications."

"Meanwhile we will see what money Captain Reynolds left at the bank," said Reynolds.

"When I was at Canterbury I had some idea of starting a milliner's shop. But I am a miserable hand at business, and am sure I should lose every penny I embarked."

"There is no particular hurry, I hope."

"I mean this, Mr. Goodhart!" she exclaimed, with energy: "the money your goodness has been instrumental in getting for me, and the money you may succeed in obtaining on my behalf, must soon be spent if I do not apply it to some practical purpose, and then I shall be reduced to my former position—I shall have to teach to eke out an income that does not support me ; and I hate teaching."

"You don't mean to leave Ramsgate yet ? "

"I don't see why I should. What can I do elsewhere ? "

"I intend to remain here for some time. The place pleases and agrees with me. Between us we may yet devise some scheme that shall result in your establishment."

The wistful expression vanished from her eyes. Her look indicated a faint inward recoil, an appearance of surprise which needed but a touch or two with the pencil of the emotions to deepen into dismay. He gazed at her calmly ; his heart was well pleased. Certainly he was not very eager that Goodhart, on the merits of her needs, should lightly win the woman out of the little horizon of whose life Reynolds had been spurned. But she was bound to be grateful ; so, inclining her head, she said—

s

"Your honourable conduct, Mr. Goodhart, and your kindness and sympathy assure me that I could not do wrong by accepting your advice."

He smiled at her, and in a breath her face changed.

"It is very curious," she said, viewing him intently, "but there are moments when you strikingly recall my husband to me. It is not the voice, nor the appearance in the least——" She paused and again searched him with her gaze.

"Resemblances are often startling, though there may be no affinity between the people," said Reynolds. "Have you a portrait of your husband?"

"Yes."

"I should like to see it. His story, and yours, make him an interesting character."

She pulled a locket out of her breast, and he recognized one of his gifts, a locket containing a portrait of him cut from a photograph. It was suspended round the neck by a thin gold chain. She unclasped the chain, and gave him the locket opened. He inspected it with a tranquil face. He was indeed acting his part phenomenally well. But then he was acting that he might conquer, and he flung his whole genius into the effort as one who must either win a life or break a heart.

"This is a fine face," said he, dwelling with affected attention upon the photograph. "I like it. It is honest, open, handsome, I think. You flatter me by finding a resemblance. Take it, Mrs. Reynolds, and compare it. Why, this is a fine young man of thirty."

She took the locket, glanced at it, and then looked at Reynolds. Their eyes met.

"It is not the face," she said. "The likeness is in characteristics of speech and manner, and sometimes you wear an expression which might certainly easily make you pass as my husband's brother. It is a family resemblance."

He asked for the locket, and again fastened his eyes upon it.

"There is thought in this face. There is much character in the mouth, and the eyes are those of a thinker. I should say this man was of a poetical cast of mind."

"Distinctly."

"A bit of a dreamer—some sailors are. I incline that way a little. The middle watch makes one so— I mean if you are gifted with the poetic impulse. To most the middle watch is a prolonged yawn and a dreary stump of a dreary deck. I cannot believe that the owner of this face deserted you."

"I never said he did!" she cried, with some vehemence.

"If you have not heard from him it is because he is dead. So! this is that shipwrecked mariner whose legacy to his wife I was instrumental in discovering! Poor fellow! There is honour, there is loyalty in this man's face. I am certain that the character this face proclaims was too good, too honest, too faithful to desert such a bride as you made him."

"Oh, Mr. Goodhart, do not persist in telling me what I have never believed and never wished to believe. Could he have written, he would," she said, with her eyes womanly with that softness of shadow which betokens the possession of the mood of tears.

"His thinking of you, and leaving you what he had, is a proof of loyalty to the last," said Reynolds, gently, returning the locket to Lucretia. "And surely it must make you happier to know that, though dead, he was yours to the end, than to suppose that he lives and has abandoned you—at a time, too, of your life when you need the support, counsel, and home which only a husband can give you."

She was looking away from him across the harbour, crying silently.

An expression of deep love, the light of a heart glowing with the purest and most exalted emotion, was upon his face as he watched her. He rose, walked away a few paces, and seemed to be interested in the manœuvring of a boat that was making for the harbour, steered by a Cockney in a cricket suit, apparently drunk. A short way down the pier, standing against the side that fronts the sea, was a young woman who held her little boy of some two or three years on top of the coping. This was one of those persons who should not visit the seaside unless attended by a sentry. It is this sort of person who, with a baby in her arms, enters a boat loaded down to her gunwales by tipsy excursionists, and screams with laughter when a young, red-faced man with a hard round hat at the back of his head gets upon a thwart or seat on straddled legs, and dangerously sways the boat from side to side to some roaring vulgar song of " Send me a letter from 'ome." This is the sort of person who, with a child, a spade, and a bucket, is always caught by the tide, and stands in a swiftly diminishing island of sand. This is the person who sits perched on a rock reading a cheap magazine whilst the flood is making, and who must be washed off and drowned if a coastguardsman is not lowered and hauled up again with the "party" in his arms. This is the party who (always with the baby) is pulled out to sea by her husband or a friend without regard to the aspect of the weather or the set of the tide, and who is as charmed as the man is who rows her by the velocity of the boat through the water, overlooking the trifling circumstance that two-thirds of the speed must be attributed to the tide, which is despatching the boat into dangerous distance and ugly waters, from which her inmates must be rescued by three or four longshoremen who put off, and who, when they have towed the boat into harbour and safety, are rewarded by the man with an offer (after much heated talk about payment) to fight them all, one after another.

Suddenly Reynolds—but not only Reynolds, everybody within the area of the vibration—was startled by a fearful scream. What had happened? The young woman holding the boy on top of the coping had relaxed her grasp whilst turning her head to critically inspect the costumes of a couple of young ladies who were passing. The straining child broke from the weakened grip, and fell like a stone into the troubled waters beneath.

This end of the pier was well covered by people moving in procession, or lounging, or sitting. The shriek of the mother appeared to paralyze every limb; the walking figures stopped dead; next followed a rush of men and women, and the coping was clothed with a mass of variegated projected shapes, in the midst of which stood the mother, yelling as the vulgar exactly know how to yell in affliction, tossing her hands, and crying, " Oh, somebody save him ! he is my only child ! Oh, somebody save him ! "

Reynolds ran and looked over, and saw in the trouble of water below a little mound of foam, due to the windmill pantomime of the drowning child. Shouting to a man next him, " Heave me that rope, there, and send a boat ! " he pulled off his coat and cap, flung them down, sprang with a sailor's grace on to the coping, and with the swimmer's art, with outstretched hands meeting cutwater fashion, went a header. He rose buoyant: he swam well; no man ever carried a cooler heart or swifter prompting brain in moments of extremity. He caught a glimpse of the vanishing child, and in a few powerful strokes of arm was beside him, had gripped him, had hoisted him breast-high out of the snappish wobble, and was making for the line which had been flung, and which he speedily got a clutch of; and there he hung, holding the child on his shoulder, lifting and falling with the tumble of sea— a white-haired man, a most noble and heroic figure truly, and amongst those who looked down was Lucretia.

The harbour boat lay at the foot of a fall of pier steps, almost abreast of the watch-house. Men are always on the look-out on Ramsgate pier. The moment those on watch—these watchmen are gallant fellows; their ranks have supplied the lifeboat with magnificent examples of British pluck and endurance in coxswains and men—knew what had happened, three of them sank down the pier-ladder into the boat, and pulled round the pier-head with the steady controlled rage of seamen who perfectly understood the significance of time—yea, of one moment too late—in all sea peril.

"The boat's coming!" they roared from the coping to Reynolds, who smiled, and spoke to the child on his shoulder, who answered him.

The boat came hopping over the foam she made.

"Catch hold of the child," cried Reynolds, and the baby was seized and lifted in; and Reynolds, putting his hands upon the gunwale, hoisted himself in his sailor's way, and with his sailor's knack to the height of his waist, and then flung a leg over, and rolled inboards. "Thanks, my lads," said he. "Now bear a hand. This youngster wants his mother. Hand him to me, and then give way with a will."

No need for the piermen to ask this white-haired, gray-bearded old gentleman, "Was you ever at sea, sir?" There is what scientific men call a natural affinity among sailors. They mutually attract one another, and are drawn together by a law which is as much ocean's secret as that of gravitation is the earth's.

The men pulled the boat round to the harbour landing-steps. A great crowd was there to witness what was to happen. Lucretia made one of that crowd, and stood very near to the mother of the child, who was crying and trembling at the head of the flight of stone stairs. When Reynolds stepped out of the boat, sopping, a soaked parcel of manhood, clasping another but a smaller parcel equally soaked, up went a cheer that was louder than the roar of the surf upon the sands.

"Oh, my ducky! Oh, my darling!" sobbed the young mother, taking the streaming child from Reynolds. "How did I come to do it? Oh, I have nearly drowned you! Oh, my sweet pet lamb!" And she kissed the child and mouthed, and then burst out weeping hysterically. "Oh, sir, how am I to thank you! How noble you are! How good you are! I shall always—always ask God to bless you."

"Now, my dear lady," said Reynolds, "your child needs attention. Walk away home with him as fast as you can. You'll know what to do. If not, send for a doctor."

He offered to make his way through the crowd, who formed a lane for him, and groaned at him in exclamations of respect and admiration. But Lucretia, who stood near, advanced with outstretched hand.

"Mr. Goodhart," she said, speaking with a vibratory note, so impassioned was the emotion that possessed her; "I cannot express how much I honour and respect you for this act. It is beautiful——" She wished to say more, but she had been crying just a little time before he jumped into the sea, the weakness of tears was still hers, and she turned away her head.

"We shall be meeting soon," said he, and walked down the pier as fast as he could, leaving a wake of wet behind him, for his pockets and boots were full, and he was buttoned up in a waistcoat that held water. A watchman ran after him with his cap and coat. He overtook the mother hurrying home with her damp, but apparently cheerful burden, and begged her to be quick, and dry the child, and get it into blankets. He then walked to a cab-stand, jumped into a cab, and was driven to the hotel.

CHAPTER XV

MR. GOODHART OFFERS MARRIAGE

ON the morning following the life-saving incident, Reynolds awoke and found himself heavy, depressed, low with malaise. He felt his pulse—seventy. He got out of bed, opened the dressing-case, and took out a clinical thermometer. His temperature was 103½°. He quite understood that this signified a return of Malta fever, whether due to his plunge last evening, or to the perception of certain secreted microscopic bacilli that a time had come when they should make their presence felt, was not of the smallest consequence. The remedy was bed, patience, and abstinence.

He kept his room all day, but his yearning after Lucretia was so great that he must needs write this note to her—

"DEAR MRS. REYNOLDS,

"I am confined to my room by a slight attack of Mediterranean fever, but hope to be well to-morrow, and in any case to be able to meet you on the day following. Possibly I shall find you on the East Cliff esplanade at five o'clock (let me definitely name the day after to-morrow), when I hope you will return with me to drink tea. I am afraid I shall not be able to tell you anything about Captain Reynolds' money by then, because before the Bank remits they will require proof of Captain Reynolds' death. But I have referred them to Lloyds' and to other authorities, and have little doubt that before a week has passed I shall have the pleasure to hand you a cheque. With kind regards,

" Yours very truly,

" JOHN GOODHART."

He used pencil and took great care to disguise his hand which he readily contrived as he wrote in bed, and his writing was a ragged scrawl. He sent this note to be delivered by hand. Next to talking to her it pleased him to write to her. Goodhart's prophecy had come to pass : the old magic had done its work : the spell was on him. How passionately was he loving her !—never more so than now—never even in days when his heart was younger by eight years, when it had not been chilled and sickened by unnatural and unwomanly revolt, when love was sweet and fresh with the glory of the rose on the bush, not the rose in the hand, nor the petal of memory betwixt the leaves in the shut volume of years. And it was his passion to possess her that determined him to go on wooing her as he now was, as Goodhart, a stranger, an acquaintance, a fast-ripening friend of deep sympathy, a man to be trusted and honoured, to whose custody, absolutely convinced that her husband Frank was dead, she might in time be coaxed and courted into committing the delicate precious charge of her virginal being.

And you will suppose that to the degree of his desire for her was his fear of detection lest the old loathing should return, like the entry of a hideous fiend, to tear and rend to pieces the machinery of a mind that was to be likened to some hall of ice far north, a moonlit vision of white pillars, and roof gleaming with cold stars, and a floor upon which no fairy that ever sang with the grasshoppers in the land of romance would choose to dance!

He lay in a bedroom from which he could view the sea shining in a blue lake-like surface, and lying alone he thought much of his term of solitude on the island, how different his condition when he had the fever there from what it was now, how he had dragged his legs of lead, and poised his head like a hot cannon-ball between his shoulders, to the foam of the cataracts' stroke, how he had lain in his cheerless crack of earth gazing with fevered eyes at the stars, and wondering how long he should live, and thinking of Lucretia as he now thought of her. His mind rambled to the old sea-chest and to the letter he had nailed to the lid, and this memory caused him to consider that he had not made a will, and if he died and nobody could prove his identity his money would be lost to Lucretia.

He deliberated how he should go to work. He would not trust a local lawyer with the secret. The gentleman might be a member of the club at Ramsgate, and some provincial lawyers talk about their clients as some provincial doctors talk about their patients, so that if he went to a lawyer in Ramsgate to make his will, his secret business might, God knows how, leak out and trickle to that one ear in the world whose reception of it might desolate his heart, and bring his fabric of self-respect down upon his head in dusty ruin.

He rose early next day, being perfectly recovered from his attack, and took the train to Deal. This little town is seated opposite the Downs. It is remarkable for the number of its public-houses. Its beach is a

shelving shore of shingle, up which the surf rushes with
a noise like the escape of steam, and down which it
shales in a conflict of foaming water and dark gleaming
pebbles which rattle as they are torn along. Boats,
called galley-punts, repose on this shingle with their
noses pointed at the sea and their sterns at tall skeleton
capstans to which they are connected by ropes ; and
when one of these boats comes ashore from a cruise, a
number of aged men, who shape themselves out of you
don't know what or where, gather about the capstan the
boat belongs to, ship bars, and begin to wind round
and round, a slow, tuneless, and melancholy circus of
very old men in broken boots, patched breeches, tall
hats discoloured by age and weather into the aspect of
bronze, and faces often so ancient that to explore them
is like opening old coffins or like watching a mask of
almost eyeless wrinkles, vital in nothing save a movement of jaw which betokens that the withered curve of
gum with its one stump of ninety-three years is still
busy with the little cube of tobacco.

The beach and esplanade are noticeable for a class
of persons called boatmen, who wear yellow trousers
and blue jerseys, from the breasts of which they will
pull down a newspaper or a parcel of letters sent ashore
by a skipper for the post, and these men, who are nearly
always starving, and therefore ask most fraudulent and
monstrous sums of money to take you off or put you
ashore, devote the greater part of their lives to the study
of that fine art of the British longshore, the art of
lounging.

No boatman in Great Britain can loaf, lounge, and
lean with such superiority of lazy, drunken, idle, sulk-
ing, dumbly-cursing postures as the Dealman. He is
born for something to lean against, to lean upon with

folded arms, to lean over, to loll at ; the whole indolence
of the man blends with the object he polishes with
breech, elbow, or hip, and he and the capstan he sprawls
upon, or he and the pillar or post he leans against,
are so much one, that a dog and his tail are not more
united.

Reynolds walked from the station to the esplanade.
The hour was a little after ten : early, but Reynolds
desired to do his business and return to entertain
Lucretia at his hotel. Ramsgate was lost to sight in
the milky softness of cliff that contained it, and that
faded in a glimmering white film in the blue air. The
sea was brushed by a soft south-west wind, and glanced
and danced in little frolicking curls, every one of which
ran with a white feather in its head, and the broad
liquid table, upbearing its burden of curtseying ships in
the Downs, was a wide and lovely tremble of sparkles
like the shivering of the tiny suns in summer trees when
the green leaves are fretted by the kisses of the breeze.

Just there, where that brig with grey hull, raking
masts, the flag of Brazil at her trysail gaff, her chocolate-
coloured girl of figure-head sinking in endless bows to the
gaunt steamer ahead, sitting hollow upon the water with
the bewildered look of a balloon that comes down from the
clouds suddenly to sea and strains and floats for a little
while aimless and imbecile,—just there lay the *Flying
Spur*, in October, 1890: and this was June, 1898.
Lucretia was on board, loathing him : Lucretia was now
yonder where the low land lifted into a rampart of
chalk. He was Goodhart, and she did not loathe him.
What would be the mood that fired her, that should
sweep her into his arms, or drag her back in renewed
access of the passion of chastity when she discovered
that he was her husband ? Which must certainly

happen before they came together, and therefore would
happen, for he meant to possess her!

A boatman who was leaning over the back of a
seat—called out—

"Put you aboard any ship out there, sir?"

"No. Do you belong to Deal?"

"Whoy, I should rather think I dew," answered
the man, grinning over the folded arms he leaned upon.

"Who's a good lawyer in this town?"

"A good lawyer?" echoed the fellow, with a large
and silly stare at another man who had indolently
strolled up, scenting half a pint. "If yer want a good
lawyer you'll find him in one of them ship's forecastles,"
with a nod at the ships in the Downs. "*They* knows
what's what, and mor'n what's what, if they're furriners.
You'll get no advice worth listening to at Deal onless
it's the magistrates', who'll lock yer up for a month if it's
the bobby's wish and 'im in with yer wife, and both
wantin' yer out of it."

He scowled at his mate. The question appeared to
have touched a sore in the man's mind: indeed, his
feelings were so strong that he even stood upright to
deliver his views.

Reynolds walked into the High Street, obtained the
address of a solicitor from a stationer who produced a
directory, and called at once at the office. He was kept
waiting, and sat listening to a bald-headed clerk on a
three legged-stool, scratching time with his pen to the
ticking of a large leering clock over his head. A man
entered: he was dressed in blue cloth, and kept his cap
on. His face was like a piece of underdone beef, blue
and red, cobwebbed with scarlet filaments, and his eyes
glowed damply like the reflection of the sun in the
Thames on a foggy day.

" Mr. Grundy in ? " he asked.

" Engaged, sir," answered the clerk.

" How long'll he be ? "

" A few minutes. This gentleman's waiting."

" Good morning," said the man, bestowing a purple nod on Reynolds, and sitting down.

Reynolds slightly started. He knew the man as one Captain Carson, had met him at several ports, and had dined with him at Singapore. His nod alarmed him. Was he recognized ? His mind speedily cleared. Captain Carson did not know him.

"Ashore on business, sir ? " said Captain Carson, pulling out a case of cigarettes, and extending it to Reynolds, who declined, then to the clerk who, with obvious regret, also declined.

"All my business is done ashore," answered Reynolds.

"Oh, I thought you belonged to my cloth. You're lucky not to be master of a ship."

And he began a story about his crew, how they all came aboard drunk, how the ship was brought to Gravesend by lumpers and runners, where she was left to swing till her men were sober enough to stand upright, how, after letting go the anchor in the Downs, they all lay aft, and said they didn't mean to proceed in the ship, as she leaked, which was a lie, as most of her principal masts were sprung, which was another lie, as she was down by the head and all her running gear rotten, and not a ratline strong enough for a rat to sling by. All lies. They were ashore, and so was he.

All the time this captain talked, Reynolds marvelled at the change that had been wrought in his own personal appearance, so that this man should not have the least idea who he was : which somehow impressed him even more than his wife's failure to detect him.

He was liberated from the obligation of following a violent attack on the character of the merchant sailor by somebody stepping out of the inner office, and the solicitor in the doorway asking him to walk in. His business was simple, and was to be easily disposed of. He wished to leave all that he owned to his wife in language unclouded by legal verbiage, so that his intention could not be misunderstood. He named the manager of the bank he did business with in London, and a gentleman who resided in Sydney, New South Wales, as executors.

"When can you let me have this will ? "

"The day after to-morrow. To-morrow is County Court, and I have a number of cases to attend to."

"A good deal of quarrelling goes on here, I believe?"

"The boatmen love the law, and numbers of petty tradesman in the district, village grocers and the like, who sell everything from a joint of beef to a bird-cage, are constantly failing, or suing or being sued."

"Kindly address the document to Mr. John Good-hart," said Reynolds, naming the hotel and town ; and, paying the fee, he walked out, exchanging a nod with Carson as he passed.

He returned to Ramsgate with a heart as light as the June day about him, that rejoiced in the blue sky, in the song of the lark. He was acting his part well, and who or what sings more sweetly and gratefully to a man than his own conscience when it is happy and at rest? His heart was putting in some special pleading for Lucretia : his concessions were liberal. If her faith had been unfaithful, she had not been falsely true. She wore his ring, and his likeness rose and fell with the

breathing of her breast and the beating of her heart.
She had remained his wife, though she believed herself a
widow. In this was she true to herself or to him ? The
solution of such a problem could signify nothing.
Few know themselves: perhaps no man, however
searching in lifelong introspection, knows himself; the
mood of the hour before dinner is not the mood of the
hour after dinner ; Lucretia before her marriage was
surely not the Lucretia she was changed into by her
marriage, or would she have married ?

At half-past five he was on the esplanade, waiting.
A pale young woman of London, holding a small boy
by the hand, came along. When she saw Reynolds she
cried out—

"Oh, Georgie, there's the gentleman that saved your
life ;" and with an emotion of gratitude that gave a
moment's refinement of beauty to the coarseness of her
prettiness, she added, "I do thank you so much, sir ;
I couldn't have borne to lose him. What would my
husband have thought ? He'd write, and gladly, to
thank you, if not too great a liberty ; but your name
and address are unknown."

Reynolds smiled, and called the little boy to him,
and taking a crown piece from his pocket, said—

"Georgie, you can be a sailor, and feel easy ; you are
not born to be drowned. Which would you like best, a
horse and cart, or a ship to swim in a pool in the
sands ?"

"A ship to swim in a pool in the sands," echoed the
boy, in a level voice.

"Then, go and buy her," said Reynolds.

The boy's small fingers hooked themselves upon the
big coin with the avariciousness of tender youth.

"I thank you kindly, sir," said the London mother.

T

"Thank the gentleman, Georgie. Every night you kneel down you will ask God to bless him, won't you? I'd like him to thank you, sir, by singin' a little song his father learnt him."

But just then, Lucretia turned the corner. The London mother's eyes followed Reynolds' gaze, and she saw it was time to go.

"I hope you are very much better, Mr. Goodhart," said Lucretia.

"Malta fever is like a brother who has gone wrong: he makes you hear of him from time to time," answered Reynolds.

She was dressed in white, and was, in truth, a very handsome, indeed beautiful, presence, princess-like, if by that term, dignity, stature, carriage, and command of person be meant. Never a man passed by who did not favour her with a glance or stare. Nor were her own sex unobservant of her.

"I hope I made my meaning clear in the scrawl I sent from my bed," he said.

"Perfectly. I thought it so very kind of you to think of me when you were ill."

"It gives me pleasure to serve you," he exclaimed, with cautious warmth, feeling his way.

"It seems strange," said she, "that one who reminds me indefinitely of my husband should have found his letter, brought his gift, and continue to act towards me as though you had been friends. I showed you his likeness—I suppose you never met him?"

"What commands did he hold?"

"Oh, he went as captain of two or three mail steamers—I think the line was the Elder Dempster. There is such a firm?"

"Certainly."

"And he also commanded several sailing-ships. One was a celebrated clipper, and he would speak with enthusiasm of her beauty under sail or lying at anchor. She was called the *Lancashire Lass.*"

"I know the ship," said Reynolds, gravely.

"My husband, when he sailed on his last voyage, in 1890, had been about eighteen years at sea."

"He must have been young when he held command."

"He was. But in these days of steam, voyages are so rapid, that, as Captain Reynolds used to say, you can pack three or four voyages into a year, and if you obtain fresh appointments, whether in the same company or others, a comparatively young sailor may claim to have seen a great deal in a short time."

"True."

"It would be strange," she exclaimed, looking thoughtfully upon the ground as they walked, "if you had met him—unconsciously, I mean—on a pier or in a street in a foreign port, and in ignorance that you had once looked at him, or he at you, you had brought home his letter."

"It may be that Reynolds and I have met in the way you suggest. Englishmen are plentiful. They are repeatedly coming across one another," said he, speaking behind his beard, mustache, and pince-nez, with a face that was purely Goodhart to her.

They entered the hotel, and were presently seated at a tea-table at an open window. He told her that he had run across to Deal in the morning, and they chatted on several no-matters till Reynolds brought the conversation back again to them both.

"I think you told me that Captain Reynolds meant to take you to sea with him when he went on his last voyage."

She raised her eyebrows and exclaimed, "Did I ? I don't remember."

" Had you gone," he continued, "you would have been shipwrecked. It's true your life might have been preserved as his was, but if he was the only survivor no sailor would give the value of that strawberry in your hand for your chances, for your husband's first care would be for you. It must have been the lowered boat, and since none lived but he, you would have gone with the rest."

"Yet my place as his wife was with him," she said, looking through the window at the sea.

It was fortunate for the concealment he sought that their eyes did not meet, whilst the sudden look that almost transformed his face stayed for a few breaths only. He took up a prawn, and seemed lost in contemplation of its workmanship, but after no very long pause, said—

"No doubt a wife's right and only place is at her husband's side."

" I have felt the truth of this since you brought me Captain Reynolds' letter," she said quietly.

" I understand. You feel, as all must see, that your husband's last thoughts were with you."

" The subject is a sad one, Mr. Goodhart."

He was very willing indeed to change the conversation ; but, though his heart was on fire with her words, he perfectly understood that, if ever a moment for the revelation of his identity was to come, it had not come yet. Memory rising between them, shaped herself spiritwise, forefinger on lip, hand lifted in command of silence. She spoke in intuition, exhorting him not to hasten, but to consider that his avowal of imposition as Goodhart might flood his wife with the disgust that had been excited by the Gravesend stratagem which had kidnapped her—to no purpose.

"I find this hotel expensive, at least for my purse," said he. "But I am so well pleased with Ramsgate, that I mean to stay on."

He looked at her significantly. She did not seem to heed him, but if any thought present in him was interpreted by her, its construction produced not the slightest change in her face.

"I shall go into lodgings. I have no home. Indeed, I have had no home since my wife left me. The colonial is more cosmopolitan than other peoples who have countries. He loves the land of his birth, and would die for her with as much enthusiasm and loyalty as any Briton for the old home; but he does not suffer as others do from contraction of mind in respect of his thoughts of his country. The roving spirit that made his sires colonists is still unquenched, though in a few generations it will be extinct. The Australian can make himself a home anywhere and be happy in it. The Briton is always yearning to return. I could make myself very happy in Ramsgate." He was again addressing her with significance of look and tone. "Where shall I find a comfortable lodging?"

"I doubt if I know as much of the place as you do."

"Shall you seek another afternoon engagement?" he asked, smiling at her.

"Yes, and I shall be thankful to find one."

"Meanwhile, as you are at liberty, it would be delightful to me to enjoy a larger share of your company than your time has permitted."

If instead of being Reynolds he had in good sooth been Goodhart, it might be held that he was pressing her a little unhandsomely. For she was under a great obligation to him, and he was still in course of obliging her; and his advance would appear as though he was taking advantage of his singular relations with her. Her colourless cheeks slightly flushed, but she smiled whilst she said—

"I must hope not to have too much time on my hands."

"Are you disengaged to-morrow afternoon?"

"Yes."

"Will you come for a drive and dine with me here?"

"I will go for a drive with pleasure, but you must excuse me for declining your kind invitation to dine."

"Now why?" he asked, with a broad, blunt candour that caused her to bring her brows a little together in the seeking, the penetrating look she fastened upon him.

"What time shall I be here, Mr. Goodhart?" she inquired, with a release of gaze that left her face charged and troubled with thought.

He named three o'clock, perceiving it was not her wish he should call for her. They lingered awhile in odds and ends of talk. She then put on her gloves, and he conducted her to the entrance of the hotel, where they parted.

At three next afternoon a carriage stood at the door of the hotel. Lucretia arrived with the punctuality of royalty. She got into the carriage, Reynolds followed, and they were driven away for a summer jaunt through Broadstairs to the North Foreland. There is no pleasanter drive in this smiling country of green lanes, and spreading orchards, and gleaming coil of river, and green slope of down, and large moist eye of violet sea betwixt the breaks of coast, than this that Reynolds and Lucretia were taking. She was dressed as on the previous day, and her enjoyment of the drive was soon expressed in a clearer brilliance of eye and in that illumination of face which is not a smile, though it produces the effect of one.

Their talk was for a long while on very little matters. She was particular in her inquiries about Sydney. She avowed a very strong leaning towards making use of the money Mr. Goodhart had kindly sent her through Mr. Wembly-Jones by trying her fortune in Australia. If more was to come, then, if the sum amounted to even a hundred pounds, she believed she would make up her mind to go out and start a school. Reynolds smiled, but offered no further opinion.

"Here," said he, as they drove through Broadstairs, "lived a man who knew human nature as well as Shakespeare. You might give offence if you said that he knew human nature better. But if you find no Lear, nor Hamlet, nor Macbeth in the works of Dickens, neither in the works of Shakespeare do you find Mrs. Gamp, nor Mr. Bumble and Mr. Squeers and Mantalini, and how many more immortals? They say he wrote 'Bleak House' in that building perched up yonder. Of course you love Dickens?"

"I remember that my husband was always quoting from him."

"The more you tell me about Captain Reynolds the higher you raise him in my esteem. I wish it had been my good fortune to have found him on the island and brought him back to you. Coachman!"

"Sir."

"You can stop at the lighthouse. We'll get out and take a turn."

This foreland cliff is not tall, but it is bold, and its face of rugged chalk stares upon the most wonderful

maritime highway in the world. Ships pass comparatively close in, and the picture is vivid with dimension,
grand and romantic in colour and shape, and profoundly
interesting, one should imagine, to even a thin thinker,
by virtue of its infinite variety and the ideas with which
contemplation of it swells and elevates the mind. As
they alighted from the carriage a bright sketch was in
full view large upon the water. It was a steel sailing-
ship, close-hauled, luffing up for the Downs, under all
plain sail, three pyramids of ascending clouds of snowy
whiteness, with many silent delicately shadowed wings
between; the foam was rolling forwards from her
sharp metal forefoot, but a steady stream of it ran along
her sides to unite at her rudder in a wake of prisms and
bells of froth and leapings and lights which struck into
the blue air, closing down with the sudden transcendent
splendour of the diamond. She was not so far off but
that you saw a figure or two moving upon her quarter-
deck.

Reynolds stood still and looked at her. Lucretia
was by his side. Within a short distance rose the
sturdy, storm-defiant figure of the lighthouse, with its
building, and its lantern, that at nightfall should change
into a roaring star, reverberating in flashes the light of
a sun.

"What a very pretty sight!" exclaimed Lucretia.
" I always think a sailing-ship makes a daintier picture
than a steamer. It may be because sails give a bland-
ness and fulness and dignity which a chimney-stack can
never supply."

"She should remind you of a ship your husband
commanded," said Reynolds, bringing his thoughts away
from a sudden vision of a ship on fire in the thick of a
living gale, and a little island close aboard.

" The *Flying Spur* ? "

" No ; that clipper you spoke of—ah ! the *Lancashire Lass.* I wonder what will be the fate of yonder craft ? Every ship has her destiny, as man has. If I were a ship, I should say, ' Let me perish by fire or foundering or in any fashion that touches not the honour of the ship ; but do not make me a coal-hulk.' Were you ever at sea in a sailing-ship ? "

" I accompanied Captain Reynolds to Falmouth in the *Flying Spur*."

" How did you enjoy the trip ? "

" I was very sick and—— " she turned her eyes a little round about her, and added, " I could not enjoy myself, for I was angry at being taken. And you cannot enjoy yourself when you are in a bad temper."

" Why should you have gone if you didn't like the idea of the trip ? . . . But, of course, Mrs. Reynolds, you went to gratify your husband. Had you persevered your sickness would have passed, and with it naturally your bad humour."

It would tease the reader to be informed of every turn of eye, every tone of speech, every shade of gravity, which was, indeed, in his case, irony and satire, the several manners he put on when he conversed with her. Sometimes he would observe her silently and intently regarding him ; but his performance was so adroit, he was so deceptive in his language about his wife having left him, by which she understood him to mean Mrs. Goodhart's death ; to his references to himself as if he were an Australian and the like, that, believing her husband dead in his island, and perceiving nothing but certain traits or opinions in this Mr. Goodhart that in any way brought up her Frank Reynolds of St.

Stephen's Church before her, she lay under as complete a deception during this drive as she had in all
their previous meetings and conversations.

They were now addressing each other with that
easiness, it need not be called familiarity or freedom,
which results from association. They roamed about for
a short while inspecting the interior of the lighthouse,
chatting with the keeper, who told them of beautiful and
strange birds swept by the storm of the night against
the radiant glass, and found dead, and of the dulness of
his life when he was lightsman aboard the Gull, and
afterwards the East Goodwin, and then the South Sand
Head light-ships; how, in his day, the old *Triton* did
the relieving work—a vessel that rolled heavily in still
waters at her berth at the West Pier; that could not
steam above four and a half knots; that could not do
six with a gale of wind astern of her, so that in heavy
weather the lightsmen, who kept watch in the lonely
hulks round about the sands and from the North Foreland to Dungeness, were sometimes obliged to wait a
fortnight and three weeks for the relief. "Hard upon
men, sir, who, in winter, consider a month's-old newspaper fresh, and have nothing to do but tend the
lights and watch for ships' flares to send up rockets for
the lifeboat."

Lucretia declined to ascend to the summit of the
lighthouse. She said she was afraid. So they returned
to the carriage and drove away towards Ramsgate.

"Won't you reconsider your decision as to dining
with me, Mrs. Reynolds?" said he.

"I am sure you'll excuse me."

"Will you drink tea at Broadstairs? It is disagreeable to me to think that you should bear the fatigue of
this long drive, and the heat, without refreshment."

" I shall enjoy a cup of tea very much indeed. But there is no fatigue—the drive is charming, and the heat, with this breeze, is delightful."

Reynolds told the coachman to stop at the best hotel in Broadstairs. There they stayed for half an hour, drinking tea and eating brown bread and shrimps. Though their talk was of anything, she could not fail to notice that Mr. Goodhart's eyes were very constant in their observation of her. She was perfectly sensible that she was in the presence of a man who admired her, and was even in love with her, and her manner grew very thinly glazed as they sat at the tea-table in the bay-window. This cold surface, though transparent enough to suffer the visual expression of any play of feeling, tranquillized her exterior to a calmness that was not remote from austerity. He recollected that much such an expression of face was hers when they had stood side by side at the altar, and walked side by side back to Mrs. Lane's modest little house. There was a tone of constraint in her voice. If she attended to his speech with a look it was soon averted. Indeed, in her eyes he saw that her spirit had hoisted its glittering storm-signals, and it was with the transport of a husband about to attempt an experiment whose success would be a death-blow to his vanity and his love, that he saw that any claims which Mr. Goodhart might have upon her gratitude would not entitle him even to a peep into that sanctuary of her heart in which the flame of the one love of her life, though burning dimly, was to be *found*, and perhaps—he could but hope it—to be fanned and fed into the sweet clear light it was when she consented to be his wife.

They left the hotel and again entered the carriage. The way before them was a short drive. Scarcely were they in the carriage, and in motion, than, planting his eyes upon her through his pince-nez, he exclaimed—

"It has given me a great, a singular pleasure, to make your acquaintance."

She bowed and smiled, but her smile was no encouragement to him to proceed.

"I am alone in the world," he continued. "I have often regretted that, since it was the will of God Mrs. Goodhart should die, her little one had not been preserved to yield the sunshine and warmth of a child's love to its parent. You too are alone, Mrs. Reynolds."

"I do not know what you would wish to say to me, Mr. Goodhart," she answered, with a visible hardening of her whole demeanour, and an undissembled shrinking of her fine figure into the corner of the seat she occupied.

"I have never felt less lonely—since the term of my loneliness began," said Reynolds, with a melancholy and solemnity of tone and look that was markedly effective in its impression on her, as he easily saw in the shining inquisitorial stare of her enlarged eyes, "than during the time I have spent in Ramsgate and in your society. I am a man of independent means. Nothing could render me so happy as to feel that I was the instrument of providing you with a settlement that should make you independent of a vocation you abhor, that should indeed keep you easy and comfortable in your circumstances for the rest of your life. It is true I am not a young man. I have no special favours of face or person to grace my suit or enrich it by that silent eloquence which women much, indeed chiefly, admire in men. I have led a hard life. The sea is an exacting calling. It has left me rugged. But it has left me an honourable man, with a heart capable of dedicating itself in lifelong affection to such a woman as you, Mrs. Reynolds. Will you be my wife ? "

She looked steadily away from him for some moments ; her face was as rigid and, in truth, as colourless as marble.

"I am sorry, Mr. Goodhart," she said, turning slowly in her stately way upon him, "that you should have asked me that question. You have been so kind to me, that the pain you cause me by obliging me to absolutely refuse you must be keener than *any* I can inflict."

"No, no."

"I should be grieved indeed to lose your friendship, but our relations could never go beyond that."

"Am I to think that you still believe your husband to be alive ? " he asked, always preserving his gravity and his melancholy.

"I was not the wife I should have been to my husband. I remember all, and before God I vow that whilst life remains I shall be his wife, and true to him."

She spoke with a vehemence that was dangerous in one so passionless, so collected, so resolved, of a deportment and exterior so admirably under control. Why did he not then and there confess himself ? His making love to her, as Goodhart, had touched the mute chords of her memory of Reynolds, and woke them into music and feeling. The hand seemed upon the second ; the mood seemed to exactly fit the wish ; the ripened fruit, to fall, seemed to need no more than the breath that is between lips meeting in a kiss. Thoughts flew through his brains with the velocity of the clouds, of the mind driven by the gales of the passions. He reasoned, "If I say I am Frank Reynolds, she, after the first convulsion and riot of feeling, might find herself possessed again by the spirit that banished me and widowed her ;

and chagrin and mortification might accompany the discovery that, for the second time, I had duped her." Memory exhorted him to hold his peace in the name of his love, his honour, and his dignity. After a silence that ran into many moments, he said, without looking at her—

"You are infinitely raised in my admiration. You do well to be loyal to a man who was manifestly loyal to you even in his lonely, dying hours. You make me feel ignoble as an intruder——"

"No, no, Mr. Goodhart," she cried, in a sobbing voice. "I thank you for the gracious way in which you have taken me."

"We shall remain friends?"

"Oh, I hope so!" she exclaimed cordially, with emotion colouring her smile with a tender sweetness her lips did not always wear in approval or mirth.

The hotel was in sight. She asked that the carriage might be stopped.

"I have thoroughly enjoyed the afternoon," she said, as they stood together at the side of the carriage. "But the pleasantest part has been the last part, because now you allow me to think of you as a friend, and, above all, we understand each other."

They shook hands, and she walked towards her lodging, whilst Reynolds re-entered the carriage to be driven to the hotel.

CHAPTER XVI

HUSBAND AND WIFE

THE Deal solicitor was punctual in sending Captain Reynolds his will. It was witnessed by the manager of the hotel and a bookkeeper, to both of whom, of course, Reynolds remained John Goodhart, Esq., because, as a rule, testators do not read aloud the contents of their wills to the people who attest them.

The possession of this will made Reynolds very happy. Happen what might to him, Lucretia would be provided for, and though they should never come together as husband and wife, he was still, though masquerading as Mr. Goodhart, the Frank Reynolds of her choice and denial, who would watch over her and provide for her by such expedients as love—such honourable and such noble love as his—"is very cunning in."

Two days after he had taken the drive with Lucretia, he went to London and called at his bank, where he had a short interview with the manager, who wrote and signed a cheque upon the bank that was countersigned by the accountant. He returned from London by a late train, and next morning took lodgings in the Augusta Road, so that by looking out of the window he could see the house in which Lucretia lived. After lunch he strolled out with the

hope of meeting her; he returned to his rooms and
wrote this note—

"I was in London yesterday, and have good news
for you. As you seem to have an aversion to invitations
to dinner, will you drink tea with me this evening
at 5.30?

"Yours sincerely,
"JOHN GOODHART."

As before, when he scrawled a letter to her in his
bed, he wrote with studious ambition of concealment
in handwriting, and was as successful in this art as
in nature he was a triumph in his representation of
Goodhart.

Within half an hour a note was left at his lodgings.
Mrs. Reynolds would do herself the pleasure to drink
tea with Mr. Goodhart. She came with the punctuality
that was one of the graces of her characteristics. Is it
necessary to describe her dress?—close fitting navy blue
serge, and sailor hat. The weather was sultry, and she
was pale, and carried a fan. A lovely bouquet of
flowers stood upon the table, and refreshed the atmosphere with the incense of half a score of different growths
of beauty. The window was still open, but the road
was a quiet one, and the lace curtains effectually screened
the occupants of the room from the inspection of the
profane and vulgar passer-by, who, with a packet of
shrimps in his pocket, which he picks at and eats as he
rolls along, his hard hat on the back of his head, and
his legs travelling somewhat tipsily in a pair of check
trousers of a pattern so enormous that a giant of fifteen
feet high could not reduce the eyesore to proportion,
holds Ramsgate to be after Margate the only place in

all England to "do himself proud in" with what he calls
a "houting."

They had not met since the day of the carriage
drive. But neither exhibited embarrassment. She was
too self-possessed to be disturbed by a feeling, that like
naïveté, may be defined in the Frenchman's expression
as "une nuance de bas, presque jamais d'élévation,"
whilst he found all the fortitude he needed in the circumstance of his being her husband.

"You have not gone very far," said she, sitting and
fanning herself and looking at the flowers on the table.

"No ; I can easily see where you live."

"What glorious flowers !"

"I was sure you would think them worth the trouble
of carrying home."

"Thanks so much. They will grace my poor room.
It needs it."

"No one will say that whilst you are its occupant."

He rang the bell for tea.

"Have you found any afternoon pupils ?"

"Not yet. I have put an advertisement this week
in a Ramsgate paper."

"I have some news for you, but I'll wait till the
servant has come and gone."

She looked about the room, and said, "Won't you
find it very dull here after life in a hotel ?"

"I dislike life in a hotel. As Dickens—the writer
your husband admired so greatly—truly says, in a
hotel nobody is glad see you, nor cares how long you
stop or when you go. You become a number ; you
lose individuality and are changed into a particle in a
stream of figures in a ledger. You can't enjoy seclusion
unless you invoke the genius of insolvency, and establish
yourself in a set of private apartments *from* a price

U

which would yield a comfortable income apiece to four or five vicars and beyond the most strenuously exerted earning-power of even a popular country medical practitioner *to* a price which, if an American girl had it in the shape of a weekly revenue, would buy her a British lord or an Italian prince. Now, in lodgings, you can dine off a chop, smoke a pipe, drink stout from the public-house, humour the landlady's cat, and live through the life of the day without that critical inspection from which all human beings suffer in the public rooms of hotels and boarding-houses. And then, Mrs. Reynolds, lodgings may be cheap."

It was manifest to him, even whilst he spoke, that the attention with which she accompanied the movements of his lips was due, not to the amiable desire to be amused, but to something lying very much deeper. When he ceased, she exclaimed—

"If my husband had been pleading on behalf of lodgings against hotels, he would have put his views just as you have—in the same spirit; I might declare, in the same words."

"Very likely," said Reynolds, quietly, looking at the tea-tray, which the servant was then placing on the table.

But his answer would not do. She was troubled; she directed at him a scrutiny that made her frown; her toe tapped the carpet, and she looked down.

"Will you give me a cup of tea?"

She drew to the table, and filled two cups in silence; but three or four times whilst she did this, she darted her brilliant gaze at him. His breathing grew a trifle laboured; the motions of his heart a little swifter. He believed that her mind was at the very touch-hole of detection, and he waited for the flash and what was to follow the flash. But the suspicion that discoloured, and even in its way distorted, her beauty soon dissolved under the warm breath of conviction. Indeed, she never had supposed, she never could suppose, the man who confronted her to be her husband. He was an Australian; his wife lay buried in Sydney; he had come to hear of Captain Reynolds by one of the hundred accidents of the sea. He had not her husband's face, nor his voice, nor enunciation. And if Frank had been alive through eight years, why did he return now? Why not earlier? She drew a breath that had the depth of a suspiration, and said—

"It is very strange."

"Coincidences *are* strange," he answered, breathing easily again. "I never allow them to weigh. They resemble dreams. We remember the two or three that come to pass, and forget the thousands that vanish unverified."

She seemed to acquiesce in this opinion by an inclination of the head. He looked at her, and thought to himself, "It is wonderful that, loving her, as I find I do, as deeply as I loved her when I married her, I should have waited eight years to return and seek her. But Goodhart was right. I did not know myself." He pulled out a pocket-book.

"I was in London yesterday," he said, "and went about your business. The bank is satisfied with my representations, and the information I obtained from Lloyds' and other sources as to Captain Reynolds, and I have much pleasure in handing you this cheque—the balance of the money your husband left at the bank before he sailed."

He extended an envelope with a large official red-wax seal; it was addressed to Mrs. Reynolds, care of

John Goodhart, Esq. She broke open the envelope,
and withdrew the cheque that was folded in a sheet of
paper, on which was lithographed "With the Manager's
Compliments." The cheque was for two hundred and
eighteen pounds. She coloured; her eyes brightened;
gratitude sweetened her beauty with the tender, smiling
light which that gentle and lovely quality casts upon
the face.

"How am I to thank you, Mr. Goodhart? I should
never have heard of this—or thought of it—but for
you."

He raised his hand in a cordial gesture of remon-
strance.

"Two hundred and eighteen pounds!" she exclaimed.
"Why, this and the money you brought to me from the
island are a fortune. I feel rich. How good of you!"
She paused, and, looking at the cheque, said, with a
sudden sorrow in tone, a sudden sorrow in look, "Poor
Frank!"

He fastened his gaze upon the ground, for he knew
just then that there was a dangerous moisture in his
eyes, and not for the life of him durst he have spoken.
Her "poor Frank!" had struck to his heart, and for a
moment or two the man wept inwardly.

"To whom shall I send a receipt for this cheque?"
she inquired, after a welcome interval of thought.

"Acknowledge it to me, and I will forward your
letter to the bank," he answered, managing his voice by
speaking low.

She asked no more questions. It did not occur to
her to inquire how it happened that the bank should
pay over her husband's money to a stranger without her
authority; how Mr. Goodhart had succeeded in satisfying the law, and, sequentially, the bank, that Captain

Francis Reynolds was dead.   Mr. Goodhart had behaved most nobly and honourably, and the money was a godsend.

"Will you give me another cup of tea, Mrs. Reynolds?"

She put the cheque in her pocket.   He took the cup from her.   Her smile was gracious as she handed it to him.   The distressed poet, scratching verses under a map of the gold-mines of El Dorado, dunned by his wife and the milkman, may, and as a matter of fact does, call money dross, filthy lucre, and the like; but there seems to exist in this dross an inherent property of such electrical vitality that, when applied, it will force laughter from anguish, illumine the sickliest countenance, inform with a passion of dance the gout itself, and liberate the virtues from the webs into which the spider Poverty coaxes them to roll them up.

"By the way," said Reynolds, looking up from some notes he had made on a piece of paper.   "Did you ever meet a man named Featherbridge?"

She started and stared hard at him, and answered, "I knew a Mr. Featherbridge."

"The man I mean," continued Reynolds, "sailed with your husband as chief mate of the *Flying Spur*."

"Yes; I knew him.   Indeed, he acted as my husband's best man at our marriage."

She spoke in a wary way, as though she distrusted this subject.   Suddenly her mood burst into impassioned life, and she cried—

"Why do you ask if I know Mr. Featherbridge? Is he alive?   Have you met him?   Have you news of my husband?"

He had by this time wholly mastered himself.

"I was in the City yesterday," he said, "and turned

into some dining-rooms near the Mansion House for
lunch. I took a seat opposite a man who, after viewing
me awhile, pronounced my name; I immediately recollected him. He was Mr. Charles Hall, member of a
firm of London shipbrokers. He had sailed with me as
passenger in a vessel I commanded. We fell into a conversation, and it was natural, perhaps, that our talk
should have large reference to the sea. He told me
that in all his experience he never remembered so many
ships posted as missing. I can scarcely tell you how it
came about, but, in speaking of missing ships, he mentioned the *Flying Spur*, in whose fate he was interested,
as his firm had negotiated the sale of her to the person
who owned her when your husband obtained command.
I told him that I had the pleasure of knowing the widow
of Captain Reynolds. 'Indeed!' said he. 'That's
strange. Reynolds' chief mate was a Mr. Featherbridge, whose mother lives where I do—a pleasant old
lady, whom my wife and I have been acquainted with
many years. The last letter Mrs. Featherbridge ever
received from her son was dated at Madeira, where the
ship had called.' Did you hear from your husband at
Madeira?"

"No," she answered.

"It was a long letter, Mr. Hall said, and it was
nearly all about Captain Reynolds and you."

Lucretia slightly coloured, but remained silent.

"Shall I proceed, Mrs. Reynolds? I don't want to
pain you. But I believed that whatever concerned your
husband after his departure would interest you, and so
I took down some notes of Mr. Hall's conversation to
help my memory if it is your wish that I should tell
you what Mr. Featherbridge wrote to his mother."

"I should be glad to hear," she said distantly.

He returned to his notes.

"You were living with your mother in Bayswater when you were married. After your marriage you locked yourself up in your bedroom and refused to see, to speak to, to have anything whatever to do with Captain Reynolds."

"It is very wonderful that Mr. Hall should remember the contents of a letter all about a stranger so very—*very* accurately!" exclaimed Lucretia, darkly, nervously, suspiciously, as though she thought that Mr. Goodhart had something of the devil in him.

He removed his glasses to polish them. Whenever he was without spectacles or pince-nez the dulled ball of left eye, lustreless, stained and veined like those marbles boys call alleys, haloed by a sort of *arcus senilis :* these and the wrinkles where he had wounded himself, the scar, the deflected arch of eyebrow utterly changing the character of the face, were very visible and instantly took the eye.

"I certainly shall not go on if I annoy you. But I thought that, knowing what your feelings are for your husband, the latest news of him down to vanishing point—for he disappears afterwards as a soap-bubble explodes—would interest you."

"It does. But you can't say he disappears. You brought news of him from the island ; news that is later than this Featherbridge letter that was posted—you say—at Madeira."

"Oh, that island news is very negative news. Its report is merely that Captain Reynolds was on the island, conceived himself dying, nailed all he was worth to the lid of a sea-chest with an appeal to the honour of the stranger who found it to hand it to you, and then we must suppose that one day or night he stiffened his spine and, looking up to God, passed out. *That's* not the news I got from Mr. Hall."

"There is no reason to believe that my husband is dead, because he was not seen on the island by the officer you sent on shore," she exclaimed, with temper in her eyes and voice.

"Shall I go on?" he asked.

"Oh, certainly," she replied, in a large, sarcastically bland manner.

He resumed his spectacles and seemed to consider his notes.

"Featherbridge told his mother that he had helped Captain Reynolds to decoy his wife to the ship. So I gathered from Hall. But her aversion was so violent, so menacing to Reynolds' character among the crew, that in despair he sent her ashore at Falmouth and proceeded on his voyage alone. Hall told me that Featherbridge, who appears to have been a gentleman and a man of education, described your husband's grief as a form of sorrow that affected him more than any sort of human misery he had witnessed. He forsook his food, his cheeks fell in, he would often in pacing halt, and stand rooted and gaze at the sea in an agony of mind; and once he clutched Featherbridge by the arm and looked him in the face with swimming eyes and after such a groan as a man gives whose heart breaks, whose spirit flies, whose whole moral being falls into ruin; he cried, 'Oh, my God, what have I done that she—the one, the only love of my life, my own, my beautiful, my dearest wife,—what have I done that she should abandon me?'"

Lucretia shrieked and sprang to her feet.

"I can endure no more—I cannot, indeed! You

will drive me madder than I then was. No more,
I beg!"

She brought her foot to the ground with a stamp
that shook the ornaments on the mantelpiece, and fanned
herself with extravagant motions.

He pocketed his glasses and his notes and put on
his pince-nez, and as she was standing he stood.

"It is too much," she exclaimed, with mounting
colour and enlarged nostril, and eye dramatized into a
fine expression of wrath in beauty by her spirit's adjustment of the mobile lid, lash, and brow, "that a matter
so sacred and personal to myself as the relations
between my husband and me should be talked about in
a London eating-house."

"Nothing of the sort, Mrs. Reynolds. Mr. Hall and I
sat apart. He spoke of you and your husband in terms
of sympathy I am sure you would appreciate. Mr.
Featherbridge——"

"I hated that man!" burst out Lucretia. "He
could look you in the face and tell a lie."

"Mr. Featherbridge," continued Reynolds, approaching her by a step or two and keeping his eyes steadfastly bent upon hers, "referred to you in his letter as
one of the most beautiful women he had ever seen, and
he declared himself utterly at a loss to understand why
you, who did undoubtedly love your husband well
enough to marry him, should, immediately after the
marriage, find something in the man of your choice,
this comely, honourable sailor who adored you, to
excite the loathing that broke his heart and widowed
you."

She fanned herself furiously. When he ceased to
speak a deep blush burned in her face. The sting of
the blood was insupportable. She went to the open

window and turned her back upon him; but, after a brief interval, without moving her figure, she looked sideways and said—

"How dared that man Featherbridge say that I loathed my husband!"

"Well, Mrs. Reynolds, I trusted that the very last news of your husband that could be given would interest you. I hope, despite my clumsy method of communicating it, we still remain friends."

He saw her swaying as she stood; in an instant she was in his arms in a swoon. He carried her to the sofa, laid her upon it, removed her hat, eased her neck, fanned her. If ever human love spoke in gesture and face it was to be interpreted in the richest eloquence of exalted emotion in that man as he stood over his unconscious wife, ministering to her, wild at heart to kiss her even once, but—not denying himself; no!—restrained by noble recognition of her rights as a woman whose heavenly offence was chastity and of her command as his wife who was a virgin.

After some little time she sighed, opened her eyes, looked at him with bewilderment, shivered like one suddenly awakened from sleep, and sitting up said—

"What has happened to me?"

"You are all right now. The heat overcame you. It is certainly very oppressive."

He stepped to a sideboard and mingled a little brandy with some soda-water. She drank, seated, upturning her rich eyes to him and thanking him with a smile which was lovely with its mingled colours of emotion as the nosegay is sweet and delightful by variety of hue.

"Do you feel better?" he asked, strait-jacketing the

deep solicitude of his soul with the demeanour of
commonplace courtesy.

"Much. It was the heat."

"You will send me an acknowledgment of the
money?"

"Oh yes. This evening."

"Do you keep a banking account in Ramsgate?"

"I have banked the money you sent me."

"Then you will be able to deal with the cheque I
gave you this afternoon. If I can ever be of service to
you in any business or other direction you may indicate,
I do beg that you will command my services."

She thanked him and rose to go, stepping to the
mantel-piece to adjust her hat and collar.

"May I see you to your door?"

"It is but a step. Good-bye, Mr. Goodhart. Believe me sincerely grateful for all your kindness."

"Do not forget your flowers, Mrs. Reynolds."

He watched her from the doorstep with anxiety
until she entered her lodging-house. He paced his
room much harassed by thought. He could not bring
himself into a resolution to confess the truth to her.
Exhibitions of loyalty of love that in her, as a wife,
wanted the consecrating element of amorousness, of
gratitude, of contrition, these had been in sufficient
abundance to furnish a basis for hope or even an
incentive to action. Yet could not he persuade himself
that if he pulled the mask off him she would not shrink
from the intimacy of wedded association as she had
shrunk eight years before; she might elude him by
silently leaving the town; and he could not find will
enough to determine him to take his chance and
challenge a new repulse, a new insult, a new degradation
to his feelings as a man and his rights as a husband.

He smiled when he opened her acknowledgment of the cheque, and kissed the signature.

They met only once in the six days that followed. She had found work for an hour and a half in the afternoon. But he was careful not to lose his hold of her. Almost every day he reminded her of his exist- ence by a gift—a box of peaches, a basket of straw- berries, a bouquet of flowers. When he met her on the day preceding the last which was to dawn, fraught with the issue of a lifetime to this couple, she thanked him for his constant kindness; indeed, she felt overwhelmed, his persistent goodness embarrassed her, she really had no claim upon him. Her manner was gracious, yet there was a constraint in it that was perceptible. It was, indeed, as though she had said to him, "I do not know if it is your intention to take advantage of my situation and the obligation you have placed me under to push kindness into persecution, but you have done so much that more must cease to be agreeable." Her meaning was as clearly intimated by her behaviour and speech as though she had pronounced it in the above words. There was a little coolness in the way she said good- bye to him. He exactly understood and took delight in what was passing in her mind, and he also judged— and rightly judged—that she was not drawn closer to Mr. Goodhart by his knowledge of her treatment of her husband.

Came the sixth day following the afternoon on which Lucretia had drunk tea with Mr. Goodhart, and received a cheque for two hundred and eighteen pounds. She had risen somewhat late. A slight headache had detained her in bed. She did not feel well enough to walk through the glaring heat of that July morning—it was about ten o'clock when she left her room—to teach three young girls, whose parents lived at the western-most extremity of the West Cliff. She sat at breakfast in a shabby parlour. Mr. Goodhart's yesterday's gift of flowers glowed on the little dingy cheffonier in which she kept her tea and sugar. A man was bawling "Fresh sawls!" in the street, and his outcry through the open window was as distracting as though he was in the room. The gilt of the cheap mantel-glass was carefully estranged by red muslin from the blow of the house-fly. Lucretia's appetite was not invited by the plain boiled egg, which she neglected for a piece of toast and butter, and a cup of tea.

The postman knocked. The landlady, very weedy in widow's weeds, entered with a letter. It was addressed to her, and the first address had been to Chepstow Place. This had been erased, and the address of the office in which Dr. Lane had purchased an annuity substituted. This had been erased, and replaced by the name and address of Wembly-Jones; which in their turn had suffered eviction, and yielded to 28, Bell Vue Road, Ramsgate. The envelope bore the Valparaiso post-mark and the Chilian stamp.

A sudden sensation of tightness, that made diffi-cult the systole and diastole of the pulse, came upon Lucretia's heart. She very well remembered that the South Pacific port to which the *Flying Spur* had sailed, was not far distant from Valparaiso, and this—though as a matter of fact it was perfectly irrelevant as a stimulus to thought—quickened in her an hysterical, and as she seemed to feel it, an affrighting imagination that this letter was from her husband. Was the address in his handwriting? But in eight years the hand-writing of some, of many, will change, more or less.

She opened the envelope. It enclosed a letter and
an envelope containing a letter, the envelope addressed
in pencil—

This envelope was pierced as though a nail had
been passed through it. Her dark eyes took on a light
and largeness of wonder with presence of alarm, the
shadow in expression of the dread of calamity, the look
of fear that is in the gaze of one to whom the shape
has come to depart no more. The letter ran thus—

"Ship *Wildfire*, Valparaiso, April 4, 1898.

"Dear Madam,
            "I am the third mate of this ship, which
sailed from Liverpool for this port in December last
year. We found ourselves becalmed off the island
of Santo Cristo three weeks ago, and the captain
sent me ashore to look for turtle and fruit. I found
neither; but, in overhauling the island, I came across
a cave in which was an old sea-chest, with the letter
I enclose, nailed to its lid. I pulled out the nail and
read the letter, but found that the bonds had been
dug up, for a shovel lay close alongside the hole in
which they had been buried. It was the hole right
enough, for it was marked as Captain Reynolds
describes. I guess he was rescued and took away the
bonds himself, for I hunted right and left for anything
like human remains, and if he had died upon the
island he was bound in due course to become a
skeleton; and there is no skeleton, nor anything
answering to a man's bones in that island. In a hollow,
not far from the cave, is Mr. John Goodhart's grave

with a cross raised by your husband as the inscription cut upon it proves. I thought it my duty to forward the enclosed, as you will naturally wish to hear about your husband, and trusting this letter may safely come in your hands,

"I am, yours truly,
"SAMUEL MURDOCH."

With no more prophetic insight, with no more apprehension by intuition of the truth, whose blaze of light was suddenly to flood her than had the letter she held been a tradesman's bill, she took the enclosure from the envelope curiously labelled "To the Honourable Stranger." The paper was very old—over a hundred years old; yellow, stained, of coarse texture; a most singular piece of paper which with its scrawl of pencil might, and could the dead write, be just such a letter as one might expect to receive from a dead man. You will remember what Reynolds wrote; how, conceiving that he must be left to perish on the island and his love for ever holding his wife in view, he, with Goodhart's gold pencil, and an old roll of paper taken from the chest in the cave, framed the appeal to "the Honourable Stranger," which Lucretia was now holding, and was now reading. Though it was but a scrawl, she knew the handwriting, and, indeed, it was contained in an envelope that she herself had addressed to him, but from which the ink had been washed by immersion, when he was in the life-belt.

She read—her face blanched into marble whiteness. She read—the blood stormed in a red-hot torrent to the roots of her hair. She read, and looked upwards and thought, "He is my husband! Had not I guessed it? Had not I suspected it in twenty shapes of look and speech and smile?" Again she read, and when she came to this part she sobbed as if her heart must break—

"My wife, Lucretia, when I left England, was living with her mother, Mrs. Lane, in Chepstow Place, Bayswater, London, W., and it is my earnest wish that she should be the recipient of these bonds and the property that may be found upon me. To which end I, a broken-hearted, desolate, dying man, humbly and affectionately greet the reader of this letter, and do entreat him, as he loves God and the truth and honour, to convey these words and the property to my wife, Lucretia Reynolds, who, for the trouble he is at in finding her, if she has removed, and in acting as my emissary, will receive fifteen hundred pounds, which he will more greatly enjoy, as money honourably and virtuously gained, than if he kept the whole sum, thereby robbing the widow, and blasting the only hope which keeps warm and alive the heart that dictates these words. Again I greet and bless you, and thank you for the noble service you will be doing me.

"FRANCIS REYNOLDS."

The truth was very clear to her now. "Mr. Goodhart" was her husband! It was her husband who had brought her the hundred and fifty pounds, not from the island, but as a gift from his love and loyalty. But oh, why had he waited all these years? Why had he not come sooner? It was her husband who had caused the Bank to send a cheque for two hundred and eighteen pounds. He had dwelt near her, and brooded over her, and courted her as Goodhart, and her heart smiled in remembrance of her triumph in *that*. Why had he not

come sooner? Why had he not revealed himself?
Her instincts as a woman pierced to the very sanctuary
where the truth was enshrined, and his motives were
as intelligible to her as though he had explained
them.

She stood rooted in thought, with her eyes on the
papers in her hand. Then took pen and ink, sat down
at the table and wrote—

"MY FRANK,
          "You are revealed to me by the enclosed.
Come to me. Come quickly, and forgive me.
                              "LUCRETIA."

She put this note and the letters she had received
into an envelope, which she addressed to John Goodhart,
Esq., and rang the bell. The landlady's daughter
appeared.

"Miss Simkins, will you please run with this at
once to Mr. Goodhart's lodgings?"

The girl of fourteen took the letter and vanished,
and Lucretia, from her window, saw her rapidly walk
to the house in Augusta Road, hand in the letter,
and leisurely return, for there were dishes to wash
and beds to make, and little Miss Simkins was in
no hurry.

Reynolds was reading a London daily paper when
the servant gave him Lucretia's letter. He read it, and
sprang to his feet, pausing for a moment in a swift
distraction or delirium of reverie upon his letter, which
he had written in the island. For into it swept, with
the velocity of sunshine, the whole of that heavy term
of ocean solitude, and for an instant the full picture was
before him, with Goodhart's grave, and the cave, and

x

the shovel, and the cook-pit,—just as at midnight the broad circle of the sea or the hills and plains of a face of country are flashed into brilliance by a dart of lightning.

He put on his cap, and in a minute or two had measured the distance that divided his own from Lucretia's lodgings. He knocked, was admitted, passed into the parlour—the door of which he closed—and stood, cap in hand, looking at his wife.

Manifestly since sending to him she had been struggling to school herself for this meeting. You saw that in her posture and demeanour as she stood at the table which remained covered with the breakfast things. But the fragile foundations and props of her woman's resolutions must sink under the weight of her woman's passions and emotions. She said, "Oh, Frank, I know you now! I see you in your changed face and—and——" But then the constricted chords in her throat refused to deliver the message of her mind. All on a sudden she sank down on her knees by the table, and, hiding her face in her arm, wept and wept.

He rushed to her side, fell upon his knees, and put his arm about her. He pressed his cheek to hers and murmured endearments, calling her his only love, his dear wife, his noble Lucretia. But it seemed that she would not have any of this just yet. For, rising in a blind way, she got round to the other side of the table, and he stood up with such a deadly chill of fear of her reception, that for a space he remained and looked like a figure in stone.

"Not yet, Frank, not yet!" she exclaimed, extending her hands towards him, but in the posture of repulsion. "Mr. Featherbridge told a lie when he wrote that

I loathed you. Loathed! Oh no, I loved you. I loathed myself! But something worked in me with a power that was stronger than love or loathing, and I could not—I could not! You violated that mad spirit in me that would have wasted itself had you given me time, had you gone your voyage, when you brought me by a falsehood to your ship. But I afterwards knew that, even when I silently left you at Falmouth, I was loving you as I had loved you when I accepted you, and I also knew that a power had worked in me which had made me false. But, oh, Frank, more faithless to myself than to you."

He moved as though to go to her; but her outstretched arms held him off."

"But what was *your* love?" she continued. "You went away and have never written, never made a sign, never come home to see if I was alive and true to you. Eight years! and I have thought you dead. Otherwise I should have known you—changed as you are, you are the Frank I loved and married. I should have known you, and you have left me alone; when, had you returned and sought me and claimed me, you would have found me your loyal wife, loving you, deploring you, accusing myself of a wickedness whose memory works in me in torment, and again and again in thinking of you, and recalling my conduct at our marriage, I could have destroyed myself."

Her arms slowly fell to her sides; her head sank.

"Lucretia," he said, in a low voice, whose tone thrilled with his love, and the thoughts her words had excited. "I did not dare seek you, because I dreaded your reception. I am a man, and have the feelings of a man, and I feared you. You might

have spurned me again—you may even yet spurn
me——"

"No," she cried, and ran to him.

And he folded her in his arms, and pressed his lips
upon hers, and thus they stood—husband and wife.

PRINTED BY WILLIAM CLOWES AND SONS, LIMITED, LONDON AND BECCLES.

CPSIA information can be obtained at www.ICGtesting.com
Printed in the USA
LVOW131613120513

333393LV00002B/388/A